On the Pampas

G. A. Henty

Contents

ON THE PAMPAS

BY

G. A. Henty

CHAPTER I.
MRS. HARDY'S RESOLUTION.

What are you thinking of, Frank?" Mrs. Hardy asked her husband one evening, after an unusually long silence on his part.

"Well, my dear, I was thinking of a good many things. In the first place, I think, I began with wondering what I should make of the boys; and that led to such a train of thoughts about ourselves and our circumstances that I hardly knew where I was when you spoke to me."

Mr. Hardy spoke cheerfully, but his wife saw at once that it was with an effort that he did so. She put down the work upon which she was engaged, and moved her chair nearer to his by the fire. "It is a serious question, Frank, about the boys. Charley is fifteen now, and Hubert fourteen. I wonder myself sometimes what we shall do with them."

"There seems no opening here in England for young fellows. The professions are crowded, even if they were not altogether beyond our means; and as to a clerk-ship, they had better have a trade, and stick to it: they would be far happier, and nearly as well paid. The fact is, Clara," and here Mr. Hardy paused a little, as if to gain courage to say what he feared would be very disagreeable to his wife--"the fact is, we are altogether too crowded here. The best thing for the children, by far, and I think the best thing for ourselves, would be to emigrate."

Mrs. Hardy gave a little sigh, but said nothing, and sat looking quietly into the fire, as her husband went on: "You see, my dear, I am just, and only just, earning enough for us to live upon. Nor is there any strong probability of an increase of business. The boys, as you say, are growing up, and I see no prospect of giving them a fair start in life. Abroad it is altogether different: we can buy land and stock it for next to nothing. We should live roughly, certainly; but at least there is no fear for the future, and we should start our boys in life with a fair certainty of success. Still, Clara, I do not of course mean that I have made up my mind upon the subject. It is far too serious a matter to decide upon hastily. I only threw out the suggestion; and if you, after thinking it over, are against it, there is an end of the matter."

Mrs. Hardy was silent for a little, and a tear sparkled on her cheek in the firelight; then she said, "I am not surprised, Frank, at what you have said. In fact I have expected it for some time. I have observed you looking over books upon foreign countries, and have seen that you often sat thoughtful and quiet. I guessed, therefore, what you had in your mind. Of course, dear, as a woman, I shrink from the thought of leaving all our friends and going to quite a strange country, but I don't think that I am afraid of the hardships or discomfort. Thousands of other women have gone through them, and there is no reason why I should not do the same. I do think with you that it would be a good thing for the boys, perhaps for the girls too; and that, when we have got over the first hardships, we too should be happier and more free from care than we are now. So you see, Frank, you will meet with no opposition from me; and if, after deliberation, you really determine that it is the best thing to do, I shall be ready to agree with you. But it is a hard thought just at first, so please do not say any more about it to-night."

Mr. Hardy was an architect, as his father had been before him. He had not, however, entered the office at the usual age, but when eighteen had gone out to the United States, to visit an uncle who had settled there. After spending some time with him, the love of adventure had taken him to the far West, and there he had hunted and shot for nearly three years, till a letter, long delayed on the way, entreated him to return to England, as his father's health was failing. He at once started for England, and found that his father was in a feeble state of health, but was still able to carry on the business. Frank saw, however, that he was unequal to the work, and so entered the office, working hard to make up for lost time. He was a good draughtsman, and was shortly able to take a great burden off his father's shoulders.

He had not been long at home, however, before he fell in love with Clara Aintree, the daughter of a clergyman; and his father making over to him a share in the business, they were married just as Frank attained his twenty-fourth year, his wife being about nineteen. Two years after the marriage Mr. Hardy senior died, and from that time Frank had carried on the business alone.

B--- was a large provincial town, but it scarcely afforded remunerative employment for an architect; and although Mr. Hardy had no competitor in his business, the income which he derived from it was by no means a large one, and the increasing expenses of his family rendered the struggle to make ends meet yearly more severe. His father had been possessed of a small private fortune, but had rashly entered into the mania of railway speculation, and at his death had left about fifteen thousand dollars to his son. This sum Frank Hardy had carefully preserved intact, as he had foreseen that the time might come when it would, for his children's sake, be advisable to emigrate. He had long looked forward to this, but had abstained from taking any step until his sons were of an age to be able to make themselves useful in a life in the bush or upon the prairies.

Frank Hardy, at the time our story begins, was about forty. He was a tall, active man, and the life he had led in America when young had hardened his muscles, and given him the full use of every faculty.

Mrs. Hardy was five years younger than her husband, and scarcely looked thirty years old. She was a high-spirited woman, well fitted to be her husband's companion in the dangers and hardships of a settler's life.

The subject of emigration once started, was frequently continued, and presently books and maps began to be consulted, and the advantages and disadvantages of the various countries and colonies to be debated. Finally, Mr. and Mrs. Hardy agreed that the Argentine Republic, in its magnificent rivers, its boundless extent of fertile land, in its splendid climate, its cheap labor, and its probable prospects, offered the greatest advantages.

The decision once arrived at, it was determined to announce it to the children, who had up to this time no idea of the great change decided upon. Breakfast was over, and the boys, whose holidays had just begun, were about to leave the table, when their father said: "Wait a moment, boys; there is something we want to talk to you about."

The boys resumed their seats. "Your mamma and I have been wondering what you boys are to become, and we do not see any openings likely to occur here. Now, what should you say to us all emigrating?"

"What, going abroad, papa!" they both exclaimed joyously.

"Yes, boys, settling in the backwoods or in the prairies."

"Oh, that would be jolly," Charley said, "I know, I papa, having fights with Indians, and all that sort of thing. Oh, it would be glorious!"

"Well, Charley," his father said, smiling, "I do not know that we shall have fights with Indians, nor do think it would be very jolly if we did. But we should have to rough it, you know; you boys would have to work hard, to help me in everything, and to look after the cattle and sheep."

"What fun! what fun!" the boys both shouted; "we should like it of all things in the world."

"And what do you think of it, Maud and Ethel?" their mamma asked the two little girls, who were looking very surprised, but rather doubtful as to the pleasure of the fights with Indians which their brothers had spoken so delightedly about. "You will have to be two very useful little women, and will have to help me just as the boys will have to help your papa. Very likely we may not be able to get a servant there, and then we shall have to do everything."

"That will be fine, mamma," said Maud, who was rather over twelve, while her sister was just eleven. "I don't think I could cook, but you should cook, and I could scrub and do all the hard work, and Ethel could wash up, and lay the table, and that sort of thing. That would be fine, mamma."

Ethel, who almost always agreed with her elder sister, did so now, and the four young ones became quite uproarious in their plans for making themselves useful. At last Mr. Hardy called for order.

"Now silence all, and listen to me. This affair is a serious business; and although I hope and believe that we shall all enjoy our life very much, still we must prepare for it, and look upon it in earnest, and not as a sort of game. I have business here which I cannot finish before another eight or nine months. Let us all make the most of our time before we start. In the first place, the language of the people among whom we are going is Spanish, and we must all learn to speak it well before we leave. For the next three months we will work together at grammar and exercises, and then I will try and get some Spanish teacher to live in the house, and speak the language with us until we go. In the next place, it will be well that you should all four learn to ride. I have hired the paddock next to our garden, and have bought a pony, which will be here to-day, for the girls. You boys have already ridden a little, and I shall now have you taught in the riding school. I went yesterday to Mr. Saris, and asked him if he would allow me to make an arrangement with his head gardener for you to go there to learn gardening. He at once agreed; and I have arranged with the gardener that you are both to be there every morning at six o'clock, and are to work until nine. At nine you will come in to breakfast. From breakfast to dinner you will have to yourselves, except upon the days you take riding lessons; and I should wish you to spend this time at your usual studies, except Latin, which will be of no use to you. From two till half-past four you are to learn carpentering. I have made an agreement with Mr. Jones to pay him so much to take you as a sort of apprentices for the next nine months. In the evening we will all work together at Spanish. It will be hard work; but if you want to be of any real use to me, it is absolutely necessary that you should be able to use a spade and to do rough carpentering. As the time draws on, too, I shall ask one of the farmers near to let you go out with his men and get some notion of plowing. Well, what do you say to all that?"

Hubert looked a little downcast at this recital of the preparatory work to be gone through, but Charley said at once, "It sounds rather hard, papa, but, as you say, we shall have to work hard out there, and it is much better to accustom one's self to it at once; besides, of course, we should be of no use at all to you unless we knew something about work."

"And what are we to learn, mamma?" Maud asked.

"Not a very great deal, my dear," Mrs. Hardy said. "Spanish to begin with, then cooking. I shall teach you at any rate, to make simple dishes and puddings, and to boil vegetables properly. I shall myself practice until I am perfect, and then I shall teach you. Besides that, it will be as well for you to learn to attend to poultry; and that is all I know of at present, except that you must both take pains to improve yourselves at sewing. We shall have to make everything for ourselves out there."

"I suppose we shan't do any more regular lessons, mamma?"

"Indeed you will, Maud. You do not imagine that your education is finished, do you? and you cannot wish to grow almost as ignorant as the poor Indians of the country. You will give up the piano, and learn Spanish instead of French, but that will be all the difference; and I shall expect you both to make as much progress as possible, because, although I shall take you both out there, and shall teach you whenever I find time, your lessons must of necessity be short and irregular. And now you can all go out into the garden and talk the matter over."

"But you have not told us yet where we are going to, papa," Charley said.

"We are going to farm upon the bunks of one of the great South American rivers--probably the Parana, in the Argentine Republic."

Mr. and Mrs. Hardy watched their children from the window. They went out in a group to the summer-house in the corner of the garden, all talking excitedly. Then Maud ran back again to the house, and in a minute or two returned with the schoolroom atlas, and opening it upon the table, they all clustered over it in eager consultation.

Mrs. Hardy turned to her husband with a smile. "You will have to get up the subject, Frank, so as to be able to answer the innumerable questions you will be asked."

"I shall always refer them to you."

There was quite a talk in B--- when it was known that Mr. Hardy was going to emigrate with his wife and family. He, and his father before him, had been so long established in the town that there were few people who did not know him, more or less.

Emigration in the year 1851 was far less common than it is now, and the interest was proportionately greater. Charley and Hubert became quite popular characters among their late schoolfellows, who, whenever they met them, would always stop to have a talk about the distant country to which they were going. The boys, however, had now but little time for talking; for upon the week after their father had first told them of his intention, they had set-to regularly at the work he had laid down for them. They rose every morning at five, had a slice of bread and a cup of milk, and were off to the gardener's, where they worked hard until half-past eight. Mr. Hardy had requested that they should be specially instructed in the raising of vegetables, and in the planting and pruning of fruit-trees. The culture of flowers could be of no utility. The digging made the boys' backs ache at first, and blistered their hands, but they stuck to it manfully, and soon became accustomed to the work, returning to breakfast with glowing cheeks and tremendous appetites.

In the afternoon they might be seen in the carpenter's shop with their coats and waistcoats off, working away with saw or plane.

Although both made good progress in both pursuits, yet their tastes differed;

Charley preferring the carpentering, while Hubert was the gardener's most promising pupil. The former was therefore christened the head carpenter by his sisters, while the latter was promoted to the post of chief gardener.

Four or five months of this work made a visible difference in the boys' appearance. They both widened out across the shoulders, their arms became strong and muscular, and they looked altogether more healthy and robust. Nor did their appearance belie them; for once when spending a holiday in the cricket-field with their former schoolfellows, wrestling matches being proposed after the game was over, they found that they were able to overcome with ease boys whom they had formerly considered their superiors in strength.

In the meantime Mr. Hardy had succeeded in obtaining the services of a young Spanish lady, who had come to England to learn the language, as governess; and of an evening the whole family worked at Spanish, and made such progress that they were soon able to establish the rule that no other language should be spoken at mealtimes. The girls here soon surpassed their brothers, as they had the advantage of morning lessons in the language, besides which young children can always pick up a language sooner than their elders; and they had many a hearty laugh at the ridiculous mistakes Charley and Hubert made in their efforts to get through a long sentence. In six months, however, all could speak with tolerable fluency.

Maud and Ethel were as amused and as diligent at learning household work as their brothers were in their departments, and might have been seen every afternoon in the kitchen, in their little white pinafores, engaged in learning the mysteries of cooking.

One day, after they had been so engaged for about four months, Mrs. Hardy said at breakfast: "I am going to try an experiment. I have given the cook leave to go out for the day. Mr. and Mrs. Partridge are coming to dinner, and I intend handing over the kitchen to the girls, and letting them make their first essay. We are going to have soup, a leg of mutton with potatoes and spinach, a dish of fried cutlets, and a cabinet pudding. I shall tell Sarah to lift any saucepan you may want on or off the fire, but all the rest I shall leave in your hands. The boys will dine with us. The hour will be half-past five, punctually."

The little girls' eyes flashed with pleasure, and they quite colored up at the thought of the importance and difficulty of the task before them. At lunch the boys pretended to eat an extra quantity, saying that they felt very doubtful about their dinner. In the afternoon Mrs. Hardy felt strongly tempted to go into the kitchen to see how things were getting on; but she restrained herself, resolving to let Maud and Ethel have entirely their own way.

The dinner was a great success, although the soup was rather hot, from Ethel, in her anxiety, having let too much pepper slip in; and the cabinet pudding came up all over the dish, instead of preserving its shape, it having stuck to the mold, and Maud having shaken it so violently that it had come out with a burst and broken up into pieces, which had caused a flood of tears on the part of the little cook. It did not taste any the worse, however. And when the little girls came in to dessert in their white frocks, looking rather shy, and very scorched in the face, from their anxious peeping into pots to see that all was going on well, they were received with a cheer by the boys; and their friends were not a little astonished to hear that the dinner they had partaken of had been entirely prepared and cooked by these little women.

After four months' gardening, Mr. Hardy placed the boys with a farmer who lived a mile distant, and made an arrangement for them to breakfast there, so that they now remained at work from six in the morning until twelve. Here they obtained some idea of harnessing and driving horses, of plowing, and of the other farming operations.

They now only went four days a week to the carpenter's, for their papa had one day said to them when they were alone with him before dinner: "Do not put on your working clothes this afternoon, boys; I am going to take you out with me, but do not say anything about it at dinner. I will tell you why afterward."

Rather surprised, they did as he told them, wondering where they could be going. Their father said nothing on the subject until they reached the town, which was a quarter of a mile distant from their house. Then he said: "Now, boys, you know we are going out to a country of which a great portion is still unsettled; and as land is a good deal cheaper at a short distance from the inhabited parts, we shall perhaps have no one within many miles of us. Now it is just possible that at first the Indians may be disposed to be troublesome. I do not suppose that they will, but it is just as well to be prepared for everything. There is no reason why you boys should not be able to shoot as straightly as a man, and I have therefore bought two carbines. They are the invention of an American named Colt, and have a revolving breech, so that they fire six shots each. There is a spare chamber to each, which is very quickly shifted in place of the one discharged; so that each of you could fire twelve shots in a very short time. They will carry up to five hundred yards. They are a new invention, but all accounts agree that they are an excellent one. I have obtained leave from Mr. Harcourt, who lives three miles from here, to put up a target at the foot of some bare hills on his property, and we will walk over there twice a week to practice. I used to be considered a first-rate shot with a rifle when I was a young man in America, and I have got down a rifle for my own use. I do not want you to speak about what we are doing to your mamma, or indeed to any one. We shall keep our rifles at a cottage near where we shoot, and no one need know anything about it. It is not likely that we shall have any trouble with the Indians, and it is of no use making your mamma uncomfortable by the thought of the probability of such a thing."

As Mr. Hardy spoke the boys were ready to dance with delight, and this was increased when they turned into the gunsmith's shop, and were shown the arms which their father had bought for this expedition.

Mr. Hardy had already an excellent double-barreled gun, and he had now purchased a long and heavy rifle carrying a conical ball. In addition to the boys' carbines, he had bought them each a light double-barreled gun. Besides these were two brace of Colt's revolving pistols. These were all new; but there were in addition two or three second-hand double-barreled guns for the use of his servants, in case of necessity, and three light rifles of the sort used for rook-shooting. Altogether, it was quite an armory. The carbines were in neat cases; and the boys carried these and a box of cartridges, while Mr. Hardy took his rifle; and so they started off to their shooting ground.

Here their father instructed them in the use of their revolving carbines, and then, after some practice with caps only, allowed them to fire a few shots each. The firing was certainly rather wild, owing to the difficulty they felt at first of firing without shutting their eyes; but after a few weeks' practice they became very steady, and in three or four months could make pretty certain of a bull's-eye at three hundred yards. Of all this Mrs. Hardy and the girls knew nothing; but there was not the same secrecy observed with reference to their shotguns. These they took home with them, and Mr. Hardy said that he understood that the plains of South America swarmed with game, and that, therefore, it was well that the boys should learn how to shoot. He insisted, however, that only one gun should be taken out at a time, to diminish the danger of accidents. After that the boys took out their guns by turns when they went to work of a morning, and many a dead blackbird soon attested to their improving skill.

CHAPTER II.
THE START.

It was nearly a year after he had made up his mind to emigrate before Mr. Hardy was able to conclude all his arrangements. Then came the great business of packing up. This is no trifling matter when a family of six persons are going to make a move to a new country. Mr. Hardy had at first thought of taking portable furniture with him, but had been told by a friend who knew the country that every requisite could be obtained at Buenos Ayres, the capital of the Argentine Republic, at a far less price than he could convey such heavy articles from England. Still the bulk of luggage was very large; and the boys, who had now left off their farming and carpentering lessons, worked at home at packing-cases, and had the satisfaction of turning their new acquirements to a useful purpose. In addition to the personal baggage, Mr. Hardy was taking with him plows and agricultural implements of English make, besides a good stock of seeds of various kinds. These had been sent on direct by a sailing ship, starting a fortnight before themselves. When their heavy baggage was packed up it too was sent off, so as to be put on board the steamer by which they were to sail; and then came a long round of visits to bid farewell to all their friends. This was a sad business; for although the boys and their sisters were alike excited and delighted at the thought of the life before them, still they could not but feel sorrowful when the time came to leave all the friends they had known so long, and the house they had lived in ever since they could remember.

This over Mrs. Hardy and the children went to Liverpool, where they were to embark; while Mr. Hardy remained behind for a day or two, to see to the sale of the furniture of the house. The day after he joined the family they embarked on board the Barbadoes, for Rio and Buenos Ayres. Greatly were the girls amused at the tiny little cabin allotted to them and their mother--a similar little den being taken possession of by Mr. Hardy and the boys. The smartness of the vessel, and the style of her fittings, alike impressed and delighted them. It has not been mentioned that Sarah, their housemaid, accompanied the party. She had been left early an orphan, and had been taken as a nursemaid by Mrs. Hardy. As time went on, and the little girls no longer required a nurse, she had remained as housemaid, and having no friends, now willingly accompanied them. Mr. Hardy had, to her great amusement, insisted upon her signing a paper, agreeing, upon her master's paying her passage, to remain with him for a year; at the end of which time she was to be at liberty to marry or to leave them, should she choose.

Knowing the scarcity of young Englishwomen in the country that they were going to, and the number of Englishmen doing well in the towns or as farmers, Mr. Hardy had considered this precaution to be absolutely necessary; as otherwise Sarah might have married and left them within a month of her arrival. At the end of a year her so doing would not matter so much, as by that time the party would-be comfortably settled in their new home; whereas during the necessary hardship at first, it would be a great comfort having a faithful and reliable servant.

The last looks which the party cast toward England, as the Welsh coast sank in the distance, were less melancholy than those of most emigrants. The young people were all full of hope and excitement; while even Mrs. Hardy felt but little disposed to give way to sorrow, as it had been arranged that in three or four years, if all went well, she should bring her daughters over to England to finish their education.

Very lovely was that first evening, and as they sat in a group together upon deck the little girls remarked that they did not think that the sea was anything like as terrible as they had expected, and that they did not feel the least seasick. Their father smiled: "Wait a little, my dears; there is an old proverb, 'Don't halloo until you are out of the wood.'"

The next day was still perfectly calm; and when, toward evening, the children were told that they were now fairly getting into the Bay of Biscay, they could scarcely believe the intelligence.

"Why, one would think, Maud," her father said, "that you were disappointed at its being calm, and that you really wanted a storm."

"Oh, papa, I do think it would be great fun; it would be so curious not to be able to walk about, and to see everything rolling and tumbling. Don't you think so, boys?"

"Yes, I think so, Maud; great fun," Charley said.

"Well, young people," the captain, who had been standing by watching the sun, now fast nearing the horizon, and who had overheard their remarks, said, "if it is any satisfaction to you, I can tell you that you are very likely to have your wish gratified. But I question if you will like it as much as you expect."

"Ah, you expect wind, Captain Trevor?" Mr. Hardy said. "I have been thinking myself that the almost oppressive stillness of to-day, and the look of the sunset, and these black clouds banking up in the southwest, meant a change. What does the glass say?"

"It is falling very rapidly," the captain answered. "We are in for a sou'wester, and a stiff one too, or I am mistaken."

Now that it appeared likely that their wishes were about to be gratified, the young Hardys did not seem so pleased as they had expected, although Charley still declared manfully that he was quite in earnest, and that he did wish to see a real storm at sea.

As the sun set the party still leaned against the bulwarks watching it, and the great bank of clouds, which seemed every moment to be rising higher and higher. There was still nearly a dead calm around them, and the heavy beat of the paddles, as they lashed the water into foam, and the dull thud of the engine, were the only sounds that broke the stillness. Now and then, however, a short puff of wind ruffled the water, and then died away again.

"Look at that great cloud, papa," Hubert said; "it almost looks as if it were alive."

"Yes, Hubert, it is very grand; and there is no doubt about there being wind there."

The great cloud bank appeared to be in constant motion. Its shape was incessantly shifting and changing; now a great mass would roll upward, now sink down again; now the whole body would seem to roll over and over upon itself; then small portions would break off from the mass, and sail off by themselves, getting thinner and thinner, and disappearing at last in the shape of fine streamers. Momentarily the whole of the heaving, swelling mass rose higher and higher. It was very grand, but it was a terrible grandeur; and the others were quite inclined to agree with Ethel, who shrank close to her father, and put her hand in his, saying, "I don't like that cloud, papa; it frightens me."

At this moment Mrs. Hardy, who had been down below arranging her cabin, came up to the group. "What a dark cloud, Frank; and how it moves. Are we going to have a storm, do you think?"

"Well, Clara, I think that we are in for a gale; and if you will take my advice, you will go down at once while it is calm, and see that the trunks, and everything that can roll about, are securely fastened up. I will come down and help you. Boys, you had better go down and see that everything is snug in our cabin."

In a quarter of an hour the necessary arrangements were completed, but even in that short time they could feel that a change was taking place. There was now a steady but decided rolling motion, and the young ones laughed as they found it difficult to walk steadily along the cabin.

Upon reaching the deck they saw that the smooth surface of the sea was broken up by a long swell, that the wind now came in short but sharp puffs, that the bank of clouds covered nearly half the sky, and that the detached scud was now flying overhead. The previous stillness was gone; and between the sudden gusts, the roar of the wind in the upper region could be heard. The sun had set now, and a pall of deep blackness seemed to hang from the cloud down to the sea; but at the line where cloud and water touched, a gleam of dim white light appeared.

In preparation for the coming storm, the sailors had put on thick waterproof coats. Many of the passengers had gone below, and those who remained had followed the sailors' example, and had wrapped themselves up in mackintoshes.

Every moment the gusts increased in frequency and power, and the regular line of swell became broken up into confused white-headed waves. The white gleam under the dark cloud grew wider and broader, and at last, with a roar like that of a thousand wild beasts, the gale broke upon them. Just before this Mr. Hardy had taken Mrs. Hardy and the girls below, promising the latter that they should come up later for a peep out, if they still wished it. Charley and Hubert were leaning against the bulwark when the gale struck them.

For a moment they were blinded and half-choked by the force and fury of the spray and wind, and crouched down behind their shelter to recover themselves.

Then, with a hearty laugh at their drenched appearance, they made their way to the mainmast, and then, holding on by the belaying pins, they were able to look fairly out on the gale. It was dark--so dark that they could scarcely see as far as the foremast. Around, the sea was white with foam; the wind blew so fiercely that they could scarcely hear each other's voices, even when they shouted, and the steamer labored heavily against the fast rising sea. Here Mr. Hardy joined them, and for some little time clung there, watching the increasing fury of the gale; then, drenched and almost confused by the strife of winds and water that they had been watching, they made their way, with great difficulty, down into the cabin.

Here the feeling of seasickness, which the excitement of the scene had kept off, increased rapidly; and they were glad to slip off their upper clothes, and to throw themselves upon their berths before the paroxysm of sickness came on.

When questioned afterward as to the events of the next thirty-six hours, the young Hardys were all obliged to confess that that time was a sort of blank in their memory--a sort of horrible nightmare, when one moment they seemed to be on their heads, and the next upon their feet, but never lying down in a comfortable position, when sometimes the top of the cabin seemed under their feet, sometimes the floor over their head. Then, for a change, everything would go round and round; the noise, too, the groaning and the thumping and the cracking, the thud of the waves and the thump of the paddles, and the general quivering, and shaking, and creaking, and bewilderment--altogether it was a most unpleasant nightmare. They had all dim visions of Mr. Hardy coming in several times to see after them, and to give them a cup of tea, and to say something cheering to them; and all four had a distinct idea that they had many times wished themselves dead.

Upon the second morning after the storm began it showed some signs of abating, and Mr. Hardy said to his sons, "Now, boys, make an effort and come upon deck; it's no use lying there; the fresh air will do you good." Two dismal groans were the only response to this appeal.

"Yes, I know that you both feel very bad, and that it is difficult to turn out; still it is worth making the effort, and you will be very glad of it afterward. Come, jump up, else I shall empty the water-jug over you. There, you need not take much trouble with your dressing," he went on, as the boys, seeing that he was in earnest, turned out of their berths with a grievous moan. "Just hold on by something, and get your heads over the basin; I will empty the jugs on them. There now you will feel better; slip on your clothes and come up."

It was hard work for Charley and Hubert to obey orders, for the ship rolled so tremendously that they could only proceed with their dressing by fits and starts, and were more than once interrupted by attacks of their weary seasickness. However, their father stayed with them, helping and joking with them until they were ready to go up. Then, taking them by the arm, he assisted them up the stairs to the deck.

Miserable as the boys felt, they could not suppress an exclamation of admiration at the magnificent scene before them. The sea was tossed up in great masses of water, which, as they neared the ship, threatened to overwhelm them, but which, as she rose on their summits, passed harmlessly under her, hurling, however, tons of water upon her deck. The wind was still blowing fiercely, but a rift in the clouds above, through, which the sun threw down a bright ray of light upon the tossing water, showed that the gale was breaking.

The excitement of the scene, the difficulty of keeping their feet, and the influence of the rushing wind, soon had the effect which their father predicted. The boys' looks brightened, their courage returned; and although they still had an occasional relapse of sickness, they felt quite different beings, and would not have returned to the blank misery of their cabins upon any consideration. They were soon able to eat a piece of dry toast, which Mr. Hardy brought them up with a cup of tea at breakfast-time, and to enjoy a basin of soup at twelve o'clock, after which they pronounced themselves as cured.

By the afternoon the force of the wind had greatly abated, and although a heavy sea still ran, the motion of the vessel was perceptibly easier. The sun, too, shone out brightly and cheeringly, and Mr. Hardy was able to bring the little girls, who had not suffered so severely as their brothers, upon deck. Two more days of fine weather quite recruited all the party; and great was their enjoyment as the Barbadoes entered the Tagus, and, steaming between its picturesque banks and past Cintra, dropped her anchor off Lisbon.

As our object, however, is to relate the adventures of our young settlers upon the Pampas of La Plata, we must not delay to describe the pleasure they enjoyed in this their first experience in foreign lands, nor to give an account of their subsequent voyage across the Atlantic, or their admiration at the superb harbor of Rio. A few days' further steaming and they arrived at the harbor of Buenos Ayres, where the two great rivers, the Uruguay and the Parana, unite to form the wide sheet of water called the river La Plata. It was night when the Barbadoes dropped her anchor, and it was not until the morning that they obtained their first view of their future home.

Very early were they astir, and as soon as it was broad daylight all four of the young ones were up on deck. Their first exclamation was one of disappointment. The shores were perfectly flat, and, seen from the distance at which they were anchored, little except the spires of the churches and the roofs of a few of the more lofty houses could be seen. After the magnificent harbor of Rio, this flat, uninteresting coast was most disappointing.

"What a distance we are anchored from the shore!" Hubert said, when they had recovered a little from their first feeling. "It must be three or four miles off."

"Not so much as that, Hubert," Maud, who was just a little fond of contradicting, said; "not more than two miles, I should think."

Hubert stuck to his opinion; and as the captain came on deck they referred the matter to him.

"The distance of objects across water is very deceiving," he said. "It is from eight to nine miles to those buildings you see."

Maud looked rather crestfallen, and Charley asked, "Why do we anchor such a long way off, captain?"

"Because the shore is so flat that there is no water for us to get in any closer. In a couple of hours you will see boats coming out to fetch you in; and unless it happens to be high tide, even these cannot get to the beach, and you will have to land in carts."

"In carts, Captain Trevor?" they all repeated; "that will be a strange way of landing."

"Yes, it is," the captain answered. "I think that we can safely say that the Argentine Republic is the only country in the world where the only way to land at its chief city is in a cart."

The captain's boat was by this time lowered, and he at once started for shore with his papers. Soon after ten o'clock he returned, followed by a number of boats.

He brought also a letter to Mr. Hardy from an old friend who had been settled for some years near Buenos Ayres, and whose advice had decided him to fix upon that country as the scene of his labors. It contained a warm welcome, and a hearty congratulation upon their safe arrival. This letter had been written two or three days previously, and had been left at the office of the steamship company. It said, however, that the writer would hear of the arrival of the steamer, and would have everything in readiness to take them out to his place upon their landing.

Mr. Hardy had been in frequent communication with his friend from the time that he had determined to emigrate, and Mr. Thompson's letters had contained the warmest assurance of a welcome, and an invitation to make his house their home until they had one of their own to go into; and now this kind letter, coming off so instantly after their arrival, cheered them all much, and made them feel less strange and to some extent at home in the new country at once.

CHAPTER III.
A NEW LIFE.

Tide was fortunately high, and the boat containing the Hardys and the lighter portion of their luggage was able to get up to the landing place without the carts being called into use. As they approached the land they were hailed in a hearty voice, and greetings were exchanged between Mr. Hardy and his friend Mr. Thompson--a sunburnt-looking man with a great beard-- in a Panama hat and in a suit of spotless white.

"Why, Mrs. Hardy," he said as they landed, "you hardly look a day older than you did when I last saw you--let me see--fourteen years ago, just as this big fellow was beginning to walk. And now, if you please, we will be off as soon as we can, for my estancia is fifteen miles away. I have made the best arrangements I could for getting out; but roads are not a strong point in this country, and we seldom trust ourselves in wheeled vehicles far out of the town. You told me in your letters, Hardy, that the young people could all ride. I have horses in any number, and have got in two very quiet ones, with side-saddles, which I borrowed from some neighbors for your girls; but if they prefer it, they can ride in the trap with Mrs. Hardy."

"Oh, no, please," Maud said; "I had much rather ride."

Ethel said nothing, and her mamma saw that she would rather go with her. Accordingly, Mrs. Hardy, Ethel. Sarah, and some of the lighter bags were packed into a light carriage, Mr. Thompson himself taking the reins, as he said he could not trust them to any one but himself. Mr. Hardy, the boys, and Maud mounted the horses prepared for them, and two of Mr. Thompson's men stowed the heavier trunks into a bullock cart, which was to start at once, but which would not reach the estancia until late at night.

As the party rode through the town they were struck with the narrowness and straightness of the streets, and at the generally European look of everything; and Mr. Thompson told them that nearly half the population of Buenos Ayres are European. The number of people upon horseback also surprised our young travelers; but horses cost only thirty shillings or two pounds, and grass is so abundant that the expense of their food is next to nothing; consequently every one rides--even shepherds look after their sheep on horseback. The horses seemed very quiet, for in front of most of the offices the horses of the merchants could be seen fastened by a head rope to a ring, grooms not being considered a necessity.

Once out of the town, the riding horses broke into a canter; for the road was so good that the horses in the light carriage were able to go along at full speed. As they proceeded they passed many houses of the rich merchants of the place, and all were charmed with the luxuriance and beauty of the gardens. Orange and lemon trees scented the air with their delicious perfumes; bananas, tree ferns, and palms towered above them; lovely butterflies of immense size, and bright little humming-birds, flitted about among a countless variety of flowers. The delight of the young ones was unbounded.

Presently they left the mansions and gardens behind and drove out fairly into the country. Upon either side the plains stretched away as far as the eye could reach, in some parts under the plow, but far more generally carpeted with bright green grass and many-colored wild flowers. Everywhere could be seen droves of horses and cattle, while dotted here and there over the plain were the estancias of the proprietors.

It was a most delightful ride. The horses went very quietly, but the boys found, to their surprise, that they would not trot, their pace being a loose, easy canter. The last five miles of the distance were not so enjoyable to the party in the carriage, for the road had now become a mere track, broken in many places into ruts, into which the most careful driving of Mr. Thompson could not prevent the wheels going with jolts that threatened to shake its occupants from their places, and they felt as if every bone in their bodies were broken by the time they drew up at their host's estancia.

Here Mrs. Thompson came out to greet them. She had been a great friend of Mrs. Hardy in their young days, and great was their pleasure at again meeting after so long a separation. Mr. Thompson had already, explained that his wife would have come over to meet them, but that at the time he had left home it was not known that the Barbadoes had arrived. She was due, and, as a measure of precaution, the horses and cart had for the last two days been in readiness, but the exact date of her arrival was of course uncertain.

Mr. Thompson's estancia was a large and picturesque building. It was entirely surrounded by a wide veranda, so that at all hours of the day relief could be obtained from the glare of the sun. In front was an extensive garden; and as Mr. Thompson had made it one of his first objects when he built his house to plant a large number of tropical trees and shrubs, these had now attained a considerable size, and afforded a delicious shade. At a short distance behind the house were the houses of the men, and the corrals, or enclosures, for the cattle.

The interior was handsomely furnished in the European style, except that the floors were uncarpeted, and were composed of polished boards. Everywhere were signs that the proprietor was a prosperous and wealthy man. Mr. Thompson had only one son, a lad of about the same age as Charles Hardy. To his care Mrs. Thompson now assigned the boys, while she conducted Mrs. Hardy and her daughters to their rooms.

In half an hour the party reassembled at dinner, to which they all did ample justice, for their long row and ride had given them the keenest of appetites. They were waited upon by an Italian man-servant; and Mrs. Thompson said that there were a good many of this nation in Buenos Ayres, and that, although they were not considered good hands for rough work, they made excellent servants many of them having been waiters in hotels or stewards on board ship before coming out.

During dinner the conversation turned chiefly upon English friends and affairs, and upon the events of the voyage. After it was over George Thompson proposed to the boys to take a stroll round the place before it became dark. The gentlemen lit their cigars and took their seats under the veranda; and the two ladies, with Maud and Ethel, went out into the garden. The conversation of Mr. Hardy and his friend turned, of course, upon the country, its position and prospects, and upon the advantage which the various districts offered to newcomers. Presently the dusk came on, followed rapidly by darkness, and in half an hour Ethel came to summon them to tea. The boys had already come in, and were full of delight at the immense herds of cattle they had seen. As they sat down to the tea-table, covered with delicate English china, with a kettle over a spirit-lamp in the center, and lit with the subdued light of two shaded moderator lamps, Maud said, "It is not one bit like what I expected, papa, after all you have told us about hardships and working; it seems just like England, except the trees and flowers and butterflies."

"Do not be afraid, Maud," her father said, laughing--for her voice had a tinge of disappointment in it--"you won't be cheated out of your hardship and your work, I promise you. Mrs. Thompson will tell you that it was a very different sort of place when she first came here."

"Yes, indeed," Mrs. Thompson said, smiling; "this was considered a very lonely place when we first settled here. We had a little hut with two rooms, and it was more than six months before I could get a woman servant to come out, and then it was only one of our shepherds' wives, who knew nothing of cooking, and who was only useful in drawing the water and sweeping the floors. In time the country became more settled, and there are stations now sixty or seventy miles beyond us."

The next week was spent in riding over the estate, which consisted of four square leagues--that is to say, was six miles each way--and in examining the arrangements of the enclosures for the cattle. At the end of that time Mr. Hardy started on a tour of inspection through the provinces most likely to suit, provided with numerous letters of introduction from his host. While he was away the boys were to assist upon the estate, and to accustom themselves to the work and duties of the life they were to lead. Into this they entered with the greatest zest, and were in the saddle from morning till night, getting more and more sunburnt from constant exposure, until, as Mr. Thompson told them, they looked like two young gauchos. The gauchos are the natives of the country. They are fine-looking men, with Spanish faces. Their dress is very picturesque. They wear loose calzoncillas or drawers, worked and fringed round the bottom. Above this is a sort of shawl, so arranged that it has the effect of very loose trousers. These shawls are generally of bright colors, woven in stripes, and sometimes of black cloth edged with scarlet. The white calzoncillas show below this garment, and above a colored flannel shirt is worn. The boots are long and are made of undressed leather. They wear a broad leathern belt, with pockets in it; in this a knife, too, is always stuck. Upon fete days they come out with gay silver ornaments upon themselves and their horse-trappings. Their saddles are very clumsy and heavy, and are seldom used by Europeans, who, as Mr. Hardy had done, generally bring English saddles from home. After an absence of a month Mr. Hardy returned with the welcome news that he had made his choice, and had bought at the public auction a tract of four square leagues, upon a river some twenty miles to the south of the town of Rosario, and consequently only a few days' journey from Buenos Ayres. Mr. Thompson looked a little grave when he heard the location of the property, but he only said that he was very glad that his friend had fixed upon a spot which would make it easy for the families to see something of each other. After the first greetings were over Mr. Hardy proceeded to satisfy the curiosity of his hearers as to the new property.

"It is six miles square," he said, "that is, about twenty-five thousand acres, and I bought it for about sixpence an acre. There is a good-sized stream runs through it; there are a good many trees, considering that it is out on the Pampas; there are several elevations which give a fine view over the plain, and upon one of these our future home will stand. A small stream falls into the larger one, and will, I think, be useful. There is an abundance of game; ducks, geese, and swans swarm upon the river. I saw a good many ostriches out on the plains. And, lastly, the soil appears to be excellent. A great point is, that it is only distant twenty miles from Rosario, a most rising town; so that the value of the land is sure to increase yearly, as new settlers come around us."

"That is a most important point," Mr. Thompson said. "Rosario is the most rising town in the country, and the land around it is certain to be very much sought after in a few years."

"Are there any settlements near, Frank?" Mrs. Hardy asked.

"The next plot to ours belongs to three young Englishmen, and the ground between us and Rosario is also principally occupied by English; so that we shall have neighbors near, and I do not suppose that it will be long before we have them all round us."

"If the advantages of the place are so great, Frank, how is it that you have got it so very cheaply? I understood from Mr. Thompson that land in a rising neighborhood, and that was likely to increase in value, was worth two or three shillings, or even more, an acre."

Mr. Hardy hesitated. "Well, Clara, the land is at present upon the extreme verge of the settlements, and the Indians are apt sometimes to be a little troublesome, and to drive off a few horses or cattle. No doubt the thing has been exaggerated; still there is something in it, and the consequence is, people are rather afraid to bid, and I have got this splendid tract of land for about twenty-five hundred dollars; and, not improbably, in ten years it may be worth ten times as much."

"A great proportion of these Indian tales are built up upon very small foundations," Mr. Thompson said cheeringly; and Mrs. Hardy's face, which had been a little serious, cleared up again, and in listening to her husband's account of his travels, she forgot all about the Indians. The boys, however, by no means did so; and as they were going to bed Charley said: "I think there is some chance of a row with the Indians, Hubert, for I noticed that Mr. Thompson looked grave when papa first said where he had bought the land. Depend upon it, we shall have some fun with them after all." They would have thought it still more likely had they heard the conversation between their father and Mr. Thompson after the ladies had gone to bed.

"Why, my dear Hardy, how came you, with a wife and family, to think of buying land so exposed to the Indian attacks? Every season, when they come down, they sweep off the horses and cattle from the outlying settlements, and murder the people if they get a chance. I look upon it as madness."

"There is a good deal in what you say, Thompson, and I thought the whole matter over before I bought it, There is a risk--a great risk, if you like; but I hear the Indians seldom attack the houses of the settlers if they are well prepared and armed. They do occasionally, but very seldom. I shall be well prepared and well armed, and have therefore no fear at all for our personal safety. As to our animals, we must protect them as well as we can, and take our chance. It is only for two or three years at most. After that we shall have settlements beyond and around us; and if emigration keeps on, as I anticipate, and if, as I believe, Rosario is to become a very large and important place, our land will eventually be worth five dollars an acre, at the very lowest. I shall take care not to invest my whole capital in animals, so that I cannot be ruined in one blow. I think that at the end of five years you will agree with me that I have done wisely."

"I have no doubt that your property will increase very much in value, as you say, Hardy, and that in the long run your speculation will be a very successful one; but it is a terrible risk, I think."

"I do not think so, Thompson. We shall be a pretty strong party: we shall have certainly two men besides ourselves. The boys could bring down their man at three hundred yards, and I should do considerable execution among a body of Indians at six or seven; so I have no fear--not the least in the world."

In another two days Mr. Hardy and the boys, accompanied by Mr. Thompson, went down to Buenos Ayres, and took up their quarters at the hotel for a night. At parting, Mr. Thompson presented them with a couple of fine dogs, which he had bred from English mastiffs: Mr. Hardy had brought a brace of fine retrievers with him. Then, with a hearty adieu and much hand-shaking, they said "Good-by" as the steamer moved off from the shore. The heavy luggage was to follow in a sailing vessel upon the following day.

CHAPTER IV.
THE PAMPAS.

The voyage up the river Parana was marked by no particular incident. The distance to Rosario from Buenos Ayres is about two hundred and fifty miles, which was performed by the steamer in about a day and a half. The river is nearly twenty miles in breadth, and is completely studded by islands. The scenery is flat and uninteresting, and the banks but poorly wooded. Our travelers were therefore glad when they arrived at Rosario. The boys were disappointed at the aspect of the town, which, although a rising place, contained under a thousand inhabitants, and looked miserably poor and squalid after Buenos Ayres. Here they were met by a gentleman to whom Mr. Thompson had introduced Mr. Hardy, and with whom he had stayed on his first visit to Rosario. He had brought horses for themselves, and bullock carts for their luggage.

"What! are these your boys, Mr. Hardy? I had not expected to have seen such big fellows. Why, they will be men in no time."

Charley and Hubert deserved Mr. Percy's commendation. They were now sixteen and fifteen years old respectively, and were remarkably strong, well-grown lads, looking at least a year older than they really were. In a few minutes the luggage was packed in two bullock carts, and they were on their way out to Mr. Percy's station, which was about halfway to the camp of Mr. Hardy. The word camp in the pampas means station or property; it is a corruption of the Spanish word campos, literally plains or meadows.

Here they found that Mr. Percy had most satisfactorily performed the commission with which Mr. Hardy had entrusted him. He had bought a couple of the rough country bullock carts, three pair of oxen accustomed to the yoke, half a dozen riding horses, two milch cows, and a score of sheep and cattle to supply the larder.

He had hired four men--a stock-keeper named Lopez, who was called the capitaz or head man, a tall, swarthy fellow, whose father was a Spaniard, and his mother a native woman; two laborers, the one a German, called Hans, who had been some time in the colony, the other an Irishman, Terence Kelly, whose face the boys remembered at once, as having come out in the same ship with themselves. The last man was an American, one of those wandering fellows who are never contented to remain anywhere, but are always pushing on, as if they thought that the further they went the better they should fare. He was engaged as carpenter and useful man, and there were few things to which he could not turn his hand. Mr. Hardy was pleased with their appearance; they were all powerful men, accustomed to work. Their clothes were of the roughest and most miscellaneous kind, a mixture of European and Indian garb, with the exception of Terence, who still clung to the long blue-tailed coat and brass buttons of the "ould country."

They waited the next day at Mr. Percy's station, and started the next morning before daylight, as they had still ten miles to travel, and were desirous of getting as early to the ground as possible.

The boys were in the highest spirits at being at last really out upon the pampas, and as day fairly broke they had a hearty laugh at the appearance of their cavalcade. There was no road or track of any kind, and consequently, instead of following in a file, as they would have done in any other country, the party straggled along in a confused body. First came the animals--the sheep, bullocks, and cows. Behind these rode Lopez, in, his gaucho dress, and a long whip in his hand, which he cracked from time to time, with a report like that of a pistol--not that there was any difficulty in driving the animals at a pace sufficient to keep well ahead of the bullock carts, for the sheep of the pampas are very much more active beasts than their English relations. Accustomed to feed on the open plains, they travel over large extent of ground, and their ordinary pace is four miles an hour. When frightened, they can go for many miles at a speed which will tax a good horse to keep up with. The first bullock cart was driven by Hans, who sat upon the top of a heap of baggage, his head covered with a very old and battered Panama hat, through several broad holes in which his red hair bristled out in a most comic fashion, and over his blue flannel shirt a large red beard flowed almost to his waist. Terence was walking by the side of the second cart in corduroy breeches and gaiters and blue coat, with a high black hat, battered and bruised out of all shape, on his head. In his hand he held a favorite shillalah, which he had brought with him from his native land, and with the end of which he occasionally poked the ribs of the oxen, with many Irish ejaculations, which no doubt alarmed the animals not a little. The Yankee rode sometimes near one, sometimes by another, seldom exchanging a word with any one. He wore a fur cap made of fox's skin; a faded blanket, with a hole cut in the middle for the head to go through, fell from his shoulders to his knees. He and Lopez each led a couple of spare horses. The mastiffs trotted along by the horses, and the two fine retrievers, Dash and Flirt, galloped about over the plains. The plain across which they were traveling was a flat, broken only by slight swells, and a tree here and there; and the young Hardys wondered not a little how Lopez, who acted as guide, knew the direction he was to take.

After three hours' riding Lopez pointed to a rather larger clump of trees than usual in the distance, and said, "That is the camp."

"Hurrah," shouted the boys. "May we ride on, papa?"

"Yes, boys, I will ride on with you." And off they set, leaving their party to follow quietly.

"Mind how you gallop, boys; the ground is honeycombed with armadillo holes, and if your horse treads in one you will go over his head."

"I don't think that I should do that," Charley, who had a more than sufficiently good opinion of himself, said; "I can stick on pretty tightly, and--" he had not time to finish his sentence, for his horse suddenly seemed to go down on his head, and Charley was sent flying two or three yards through the air, descending with a heavy thud upon the soft ground.

He was up in a moment, unhurt, except for a knock on the eye against his gun, which he was carrying before him; and after a minute's rueful look he joined heartily in the shouts of laughter of his father and brother at his expense, "Ah, Charley, brag is a good dog, but holdfast is a better. I never saw a more literal proof of the saying. There, jump up again, and I need not say look out for holes."

They were soon off again, but this time at a more moderate pace. This fall was not, by a very long way, the only one which they had before they had been six months upon the plains; for the armadillos were most abundant, and in the long grass it was impossible to see their holes. In addition to the armadillos, the ground is in many paces honeycombed by the bischachas, which somewhat in size and appearance resemble rabbits, and by a little burrowing owl.

The Hardys soon crossed a little stream, running east to fall into the main stream, which formed the boundary of the property upon that side; and Mr. Hardy told the boys that they were now upon their own land. There was another hurrah, and then, regardless of the risk of falls, they dashed up to the little clump of trees, which stood upon slightly rising ground. Here they drew rein, and looked round upon the country which was to be their home. As far as the eye could reach a flat plain, with a few slight elevations and some half-dozen trees, extended. The grass was a brilliant green, for it was now the month of September. Winter was over, and the plain, refreshed by the rains, wore a bright sheet of green, spangled with innumerable flowers. Objects could be seen moving in the distance, and a short examination enabled Mr. Hardy to decide that they were ostriches, to the delight of the boys, who promised themselves an early hunt.

"Where have you fixed for the house, papa?" Hubert asked.

"There, where those three trees are growing upon the highest swell you can see, about a mile and a half further. We will go on at once; the others will see us."

Another ten minutes took them to the place Mr. Hardy had pointed out, and the boys both agreed that nothing could be better.

At the foot of the slope the river which formed the eastern boundary flowed, distant a quarter of a mile or so from the top of the rise. To the right another stream came down between the slope and another less elevated rise beyond. This stream had here rather a rapid fall, and was distant about three hundred yards from the intended site of the house. The main river was thirty or forty yards across, and was now full of water; and upon its surface the boys could see flocks of ducks, geese, and other birds. In some places the bank was bare, but in others thick clumps of bushes and brushwood grew beside it.

They now took off the saddles and bridles from their horses, and allowed them to range as they pleased, knowing that the native horses were accustomed to be let free, and that there was no fear of their straying away. "Now, boys," Mr. Hardy said, "let us begin by getting our first dinner. You go straight down to the water; I will keep to the right. You take Dash, I will take Flirt."

In another ten minutes the reports of the guns followed close upon each other, and the boys had the satisfaction of knocking down two geese and eight ducks, which Dash brought ashore, beside others which escaped. In five minutes more they heard a shout from their father, who had bagged two more geese and three ducks. "That will do, boys; we have got plenty for the next day or two, and we must not alarm them by too much slaughter."

"Four geese and eleven ducks, papa, in five minutes," the boys said, when they joined Mr. Hardy; "that is not bad shooting to begin with."

"Not at all, boys. What with wild fowl and armadillos, I think that at a pinch we could live for some time upon the produce of the estate."

"You don't mean to say, papa, that they eat the armadillos?" Hubert said with a look of suspicion.

"They do indeed, Hubert, and I am told that they are not at all bad eating. Now let us go up to the rise again; our carts must be nearly up."

By the time they reached the three trees they found that the rest of the cavalcade was within a quarter of a mile, and in a few minutes they came up.

The cattle and sheep required no attending. Immediately they found that they were not required to go any further, they scattered and began to graze. The oxen were unyoked from the carts, and all hands set-to to unload the miscellaneous collection of goods which had been brought up. Only the things which Mr. Hardy had considered as most indispensable for present use had been brought on, for the steamer from Buenos Ayres did not carry heavy goods, and the agricultural implements and other baggage were to come up in a sailing vessel, and were not expected to arrive for another week.

The carts contained three small portmanteaus with the clothes of Mr. Hardy and the boys, and a large case containing the carbines, rifles, and ammunition. There was a number of canisters with tea, coffee, sugar, salt, and pepper; a sack of flour; some cooking pots and frying pans, tin plates, dishes, and mugs; two sacks of coal and a quantity of firewood; shovels, carpenter's tools, a sickle, the framework of a hut with two doors and windows, three rolls of felt, a couple of dozen wooden posts, and two large coils of iron wire. While the others were busy unloading the German had cut some turf and built a rough fireplace, and had soon a bright fire blazing.

"Shall we pluck the ducks?" Charley asked.

"I reckon we can manage quicker than that," the Yankee said; and taking up one of the ducks, he cut off its head and pinions; in another minute he had roughly skinned it, and threw it to the German, who cut it up and put the pieces into the frying pan. A similar process was performed with the other ducks, a little pepper and salt shaken over them, and in a wonderfully short time the first batch was ready. All drew round and sat down on the grass; the tin plates were distributed but were only used by Mr. Hardy and his sons, the others simply taking the joints into their hands and cutting off pieces with their knives. The operation of skinning the fowls had not been pleasant to look at, and would at any other time have taken away the boys' appetites; but their long ride had made them too hungry to be particular. The result of this primitive cooking was pronounced to be excellent; and after drinking a mug of tea all felt ready for work.

"What is to be done first, papa?"

"The first thing is to get these posts into the ground, and to get up a wire fence, so as to make an enclosure for the animals at night. We will put in five posts each side, at ten yards apart; that will take eighteen posts. With the others we can make a division to separate the sheep from the cattle. Unless we do this some of them may take it into their heads to start off in the night and return to their old home."

A spot was soon chosen between the house and the stream on the right. The distance was soon measured and marked; and while Hans carried down the heavy posts one by one on his shoulder, the others went to work. The soil was soft and rich, and the holes were dug to the required depth in a shorter time than would have been considered possible. The wire was stretched and fastened, and before sunset everything was in readiness. The animals were driven in, and the entrance, which was narrow, was blocked up with brushwood from the river. Then followed another half-hour's work in getting up a small shelter with the cases and some of the felting, for Mr. Hardy and his sons. By this time all were really tired, and were glad when Hans summoned them to another meal, this time of one of the sheep. Then Mr. Hardy, and the boys, taking their mugs of tea, retired into the shelter prepared for them, and sat and talked over the events of the day, and as to the work for to-morrow; and then, wrapping themselves up in their blankets, lay down to sleep, listening for some time dreamily to the hum of conversation of the men, who were sitting smoking round the fire, and to the hoarse roar of the innumerable frogs in the stream below.

In the morning they were up and abroad with daylight, and a cup of hot coffee and a piece of bread prepared them for work. Mr. Hardy, his boys, and the Yankee set-to upon the framework of the two huts; while the others went down to the stream and cut a quantity of long, coarse rushes, which they made into bundles, and brought up to the place of the house in a bullock cart. The framework for the huts, which were each about fifteen feet square, was all ready fitted and numbered: it took, therefore, a very short time to erect; and when one was done Mr. Hardy and the Yankee set-to to erect the other at a distance of from forty to fifty yards, while Charley and Hubert drove in the nails and secured the work already done.

By dinner-time the work was complete, and a perfect stack of rushes had been raised in readiness. A great number of long rods had been cut from the bushes, and as the most of them were as flexible and tough as willows they were well suited for the purpose.

After dinner the whole party united their labor to get one of the huts finished. The rods were split in two, and were nailed at intervals across the rafters of the roof. Upon them the long rushes were laid, and over all the felt was nailed. The sides were treated in the same way, except that the rushes were woven in and out between the wattles, so as to make quite a close, compact wall, no felt being nailed on it. The other house was treated in the same way; and it was not until the third night that both huts were finished and ready for occupancy.

Mr. Hardy and his sons then took possession of the one near the brow of the hill. This was to be merely a temporary abode, to be removed when the house was built. The men had that lower down, and rather nearer to the cattle. Beds of rushes were piled up in three corners, and the boys thought that they had never passed such a delicious night as their first in their new house. The next day Mr. Hardy told his boys that they should take a holiday and ride over the place.

The press of work was over, and things would now settle down in a regular way. Hans and Terence had taken a contract to dig the holes for the posts of the strong fence which was to surround the house, including a space of a hundred yards square. This precaution was considered to be indispensable as a defense against the Indians. Seth, the Yankee, had similarly engaged to dig a well close to the house. No supervision of them was therefore necessary. Lopez was to accompany them. Each took a double-barreled gun and a revolver. The day was very fine--about as hot as upon a warm day in June in England. Mr. Hardy proposed that they should first ride westerly as far as the property extended, six miles from the river; that they should then go to the south until they reached that boundary, and should follow that to the river, by whose banks they should return, and bring back a bag of wild fowl for the larder. Quite a pack of dogs accompanied them--the two mastiffs, the setters, and four dogs, two of which belonged to Lopez, and the others to Hans and Seth: these last, seeing that their masters had no intention of going out, determined to join the party upon their own account.

These dogs were all mongrels of no particular breed, but were useful in hunting, and were ready to attack a fox, an animal which swarms upon the pampas, and does great damage among the young lambs.

For the first three or four miles nothing was seen save the boundless green plain, extending in all directions; and then, upon ascending a slight rise, they saw in the dip before them two ostriches. Almost simultaneously the creatures caught sight of their enemies, and went off at a prodigious rate, followed by the dogs and horsemen. For a time their pace was so fast that their pursuers gained but little upon them. Presently, however, the dogs gained upon one of them, and, by their barking and snapping at it, impeded its movements. The horsemen were close together, and the boys had drawn out their revolvers to fire, when their father cried, "Don't fire, boys! Watch Lopez."

At this moment the gaucho took from the pommel of his saddle two balls like large bullets, connected with a long cord. These he whirled round his head, and launched them at the ostrich. They struck his legs, and twined themselves round and round, and in another moment the bird was down in the dust. Before Lopez could leap to the ground the dogs had killed it, and the gaucho pulled out the tail feathers and handed them to Mr. Hardy. "Is the flesh good?" Mr. Hardy asked.

"No, senor; we can eat it when there is nothing else to be had, but it is not good."

"I am rather glad the other got away," Hubert said. "It seems cruel to kill them merely for the sake of the feathers."

"Yes, Hubert; but the feathers are really worth money," Mr. Hardy said. "I should be the last person to countenance the killing of anything merely for the sake of killing; but one kills an ostrich as one would an animal with valuable fur. But what is that?"

As he spoke the dogs halted in front of a patch of bush, barking loudly. The retrievers and the native dogs kept at a prudent distance, making the most furious uproar; but the mastiffs approached slowly, with their coats bristling up, and evidently prepared for a contest with a formidable antagonist. "It must be a lion!" Lopez exclaimed. "Get ready your revolvers, or he may injure the dogs."

The warning came too late. In another instant an animal leaped from the thicket, alighting immediately in front of Prince and Flora. It was as nearly as possible the same color as the mastiffs, and perhaps hardly stood so high; but he was a much heavier animal, and longer in the back. The dogs sprang upon it. Prince, who was first, received a blow with its paw, which struck him down; but Flora had caught hold. Prince in an instant joined her, and the three were immediately rolling over and over on the ground in a confused mass. Mr. Hardy and Lopez at once leaped from their horses and rushed to the spot; and the former, seizing his opportunity, placed his pistol close to the lion's ear, and terminated the contest in an instant. The animal killed was a puma, called in South America a lion; which animal, however, he resembles more in his color than in other respects. He has no mane, and is much inferior in power to the African lion. They seldom attack men; but if assailed are very formidable antagonists. The present one was, Lopez asserted, a remarkably large one.

Mr. Hardy's first care was to examine the dogs. Prince's shoulder was laid open by the stroke of the claws, and both dogs had numerous scratches. Flora had fortunately seized him by the neck, and he had thus been unable to use his teeth.

Mr. Hardy determined to return home at once, in order to dress Prince's shoulder; and leaving Lopez to skin the puma, the rest took their way back. When they arrived the wounds of the dogs were carefully washed, and a wet bandage was fastened with some difficulty upon Prince's wound. Leaving all the dogs behind, with the exception of the retrievers, Mr. Hardy and the boys started for a walk along the river, leading with them a horse to bring back the game, as their former experience had taught them that carrying half a dozen ducks and geese under a broiling sun was no joke. They were longer this time than before in making a good bag; and after-experience taught them that early in the morning or late in the evening was the time to go down to the stream, for at these times flights of birds were constantly approaching, and they could always rely upon coming home laden after an hour's shooting. Upon the present occasion, however, they did not do badly, but returned with a swan, three geese, and twelve ducks, just in time to find the men preparing for dinner.

The next morning the two bullock carts were sent off with Hans and Terence to Rosario, to fetch the posts for the fence, together with two more coils of wire, which had been left there from want of room in the carts when they came up. Charley was sent with them, in order that he might find out if the sailing vessel had arrived with the plows and heavy baggage. While he was away, Mr. Hardy and Hubert were occupied in making a complete exploration of the property, and in erecting a storehouse for the goods.

In five days Charley returned with the carts he had taken, and with four others which he had hired at Rosario, bringing the heavy baggage, which had come in the day after he had arrived there. The goods were placed for the present in the new store, and then all hands set to work at the fence. Hans and Terence had already dug the holes; and the putting in the posts, ramming the earth tightly round them, and stretching the wires, took them two days.

The usual defense in the outlying settlements against Indians is a ditch six feet wide and as much deep; but a ditch of this width can be easily leaped, both by men on horseback and on foot. The ditch, too, would itself serve as a shelter, as active men could have no difficulty in getting out of it, and could surround the house by creeping along the bottom of the ditch, and then openly attack all round at once, or crawl up unperceived by those who were upon the watch on the other side.

The fence had none of these disadvantages. It was six feet high. The wires were placed at six inches apart for four feet from the bottom, and at nine inches above that. Then the upper wires were not stretched quite so tightly as the lower ones, rendering it extremely difficult to climb over. In this way an attacking party would have no protection whatever, and would, while endeavoring to climb the fence, be helplessly exposed to the fire of those in the house. Those who got over, too, could receive no assistance from their comrades without, while their retreat would be completely cut off.

The gateway to the fence was an ordinary strong iron gate which Mr. Hardy had bought at Rosario, and to which strong pointed palings, six feet long, were lashed side by side, with intervals of six inches between them. This was the finishing touch to the fortification; and all felt when it was done that they could withstand the attack of a whole tribe of Indians.

The carts were again sent off to Rosario to bring back some more wood, from which to make the framework of the house. Hubert this time accompanied them, as Mr. Hardy wished the boys to become as self-reliant as possible. He was also to hire three peons, or native laborers. Before he started the plan of the future house was discussed and agreed upon. In the middle was to be the general sitting-room, fifteen feet square; upon one side was the kitchen, fifteen by ten and a half; upon the other, the servants' bedroom, of the same size; behind were three bedrooms, twelve feet by fifteen each, all opening from the sitting-room. The house, therefore, was to form a block thirty-six feet by thirty.

Upon the side next to the kitchen, and opening from it, a small square tower with two stories in it was to stand. It was to be ten feet square; the lower room to be a laundry and scullery, and the one above, approached by straight wooden steps, to be the storehouse. The roof was to be flat, with a parapet three feet high. From this a clear view could be had over the country for miles, and the whole circuit of the fence commanded in case of attack. The walls of the house were to be of adobe or mud the internal partitions of sun-baked bricks.

CHAPTER V
THE SETTLER'S HOME.

Just before commencing the house Mr. Hardy heard that a sale of stock was to take place at an estancia about twenty miles to the west of Rosario, in consequence of the death of its owner. He therefore took Lopez and the newly hired peons, and started. He was likely to be away five days. The boys were to do what work they judged best in his absence. They determined to set about brickmaking. Fortunately, Hans was accustomed to the work and knew the way that the natives of the country set about it; the American, Seth, knew nothing about it, but he was always willing to turn his hand to anything. First, a piece of ground was cleared of grass, and was leveled for the reception of the bricks when made; then some planks were knocked together so as to form a rough table. Two brick molds were made, these being larger than those used in England. A piece of ground was chosen near. The turf was taken off, the soil was dug up, and the peons drove the bullocks round and round upon it, trampling it into a thick mud, some water being thrown in when necessary.

As it was sufficiently trampled Terence carried it in a trough and emptied it on to the table close by, where Hans and Seth fashioned it in the molds, turning the bricks out on to a plank a foot wide and six feet long. When this was full the boys took each an end and carried it off to the prepared ground, where they carefully removed the bricks with two little slabs of wood, and placed them on the ground to dry, returning with the empty plank to find, another one filled for them. It was hard work for all, and from eleven until three the heat was too great to allow them to work at it; but they began with daylight, and taking a nap during the heat of the day, were ready to work on again as long as it was light.

The bricks were, of course, to be dried by the sun, as fuel was too scarce for them to think of burning them; but this was of little consequence, especially as they were to be used indoors, the heat of the sun being quite sufficient to make very fair bricks without the use of fire.

By the afternoon of the fifth day they had made a quantity of bricks which would, they calculated, be ample for the construction of the partition walls of their house.

The boys had just deposited the last brick upon the drying ground, and were moving away, when Hubert cried, "Stop, Charley, don't move a step."

Startled by the suddenness and sharpness of the cry, Charley stood without moving, and was surprised to see his brother pick up one of the wet bricks in both hands, and dash it upon the ground immediately in front of where they were walking.

"I've killed him!" Hubert cried triumphantly; and Charley, looking down, saw a snake of about three feet long writhing in the grass, his head being completely driven into the ground under the force of the lump of wet clay. Two or three stamps of their heavy boots completed the work. And the men coming up to see what was the matter, Hans said that Charley, who would have trodden upon the reptile in another instant had not his brother called out, had had a very narrow escape, for that the snake was the *vivora de la crux*, so called from a mark like a cross upon his head, and that his bite was almost always mortal.

It was a pretty snake, with bands of red, white, and black upon his body. Charley grew very pale at the thought of the narrow escape he had had, and wrung his brother very hard by the hand; while Hubert was half-inclined to cry at the thoughts of what might have happened.

The sun was just setting when they saw a crowd of objects in the distance; and the boys at once saddled their horses and rode off, to meet their father and to assist to drive in the animals. They found, upon reaching him, that he had bought a thousand sheep, fifty cattle, and twenty horses; three of these last being remarkably well bred, and fast, and bought specially for their own riding. Upon their arrival at the house the sheep were turned into the enclosure, the horses were picketed, and the cattle left to roam at their will, as it was not thought probable that they would attempt to return to their distant homes, especially after two days' fatiguing march.

Mr. Hardy was very much pleased at the sight of the long rows of bricks lying in front of the house, and gave great credit to all for the amount of work which had been done during his few days' absence. The next morning he assigned to every one their share of the future work. Lopez and one of the peons went out with the horses, cattle, and sheep. After a time it would not be necessary to have two men employed for this work, as the cattle and horses, when they once became accustomed to their new home, would never wander very far. Charley, Hubert, and Terence were to take three yoke of oxen and the three plows, and to commence to get the land in order for cultivation; the ground selected as a beginning being that lying below the house near the river. Mr. Hardy, Hans, and the two peons were to work at the house, and Seth was to finish the well, which, although begun, had been stopped during the press of more urgent work, and the water required had been fetched from the stream in a barrel placed in a bullock cart. The way in which adobe or mud houses are constructed is as follows: The mud is prepared as for brick-making; but instead of being made into bricks, it is made at once into the wall. The foundation having been dug out and leveled, two boards are placed on edge eighteen inches or two feet apart. These are kept in their places by two pieces of wood nailed across them. The space between these boards is filled with mud. in which chopped hay and rushes have been mixed to bind it together. The boards are left for a day or two, while the builders proceed with the other part of the wall. They are then taken off, and the heat of the sun soon dries the wall into a mass almost as hard as a brick. The boards are then put on again higher up, and the process repeated until the walls have gained the desired height.

In a fortnight's time the walls were finished, and the bullock carts were dispatched to Rosario to fetch lime, as Mr. Hardy had determined to plaster the inside walls to keep in the dust, which is otherwise continually coming off mud walls. By this time a considerable extent of land was plowed up, and this was now planted with maize, yam or sweet potato, and pumpkins: a small portion, as an experiment, was also planted with potato seeds, but the climate is almost too warm for the potato to thrive.

Upon the return of the carts with the lime the partition walls were built with the bricks. The walls finished, all hands went to work at the roof. This Mr. Hardy had intended to have had regularly thatched; but during his last visit to Rosario he had heard that the Indians frequently endeavored in their attacks to set fire to the roofs, and he therefore determined to use tiles. The carts had to make two journeys to Rosario to get sufficient tiles and lath. But at last all was finished; the walls were plastered inside and whitewashed out; the floor was leveled, beaten down hard, and covered with a mixture of clay and lime, which hardened into a firm, level floor.

It was exactly two months from the date of their arrival at the farm that the doors were hung and the finishing touch put to the house, and very pleased were they all as they gave three cheers for their new abode. The tower, they all agreed, was an especial feature. It was built of adobe up to the height of the other walls, but the upper story had been built of bricks two thick and laid in mortar. The top had been embattled; and the boys laughed, and said the house looked exactly like a little dissenting chapel at home.

It was a joyful day when a fire was first lighted in the kitchen chimney, which, with that in the sitting-room, was lined with bricks; and the whole party sat down to a dinner of mutton and wild fowl of three or four sorts.

The same evening Mr. Hardy told the boys that he should start the next day to bring up their mamma and the girls, who were all getting very impatient indeed to be out upon the pampas. He explained to them that he should bring up iron bed-steads with bedding, but that he relied upon them to increase their stock of tables and benches, and to put up shelves, which would do until regular cupboards and closets could be made. Mr. Hardy thought that he should not be away much more than a week, as, by making a long ride to Rosario the next day he should catch the boat, which left the following morning for Buenos Ayres; and as he had already written to Mr. Thompson saying when he should probably arrive, there would be no time lost. The next morning he started before daylight, the last words of the boys being: "Be sure, papa, to bring the mosquito curtains for us all; they are getting worse and worse. We hardly closed an eye all last night."

Hot as the weather now was, the boys worked incessantly at their carpentering for the next week, and at the end had the satisfaction of seeing a large table for dining at in the sitting-room, and a small one to act as a sideboard, two long benches, and two short ones. In their mother and sisters' rooms there were a table and two benches, and a table and a long flap to serve as a dresser in the kitchen. They had also put up two long shelves in each of the bedrooms, and some nails on the doors for dresses. They were very tired at the end of the week, but they looked round with a satisfied look, for they knew they had done their best. The next morning they were to ride to Rosario to meet the party. The carts had gone off under the charge of Terence that day.

It was indeed a joyful meeting when Mr. and Mrs. Hardy and the girls stepped off the steamer; but the first embrace was scarcely over when the boys exclaimed simultaneously, "Why, girls, what is the matter with your faces? I should not have known you."

"Oh, it's those dreadful mosquitoes; there were millions on board the steamer last night. I really thought we should have been eaten up. Didn't you, mamma?"

"Well, my dear, I thought that they would perhaps leave something of us till morning, but I felt almost inclined to go mad and jump overboard. It was a dreadful night. I do hope they are not so bad here, Frank."

"No, Clara, they are nothing like so bad as they were last night; but still, as we are so close to the river, they will, no doubt, be troublesome, and I question whether the beds at the hotel have mosquito curtains; but if you take my advice, and all sleep with the sheet over your heads, you will manage to do pretty well. It is better to be hot than to be bitten all over."

In spite, however, of the expedient of the sheets, all the party passed a bad night, and were quite ready to get up before daylight to start for their ride to Mr. Percy's estancia. They were all to ride, with the exception of Sarah, who took her place in one of the bullock carts; and they would therefore reach the estancia before the heat of the day fairly set in. Terence having been told that Sarah was going to ride, had cut some boughs, with which he made a sort of arbor over the cart to shade her from the sun--a general method of the country, and at which Sarah was much gratified. She had at first felt rather anxious at the thought of going without her mistress; but Terence assured her: "Sure, miss, and it's meself, Terence Kelly, that will take care of ye; and no danger shall come near your pretty face at all, at all; ye'll be quite as safe as if ye were in the auld country. And as for the bastes, sure and it's the quietest bastes they are, and niver thought of running away since the day they were born."

So Sarah took her place without uneasiness, and the others started at a hand canter for Mr. Percy's estancia.

While at Mr. Thompson's both Mrs. Hardy and the girls had ridden regularly every day, so that all were quite at their ease on their horses, and were able to talk away without ceasing of all that had happened since they parted. The only caution Mr. Hardy had to give, with a side look at Charley, was, "Look out for armadillo holes; because I have known fellows who were wonderful at sticking on their horses come to grief at them."

At which Hubert laughed; and Charley said, "Oh, papa!" and colored up and laughed, as was his way when his father joked him about his little weaknesses.

They had not gone more than halfway before they met Mr. Percy, who had ridden thus far to welcome his guests, for English ladies are very scarce out on the pampas, and are honored accordingly. One of the first questions the girls asked after the first greetings were over was, "Have you many mosquitoes at your estancia, Mr. Percy?"

"Not many," Mr. Percy said; "I have no stream near, and it is only near water that they are so very bad."

After waiting during the heat of the day at Mr. Percy's, the boys rode on home, as six guests were altogether beyond Mr. Percy's power of accommodating.

The next morning the boys were up long before daylight, and went down to the stream, where, as day broke, they managed to shoot a swan and five wild ducks, and with these they returned to the house. Then they swept the place with the greatest care, spread the table, arranged the benches, set everything off to the best advantage, and then devoted their whole energies to cooking a very excellent breakfast, which they were sure the travelers would be ready for upon their arrival. This was just ready, when, from the lookout on the tower, they saw the party approaching. The breakfast was too important to be left, and they were therefore unable to ride out to meet them. They were at the gate, however, as they rode up.

"Hurrah, hurrah!" they shouted, and the girls set up a cheer in return.

The men ran up to take the horses, and in another minute the whole party were in their new home. The girls raced everywhere wild with delight, ascended to the lookout, clapped their hands at the sight of the sheep and cattle, and could hardly be persuaded to take their things off and sit down to breakfast.

Mrs. Hardy was less loud in her commendation of everything, but she was greatly pleased with her new home, which was very much more finished and comfortable than she had expected.

"This is fun, mamma, isn't it?" Maud said. "It is just like a picnic. How we shall enjoy it, to be sure! May we set-to at once after breakfast, and wash up?"

"Certainly, Maud; Sarah will not be here for another two hours, and it is as well that you should begin to make yourselves useful at once. We shall all have to be upon our mettle, too. See how nicely the boys have cooked the breakfast. These snatch-cock ducks are excellent, and the mutton chops done to a turn. They will have a great laugh at us, if we, the professed cooks, do not do at least as well."

"Ah, but look at the practice they have been having, mamma."

"Yes, Maud," Hubert said; "and I can tell you it is only two or three things we can do well. Ducks and geese done like this, and chops and steaks, are about the limits. If we tried anything else, we made an awful mess of it: as to puddings, we never attempted them; and shall be very glad of something in the way of bread, for we are heartily sick of these flat, flabby cakes."

"Why have you only whitewashed this high middle wall halfway up, Frank?"

"In the first place, my dear, we fell short of whitewash; and, in the next place, we are going to set to work at once to put a few light rafters across, and to nail felt below them, and whitewash it so as to make a ceiling. It will make the rooms look less bare, and, what is much more important, it will make them a great deal cooler."

"You get milk, I hope?"

"Yes," Charley said; "two of the cows of the last lot papa bought are accustomed to be milked, and Hubert and I have done it up till now; but we shall hand them over to you, and you girls will have to learn."

Maud and Ethel looked at each other triumphantly. "Perhaps we know more than you think," Ethel said.

"Yes," Mrs. Hardy said; "the girls are going to be two very useful little women. I will tell you a secret. While you boys were at work of a morning, the girls, as you know, often walked over to Mr. Williams the farmer's, to learn as much as they could about poultry, of which he kept a great many. Mrs. Williams saw how anxious they were to learn to be useful, so she offered to teach them to milk, and to manage a dairy, and make butter and cheese. And they worked regularly, till Mrs. Williams told me she thought that they could make butter as well as she could. It has been a great secret, for the girls did not wish even their papa to know, so that it might be a surprise."

"Very well done, little girls," Mr. Hardy said; "it is a surprise indeed, and a most pleasant one. Mamma kept your secret capitally, and never as much as whispered a word to me about it."

The boys too were delighted, for they had not tasted butter since they arrived, and they promised readily enough to make a rough churn with the least possible delay.

By ten o'clock the carts arrived with Sarah and the luggage, and then there was work for the afternoon, putting up the bedsteads, and getting everything into order. The mosquito curtains were fitted to the beds, and all felt gratified at the thought that they should be able to set the little bloodsuckers at defiance. The next day was Sunday, upon which, as usual, no work was to be done. After breakfast the benches were brought in from the bedrooms, and the men assembling, Mr. Hardy read prayers, offering up a special prayer for the blessing and protection of God upon their household. Afterward Mrs. Hardy and the girls were taken over the place, and shown the storehouse, and the men's tent, and the river, and the newly planted field.

"The ground is getting very much burned up, papa," Charley said. "It was damp enough when we put in the crops, and they are getting on capitally; but I fear that they were sown too late, and will be burned up."

"Ah, but I have a plan to prevent that," Mr. Hardy said. "See if you can think what it is."

Neither of the boys could imagine.

"When I first described the place to you, I told you that there was a main stream with a smaller one running into it, and that I thought that this last would be very useful. I examined the ground very carefully, and I found that the small stream runs for some distance between two slight swells, which narrow in sharply to each other just below the house. Now I find that a dam of not more than fifty feet wide and eight feet high will make a sort of lake a quarter of a mile long, and averaging fifty yards wide. From this the water will flow over the whole flat by the river in front of the house and away to the left, and we shall be able to irrigate at least three or four hundred acres of land. Upon these we shall be able to raise four or five crops a year; and one crop in particular, the alfalfa, a sort of lucern for fattening the cattle in time of drought, when the grass is all parched up. At that time cattle ordinarily worth only fifteen dollars can be sold, if fat, for forty-five or fifty dollars. So you see, boys, there is a grand prospect before us."

The boys entered enthusiastically into the scheme, and the party went at once to inspect the spot which Mr. Hardy had fixed upon for the dam. This, it was agreed, should be commenced the very next day; and Mr. Hardy said that he had no doubt, if the earth was properly puddled, or stamped when wet, that it would keep the water from coming through.

In the afternoon Mrs. Hardy, Maud, and Ethel were taken a ride round the property, and were fortunate enough to see some ostriches, to the great delight of the girls.

At tea Mr. Hardy said: "There is one very important point connected with our place which has hitherto been unaccountably neglected. Do any of you know what it is?"

The boys and their sisters looked at each other in great perplexity, and in vain endeavored to think of any important omission.

"I mean," their father said at last, "the place has no name. I suggest that we fix upon one at once. It is only marked in the government plan as Lot 473. Now, what name shall it be?"

Innumerable were the suggestions made, but none met with universal approbation. At last Mrs. Hardy said: "I have heard in England of a place called Mount Pleasant, though I confess I do not know where it is. Now, what do you say to Mount Pleasant? It is a mount, and we mean it to be a very pleasant place before we have done with it."

The approval of the suggestion was general, and amid great applause it was settled that the house and estate should hereafter go by the name of "Mount Pleasant."

In the morning the boys were at work at two wheelbarrows, for which Mr. Hardy had brought out wheels and ironwork; and Mr. Hardy and the men went down to the stream, and began to strip off the turf and to dig out a strip of land twenty-five feet wide along the line where the dam was to come. The earth was then wetted and puddled. When the barrows were completed they were brought into work; and in ten days a dam was raised eight feet high, three feet wide at the top, and twenty-five feet wide at the bottom. In the middle a space of two feet wide was left, through which the little stream at present ran. Two posts, with grooves in them, were driven in, one upon either side of this; and thus the work was left for a few days, for the sun to bake its surface, while the men were cutting a trench for the water to run down to the ground to be irrigated.

A small sluice was put at the entrance to this, to regulate the quantity of water to be allowed to flow, and all was now in readiness to complete the final operation of closing up the dam. A quantity of earth was first collected and puddled, and piled on the top of the dam and on the slopes by its side, so as to be in readiness, and Mrs. Hardy and the girls came down to watch the operation.

First a number of boards two feet long, and cut to fit the grooves, were slipped down into them, forming a solid wall, and then upon the upper side of these the puddled earth was thrown down into the water, Terence standing below in the stream and pounding down the earth with a rammer. The success was complete: in a couple of hours' time the gap in the dam was filled up, and they had the satisfaction of seeing the little stream overflowing its banks and widening out above, while not a drop of water made its escape by the old channel.

While this work had been going on the boys had been engaged up at the house. The first thing was to make a churn, then to put up some large closets and some more shelves, and the bullock carts had to be sent to Rosario for a fresh supply of planks. This occupied them until the dam was finished. The girls had tried their first experiment at butter, and the result had been most satisfactory. The dinners, too, were pronounced to be an immense improvement upon the old state of things.

Soon after the dam was finished Hans, who had been too long a rover to settle down, expressed his desire to leave; and as Mr. Hardy had determined to lessen his establishment--as, now that the heavy work was over, if was no longer necessary to keep so many hands--he offered no objection to his leaving without the notice he had agreed to give. Wages were high, and Mr. Hardy was desirous of keeping his remaining capital in hand, in case of his sheep and cattle being driven off by the Indians. One of the peons was also discharged, and there remained only Lopez, Seth, Terence, and two peons.

CHAPTER VI.
A TALE OF THE MEXICAN WAR.

Mr. Hardy was rather surprised at Seth Harper, the Yankee, having remained so long in his service, as the man had plainly stated, when first engaged, that he thought it likely that he should not fix himself, as he expressed it, for many weeks, However, he stayed on, and had evidently taken a fancy to the boys; and was still more interested in the girls, whose talk and ways must have been strange and very pleasant to him after so many years' wandering as a solitary man. He was generally a man of few words, using signs where signs would suffice, and making his answers, when obliged to speak, as brief as possible. This habit of taciturnity was no doubt acquired from a long life passed either alone or amid dangers where an unnecessary sound might have cost him his life. To the young people, however, he would relax from his habitual rule of silence. Of an evening, when work was over, they would go down to the bench he had erected outside his hut, and would ask him to tell them tales of his Indian experiences. Upon one of these occasions Charley said to him: "But of all the near escapes that you have had, which was the most hazardous you ever had? which do you consider was the narrowest touch you ever had of being killed?"

Seth considered for some time in silence, turned his plug of tobacco in his mouth, expectorated two or three times, as was his custom when thinking, and then said, "That's not altogether an easy question to answer. I've been so near wiped out such scores of times, that it ain't no easy job to say which was the downright nearest. In thinking it over, I conclude sometimes that one go was the nearest, sometimes that another; it ain't no ways easy to say now. But I think that, at the time, I never so much felt that Seth Harper's time for going down had come, as I did in an affair near San Louis."

"And how was that, Seth? Do tell us about it," Maud said.

"It's rather a long story, that is," the Yankee said.

"All the better, Seth," Charley said; "at least all the better as far as we are concerned, if you don't mind telling it."

"No, I don't mind, no how," Seth answered. "I'll just think it over, and see where to begin."

There was a silence for a few minutes, and the young Hardys composed themselves comfortably for a good long sitting, and then Seth Harper began his story.

"Better than five years back, in '47, I were fighting in Mexico. It wasn't much regular up and down fighting we had, though we had some toughish battles too, but it were skirmishing here, skirmishing there, keeping one eye always open, for man, woman, and child hated us like pison, and it was little mercy that a straggler might expect if he got caught away from his friends. Their partisans chiefs, half-soldier, half-robber, did us more harm than the regulars, and mercy was never given or asked between them and us. Me and Rube Pearson worked mostly together. We had 'fit' the Indians out on the prairies for years side by side, and when Uncle Sam wanted men to lick the Mexicans, we concluded to go in together. We 'listed as scouts to the 'Rangers,' that is, we agreed to fight as much as we were wanted to fight, and to go on in front as scouts, in which way we had many a little scrimmage on our own account; but we didn't wear any uniform, or do drill, which couldn't have been expected of us. We shouldn't have been no good as regulars, and every one knew that there were no better scouts in the army than Rube Pearson and Seth Harper. Lor', what a fellow Rube was, to be sure! I ain't a chicken," and the Yankee looked down at his own bony limbs, "but I was a baby by the side of Rube. He were six feet four if he were an inch, and so broad that he looked short unless you saw him by the side of another man. I do believe Rube Pearson were the strongest man in the world. I have heard," Seth went on, meditating, "of a chap called Samson: folks say he were a strong fellow. I never came across any one who had rightly met him, but a good many have heard speak of him. I should like to have seen him and Rube in the grips. I expect Rube would have astonished him, Rube came from Missouri--most of them very big chaps do. I shouldn't wonder if Samson did, though I never heard for certain."

The young Hardys had great difficulty to prevent themselves from laughing aloud at Seth's idea on the subject of Samson. Charley, however, with a great effort, steadied himself to say, "Samson died a great many years ago, Seth. His history is in the Bible."

"Is it, though?" Seth said, much interested. "Well now, what did he do?"

"He carried away the gates of Gaza on his back, Seth."

Seth remained thoughtful for some time. "It all depends on how big the gates were," he said at last. "That gate down there is a pretty heavyish one, but Rube Pearson could have carried away two sich as that, and me sitting on the top of them. What else did he do?"

"He was bound in new cords, and he broke them asunder, Seth."

Seth did not appear to attach much importance to this, and inquired, "Did he do anything else?"

"He killed three hundred men with the jawbone of an ass."

"He killed--" Seth began, and then paused in sheer astonishment. Then he looked sharply round: "You're making fun of me, lad."

"No, indeed, Seth," Charley said; "it is quite true."

"What! that a man killed three hundred men with the jawbone of an ass? It couldn't have been; it was sheer impossible--unless they were all asleep, and even then it would be an awful job."

"I don't know how it was, Seth, but the Bible tells us, and so it must be true. I think it was a sort of miracle."

"Oh, it was a miracle!" Seth said thoughtfully, and then remained silent, evidently pondering in his own mind as to what a miracle was, but not liking to ask.

"It was a very long time ago, Seth, and they were no doubt a different people then."

"Was it a very, very long time back?" Seth asked.

"Yes, Seth; a very, very, very long time."

"Ah!" Seth said in a thoughtful but more satisfied tone, "I understand now. I expect it's that. It's the same thing among the Indians: they have got stories of chiefs who died ever so long ago, who used to be tremendous fellows--traditions they call 'em. I don't expect they were any braver than they are now; but a thing grows, you see, like a tree, with age. Lor' bless 'em! if they tell such tales now about a Jew, what will they do some day about Rube Pearson?"

The young Hardys could stand it no longer, but went off into a scream of laughter, which even the surprised and offended looks of the ignorant and simple minded, but shrewd, Yankee could not check. So offended was he, indeed, that no entreaties or explanations were sufficient to mollify him, and the story was abruptly broken off. It was not for two or three days that the boys' explanation and assurance sufficed; and then, when Charley had explained the whole history of Samson to him, he said:

"I have no doubt that it is all true, and I wish I could read it for myself. I can just remember that my mother put a great store on her Bible, and called it the good book. I can't read myself, and shouldn't have time to do it if I could; so it's all one as far as that goes. I am just a hunter and Indian fighter, and I don't know that for years I have ever stopped so long under a roof as I have here. My religion is the religion of most of us out on the prairies. Be honest and true to your word. Stick to a friend to death, and never kill a man except in fair fight. That's about all, and I hope it will do; at any rate, it's too late for me to try and learn a new one now. I listen on a Sunday to your father's reading, and I wish sometimes I had been taught; and yet it's better as it is. A man who acted like that wouldn't be much good for a rough life on the prairies, though I have no doubt it could be done in the settlements. Now I must go on with my work. If you and the others will come over to the hut this evening I will go on with that yarn I was just beginning."

After tea the young Hardys went down to the hut, outside which they found Seth awaiting their arrival. They were now comfortably seated, and Seth, without further introduction, went on.

"One day our captain sent for Rube and me, and says, 'I've got a job for you two scouts. It's a dangerous one, but you won't like it any the worse for that, I know.'

"'Not a bit,' said Rube with a laugh. He was the lightest-hearted fellow, was Rube; always gay and jolly, and wouldn't have hurt a squirrel, except in stand-up fight and as a matter of business.

"'What is it, Cap?' said I; 'you've only got to give us the word, and we're off.'

"'I've had a message,' he said, 'from Colonel Cabra of their service, that he is ready to turn traitor, and hand us over some correspondence of Santa Anna, of which he has somehow got possessed. Being a traitor, he won't trust any one, and the only plan we can hit upon is, that he shall make a journey to San Miguel, thirty miles north of this, as if on business. I am to make an expedition in that direction, and am to take him prisoner. He will then hand over the papers. We shall bring him here, and, after keeping him for a time, let him go on parole. No suspicion will therefore at any future time arise against him, which there might be if we met in any other way. The papers are very important, and the affair must not be suffered to slip through. The country between this and San Miguel is peaceful enough, but we hear that El Zeres' band is out somewhere in that direction. He has something like two hundred cutthroats with him of his own, and there is a rumor that other bands have joined him. Now I want you to go on tomorrow to San Miguel. Go in there after dusk, and take up your quarters at this address; it is a small wine-shop in a street off the market. Get up as Mexicans; it only requires a big cloak and a sombrero. You can both speak Spanish well enough to pass muster. Stay all next day, and till daybreak on the morning afterward, and then ride back on this road. You will find cut in the first place whether Cabra has arrived, and in the next place whether El Zeres is in the neighborhood. I shall only bring forty men, as I do not wish it to be supposed that I am going on more than a mere scouting expedition. You understand?'

"'All right, Cap; we'll do it,' I said, and we went off to our quarters.

"I can't say I altogether liked the job. It was a long way from headquarters, and, do what they may, two men can't fight more than, say, ten or a dozen. I was rather surprised to see by Rube's face that he rather liked it; but I did not find out till late that night what it was pleased him--then the truth came out.

"'We had better start early, Seth,' said he; 'say at daybreak.'

"'What for, Rube?' I said; 'the Cap said we were to go in after dusk. It's only thirty miles; we shan't want to start till three o'clock.'

"Rube laughed. 'I don't want to get there before dusk, but I want to start at daybreak, and I'll tell you why. You remember Pepita?'

"'There,' said I, 'if I didn't think it had something to do with a woman. You are always running after some one, Rube. They will get you into a scrape some day.'

"Rube laughed. 'I am big enough to get out of it if it does, Seth; but you know I did feel uncommon soft toward Pepita, and really thought of marrying and taking her back to Missouri.'

"'Only she wouldn't come, Rube?'

"'Just so, Seth,' said he, laughing. So we agreed we would be the best friends; and she asked me, if ever I went out to San Miguel, to go and see her. She said her father was generally out, but would be glad to see me if he were in. She lives in a small hacienda, a league this side of the town.

"I saw that it was of no use to argue, but I didn't like it. The Mexican women hated us worse than the men did, and that warn't easy to do; and many of our fellows had been murdered after being enticed by them to out-of-the-way places. Still, in the present case, I did not see that the girl could have expected that Rube would be there unless the rest of us were near at hand, and I did not attempt to oppose Rube's wishes."

"So next morning off we started, and by ten o'clock we rode up to the door of the place which Rube said answered to the description Pepita had given him. It was a pretty place, with trees round it, and might have been the residence of a small proprietor such as Pepita had described her father to be. As we rode up to the door it opened, and I saw at once that Rube were right, for a dark-eyed Mexican girl came out and looked at us inquiringly.

"'What can I do for you, senors?' she asked.

"'Don't you remember me, Donna Pepita?' Rube said, laughing, as he lifted the sombrero which had shaded his face.

"The girl started violently. 'Ah, Signor Americano, is it you? I might have known, indeed,' she said, smiling, 'by your size, even wrapped up. This, of course, is Signor Seth--you are always together. But come in,' she said.

"'Who have you got inside, Donna Pepita?' Rube asked. 'I know that I can trust you, but I can't trust others, and I don't want it known I am here.'

"'The house is empty,' Pepita said. 'My father is out. There is only old Jacinta at home.'

"At this moment an old woman made her appearance at the door, and at a word from Pepita took our horses, while Pepita signed to us to enter.

"'Excuse me, signora,' I said. 'We will go first and see our horses stabled. It is our custom; one never knows when he may want them.'

"I thought Pepita looked annoyed, but it was only for a moment, and then she said something in one of the country dialects to the old woman. She nodded her head, and went off round to the back of the house, we leading our horses, and following her. The stables, I observed, were singularly large and well kept for a house of its size; but, to my surprise, instead of going to the long range of buildings, the old woman led the way to a small shed."

"'Ain't these stables?' said I.

"She shook her head, and said in Spanish, 'They were once, but we have only two horses. Now they are used as a store for grain; the master has the key.'

"I could not contradict her, though I believed she was telling me a lie. However, we fastened our horses up in the shed, put the pistols from our holsters into our belts, and, taking our rifles in our hands, entered the house.

"Pepita received us very warmly, and busied herself assisting the old woman to get us something to eat; after which she and Rube began love-making, and it really seemed as if the girl meant to change her mind, and go back with Rube, after all. There was nothing, in fact, to justify my feeling uneasy, except that, while Pepita had promised me when I entered the house not to tell the old woman who we were, I was convinced that she had done so by the glances of scowling hatred which the old hag threw at us whenever she came into the room. Still I was uneasy, and shortly made some excuse to leave the room and saunter round and about the house, to assure myself that Pepita had spoken truly when she had said that there was no one there except the old woman and herself. I found nothing to excite the smallest suspicion, and was therefore content to return to the room and to throw myself lazily down and go off for a siesta, in the wakeful intervals of which I could hear that Pepita had given way, and that the delighted Rube was arranging with her how she should escape and join him when the army retired; for of course neither had any idea that her father would consent to her marrying one of the hated enemies of his country.

"At three o'clock I roused myself and soon after the old woman came into the room with some lemonade. I observed that Pepita changed color, but she said nothing, and a moment after, making some excuse, she left the room. I was about to speak to Rube on the subject, when the window was darkened with men, Five or six shots were fired at us, and with a yell a crowd of Mexicans rushed into the room.

"As they appeared Rube sprang up with the exclamation, 'Trapped, by thunder!' and then fell flat on his back, shot, I believed, through the head.

"I rushed to my rifle, seized it, but before I could get it to my shoulder it was knocked from my hand. Half a dozen fellows threw themselves upon me, and I was a prisoner. I didn't try to resist when they laid hands on me, because I knew I should have a knife in me at once; and though I knew my life was not worth an hour's purchase--no, nor five minutes'--after I was caught, still upon the whole it was as well to live that five minutes as not.

"There was such a hubbub and a shouting at first that I couldn't hear a word, but at last I picked up that they were a party of the band of El Zeres, who was in the neighborhood, and had been fetched by a boy that traitress Pepita had dispatched for them directly we arrived. Pepita herself was wife of one of the other chiefs of the band. Much fun was made of poor Rube and myself about our courting. I felt mad with myself for having been caught so foolishly. I couldn't feel angry with Rube, with him lying dead there, but I was angry with myself for having listened to him. I oughtn't to have allowed him to have his own way. I warn't in love, and I ought to have known that a man's head, when he's after a gal, is no more use than a pumpkin. While I was thinking this out in my mind I had my eyes fixed upon poor Rube, whom no one thought of noticing, when all of a sudden I gave quite a start, for I saw him move. I couldn't see his face, but I saw a hand stealing gradually out toward the leg of a man who stood near. Then there was a pause, and then the other hand began to move. It wasn't at all like the aimless way that the arms of a badly hit man would move, and I saw at once, that Rube had been playing 'possum' all along."

"Doing what, Seth?" Ethel asked.

"Just pretending to be dead. I held my breath, for I saw he had come to the conclusion that he could not be overlooked much longer, and was going to make a move.

"In another minute there was a crash and a shout as the two men fell to the ground with their legs knocked clean from under them, catching hold of other men and dragging them down with them. From the midst of the confusion Rube leaped to his feet and made a rush for the window; one man he leveled with a blow of his fist; another he caught up as if he had been a baby, and hurling him against two others, brought them on the ground together, and then leaping over their bodies, dashed through the window before the Mexicans had recovered from their astonishment. I could have laughed out loud at the yell of rage and amazement with which they set off in pursuit; but two or three of them remained to guard me, and I might have got a knife in my ribs, so I kept quiet. I did just feel so glad to see Rube was alive, that I hardly remembered that it warn't likely that either he or I would be so long, for I did not for a moment expect that he would make good his escape. The odds were too great against it, especially in broad daylight. Even on horseback it would be next to impossible. No one but Rube would have attempted such a thing; but he never stopped to think about odds or chances when his dander was up. In less than no time I heard a shot or two, then was a silence for a time, then a shout of triumph. I knew it was all over, and that Rube was taken again.

"He told me afterward that he had made a dash round to the stable, where he had found seven or eight Mexicans looking after the horses; that he had knocked down one or two who were in his way, had leaped upon the nearest animal, and had made off at the top of his speed, but that a dozen others were after him in an instant; and seeing that he would be lassoed and thrown from his horse, he had stopped and thrown up his arms in token of surrender. Rube's hands were bound tightly behind him, and he was led back into the room.

"He gave a loud laugh when he saw me: 'That was a boy's trick; wasn't it, Seth? But I couldn't have helped it if I had been shot a minute afterward. There were those fellows' legs moving about me just as if I was a log of wood. The thoughts came across me, "A good sharp rap above the ankle and over you'd go;" and when I'd once thought of it, I was obliged to do it. It was fun, though, Seth; wasn't it?'

"'It was, as you say, Rube, a boy's trick, and just at present is hardly the time for that. But don't let us say anything we don't want overheard, Rube; some of these fellows may understand.'

"'Right you are, Seth. I am main sorry, old hoss, that I've got you into this scrape, but I expect we shall get out again somehow. I don't think Rube Pearson is going to be wiped out yet.

"I hoped not too. I warn't a bit tired of life, but I did not see my way out of it. However, I had one comfort: I knew if any two men could get out of an ugly mess, those two men were Rube and I.

"We were now told to sit down on the ground in one corner of the room, two fellows taking up their station by our sides. Then there was a hot discussion about our fate, which warn't exactly pleasant to listen to. Some were in favor of hanging us at once, but the majority were for taking us to the main body under El Zeres himself, because the chief would be so glad to have us in his power. He had frequently vowed vengeance against us, for we were known as the most active scouts in the army, and had led troops in his pursuit many a time, and had once or twice come very near to catching him. He had vowed solemnly to his patron saint that if we fell into his hands he would put us to death with unheard-of tortures; and as El Zeres was rather celebrated that way--and it was the anticipation of an unusual treat which decided the majority to reserve us--it warn't altogether pleasant to listen to. But we put a good face on the matter, for it would never have done to let those Mexican varmints see that two backwoodsmen who had 'fit' them and beaten them time after time were afraid to die when their time came. Presently there was a little stir, and Pepita came into the room. I rather think that, though the girl hated us like pison, she didn't like to come into the room where one of us was, she thought, laying dead. Now she came in, looking, I will say for her, uncommonly pretty. She came straight up to us, and looked us full in the face. I paid no attention to her, but Rube nodded quite cheerfully.

"'Well, signora, so you were making fools of us, after all! Well, I ain't the first chap that's been fooled by a pretty woman; that's one comfort, anyhow. I suppose our engagement is to be considered at an end, eh?' and he laughed.

"'American dog!' the girl said, with her eyes flashing with rage, 'did you think you were so good-looking that the women of the nation you tread upon are all to lose their hearts to you? We are Mexicans, and we hate you!' and she stamped her foot with passion.

"Rube laughed unconcernedly. 'Well, signora, after what you now permit me to see of you, I am really thankful that you are so kind and lenient. Thunder! what a fate mine would have been if you had taken it into your head to marry me!'

"There was a general laugh among the men at the cool way in which Rube treated the girl, and the enraged Pepita struck him a box on the ear. It was a hearty one; but Rube's face hardly changed, and he said, still smiling:

"'We have a custom in the States, Pepita, that when a gal boxes a man's ears, he has a right to give her a kiss. You are reversing that; I had the kisses this afternoon, and now I have got the box on the ear.'

"There was again a roar of laughter among the Mexicans, and the enraged woman drew a knife, and would have stabbed Rube to the heart had she not been seized by the men standing round her and forced from the room. We were kept in that room under a guard so watchful that any attempt to escape was out of the question, until three o'clock the next morning. The horses were then saddled, and we were soon off, Rube and I riding in the midst of the party with our hands tied before us, so that we could just hold the bridle. We had found out from the conversation that El Zeres with his band was about twenty-five miles distant.

"Upon our ride I found an opportunity for the first time since our capture for a talk with Rube.

"'What do you think of it, Seth?'

"'Looks bad, Rube,' I said. 'If we find El Zeres in camp, I expect he will make short work of us; if he is away I suppose we shall get till to-morrow morning. If we are to escape at all it must be to-night.'

"'Escape!' Rube said scoffingly; 'of course we are going to escape. The question is, Which one of all the ways open to us are we to choose?' and he laughed merrily.

"'I don't quite see all the ways yet, Rube; however, we shall see what sort of a place we are put in to-night, and can then come to some conclusion. There comes the sun.'

"It was about nine o'clock when we rode into camp; and as we approached it we acknowledged that a better place against a sudden surprise could hardly have been chosen. The ground was flat for miles round; but the site of the camp rose in a slight mound, of nearly circular form and perhaps one hundred yards across; the central part was thirty feet or so above the general level. Round this the band of El Zeres was encamped. Rube and I guessed them at four hundred strong. There was an attempt at military order, for, by the bundles of wearing apparel, etc., it was evident that the men slept round a series of bivouac fires, extending in a circle round the foot of the mound. Within the line of fires the horses were picketed in two rows. In the center of the circle, upon the highest point of the rise, was a small house. As we approached we could see a stir in the camp: a party of men were mounting their horses as if for an expedition.

"'I hope El Zeres is on the point of starting somewhere, Rube,' I said, 'and that he is in too great a hurry to stop to amuse himself with us as he has threatened: it will give us another day.”

"'I hope so,' Rube said; 'it's hard if we don't manage to make tracks if we get twenty-four hours.'

"On reaching the camp we were ordered to alight; and upon its being known who we were, there was as many shouts of triumph as if we had been generals.

"'We are quite celebrated characters, Seth,' Rube said, with his usual laugh.

"'Ah,' said I, 'we could do without such celebrity just at present.'

"'I don't know,' Rube said. 'If we were mere American soldiers they would cut our throats at once: as it is they may keep us for a more ceremonial killing.'

"As we were talking we were being led up toward the central hut, which was evidently the abode of the chief. He was standing at the door, tapping his riding-boot impatiently with a heavy whip; a man was holding his horse in readiness. One of the other leaders was standing talking to him. 'Jehoshophat!' said I, 'he is going out. We are safe for awhile.'

"El Zeres was a slight, wiry man, with a small wicked-looking eye, which gave one the 'squerms' to look at, and a thin mouth curved up in a cruel smile. He was the savagest and most bloodthirsty of all the Mexican partisans. The man with him was a tall, swarthy, ferocious-looking villain.

"El Zeres looked at us for some time without a word. Then he said, 'I've got you at last; I've been on the lookout for you for a long time past.'

"'It hasn't been our fault we haven't met before,' said Rube; which was true enough, for we had given him a close chase several times. El Zeres only gave an evil smile, but the other Mexican exclaimed savagely, 'You dog, do you dare to answer?' and struck Rube across the face with all his force with his heavy whip.

"Rube turned quite white, and then with a tremendous effort he broke the cowhide thongs which fastened his hands--not new rope, mind you, but cowhide--just as if it had been so much grass, and went right at the fellow who had struck him. The Mexicans gave a cry of astonishment, and threw themselves upon Rube, El Zeres shouting at the top of his voice, 'Don't draw a knife, don't draw a knife; I'll hang any man who injures him.'

"Rube had got the fellow by the throat with both hands, and though the crowd of men who threw themselves upon him pulled him to the ground, he never let go, but brought the man down too. I knew it was all over with him. I was quite mad to join in and help; but though I tugged and strained at my thongs till they cut right into my wrists, I could not succeed. For awhile they lay in a struggling mass on the ground, and then Rube shook himself free of them for a moment and got to his feet. A dozen men were upon him in a moment; but he was blind with rage, and would not have minded if it had been a thousand. Those who came in front went down as if shot before the blows of his fists; but others leaped on him from behind, and then the struggle began again. I never saw sich a thing before, and never shall again. It was downright awful. They could not hold his arms. Their weight, over and over again, got him upon the ground, and over and over again he was up on his feet; but his arms, somehow, they could not hold, and the work he did with them was awful. Anything he hit went down, and when he could not hit he gripped. It was like a terrier with rats: he caught 'em by the throat, and when he did it was all up with them. Some of them made a grab for their knives, but they had no time to use them. In a moment their eyes would seem to start from their heads; and then, as he threw 'em away, they fell in a dead lump."

How long this went on I can't say--some minutes, though--when a Mexican snatched the lasso, which every Mexican carries, from the saddle of El Zeres' horse, and dropped the noose over Rube's neck. In another moment he was lying half-strangled upon the ground, and a dozen hands bound his hands behind him and his feet together with cowhide thongs. Then they stood looking at him as if he was some devil. And no wonder. Seven Mexicans lay dead on the ground, and many more were lying panting and bleeding around. The Mexicans are an active race of men, but not strong--nothing like an average American--and Rube at any time was a giant even among us scouts; and in his rage he seemed to have ten times his natural strength. El Zeres had never moved; and except shouting to his men not to use their knives, he had taken no part whatever in it--watching the struggle with that cruel smile, as if it had only been a terrier attacked by rats. When it was over he mounted his horse, and said to one of his lieutenants who was standing near: 'I must go now. I leave these men in your charge, Pedro. Fasten that one's hands behind him; then take them inside. Put them in the inner room. Clear my things out. Take ten picked men, and don't let any one in or out till I return. I shall be back before daybreak. I shall amuse myself to-day with thinking how I shall try the nerves of these Americanos. I can promise you all a handsome amusement of some sort, anyhow.' And he rode off.

"I have often faced death, and ain't afraid of it; but the unruffled face and the cruel smile of that man made my flesh creep on my bones, as I thought of what Rube and I had got to go through the next day. And now," Seth said, breaking off, "it's getting late, and I haven't talked such a heap for years. I will finish my yarn another night."

Very warm were the young Hardys in their thanks to Seth for this exciting story from his own experience, and great was the discussion among themselves that arose as to how the two Americans could possibly have made their escape from their terrible predicament.

CHAPTER VII.
SETH CONTINUES HIS NARRATIVE
OF THE MEXICAN ADVENTURE.

The next evening the young Hardys again took their seats by Seth, and, without any delay, he went on with his story.

"After El Zeres had ridden off, the lieutenant, Pedro, selected ten from the men around--for pretty well the whole camp had gathered round us--and told them, in the first place, to clear the house of the hammock and other belongings of El Zeres, and when this was done to carry Rube in. Bound and helpless as he was, there was a visible repugnance on the part of the men to touch him, so great was the fear which his tremendous strength had excited. However, six of them took him up and carried him into the hut--for it was little more--and threw him down like a log in the inner room. I walked in of my own accord, and sat down on the ground near him. I heard Pedro give orders to some of the men outside to take away the dead bodies and bury them, and for the rest to go down to their campfires. Then he entered the house with his other four men.

"The house was just the ordinary Mexican hut. It contained two rooms, or rather, one room partially divided into two, the inner compartment forming the sleeping-room of the family. There was no door between the rooms, nor was there any window; the light entering through the wide opening into the outer room. The outer room had no regular windows, only some chinks or loopholes, through which a certain amount of light could come; but these were stopped up with straw, for the Mexicans are a chilly people; and as the door was always open, plenty of light came in through it. The house was not built of adobe, as are most Mexican huts, but of stones, with the interstices plastered with mud."

"Never in my life did I feel that the game was up as I did when I sat down there and looked round. The men were seated on the ground in the next room, in full view of us, and every now and then one walked in to look at us. Helpless as we were, they had an uneasy doubt of what we might do. Rube still lay at full length on the ground. For a quarter of an hour I did not speak, as I thought it best to let him cool and quiet down a bit; and I thought and thought, but I couldn't, for the life of me, think out any plan of getting clear away. At last I thought I would stir Rube up."

'How do you feel, Rube?'

'Well, I feel just about tired out,' Rube said; 'just as if I had walked a hundred miles right on end. I've been a fool again, Seth, sure enough; but I've given some of them goss, that's a comfort. I'll just take a sleep for a few hours, and then we'll see about this business. 'Hello, there!' he shouted in Spanish; 'water.' For awhile no one attended to him; but he continued to shout, and I joined him, so that the men in the next room were obliged to leave off their talk to do as we wanted them. One of them got up and took a large copper pan, filled it with water from a skin, and placed it down between us; and then giving me a hearty kick--even then he did not dare kick Rube--went back to his pillow. It took some trouble and much rolling over before we could get so as to get our mouths over the pan to drink. When we had satisfied our thirst we rolled over again, made ourselves as comfortable as we could under the circumstances--which warn't saying much--and in a short time were both asleep, for we had only been four hours in bed for two nights. I was pretty well accustomed to sleep on the ground, and I slept without waking for nearly seven hours; for when I did so I saw at once it was nearly sunset. I can't say it was an agreeable waking, that; for I felt as if my shoulders were out of joint, and that I had two bands of red-hot iron round my wrists. My first move was to roll over and have another drink. Then I sat up and looked round. Rube was sitting up, looking at me.

'So you are awake, Seth?'

'Yes,' said I. 'Are you all right now, Rube?'

'As right as can be,' Rube said in his ordinary cheerful tone; 'except that I feel as if a fellow was sawing away at my ankles and wrists with a blunt knife.'

'That's about the state of my wrists,' I said.

'I don't mind my wrists so much,' he said; 'it's my feet bothers me. I shall be such a time before I can walk.'

'You needn't bother about that, Rube,' said I. 'It isn't much more walking your feet have got to do.'

'I hope they've got more to do than they've ever done yet, old hoss,' Rube said; 'at any rate, they've got a good thirty miles to do to-night.'

'Are you in earnest, Rube?' said I.

'Never more so,' said he. 'All we've got to do is to get away, and then tramp it.'

'How do you mean to get away, Rube?'

'Easy enough,' Rube said carelessly. 'Get our hands loose first, then our legs, then kill them fellows and make tracks.'

Now it ain't very often that I larf out. I don't suppose I've larfed right out three times since I was a boy; but Rube's coolness tickled me so that I larfed out like a hyena. When I began, Rube he began; and when he larfed it was tremendous. I don't think Rube knew what I war larfin' at; but he told me afterward he larfed to see me larf, which, in all the time we had been together, he hadn't seen. What made us larf worse was that the Mexicans were so startled that they seized their rifles and rushed to the doorway, and stood looking at us as if we were wild beasts. Keeping the guns pointed at us, they walked round very carefully, and felt our cords to see that they were all right; and finding they were, went back into the next room, savage and rather scared. Our larfing made them terribly uneasy, I could see; and they had an idea we couldn't have larfed like that if we hadn't some idea of getting away. When we had done I said:

'Now, Rube, tell me what you have planned out, that is, if you're downright in arnest.'

'In arnest!' says he, almost angry; 'of course I'm in arnest. Do you think I'm going to be fool enough to stop here to be frizzled and sliced by that El Zeres to-morrow? 'No, it's just as I said: we must get our hands free; we must kill all these fellows, and be off.'

'But how are we to get our hands free, Rube?'

'That's the only point I can't make out,' he said. 'If these fellows would leave us alone, it would be easy enough; we could gnaw through each other's thongs in ten minutes; but they won't let us do that. All the rest is easy enough. Just think it over, Seth.'

I did think it over, but I did not see my way to getting rid of our thongs. That done, the rest was possible enough. If we could get hold of a couple of rifles and take them by surprise, so as to clear off four or five before they could get fairly on their legs, I had little doubt that we could manage the rest. No doubt they would shut the door as it got later, and it was possible that the row might not be heard. If that was managed, I was sure we could crawl through the lines and get off. Yes, it was straightforward enough if we could but get rid of our cords. As I was thinking it over my eye fell upon the pan of water. An idea came across me.

'I don't know, Rube, that it would stretch them enough to slip our hands out, but if we could wet these hide thongs by dipping them in water, we might stretch them a bit, anyhow, and ease them,'

'That would be something, Seth, anyhow.'

We shuffled by turn, next to the pan, and leaned back so that our wrists were fairly in the water. The water relieved the pain, and I could feel the thongs give a little, but it was only a little; they had been tied too carefully and well to render it possible to unloose them. We came to this conclusion after an hour's straining, and at the cost of no little pain. We agreed it was no use, and sat thinking over what was the next thing to do, and taking it by turns to cool our wrists. We did not altogether give up hope, as we agreed that we must try, in the short intervals between the visits of the Mexicans, to untie the knots of each other's cords with our teeth. It was possible, anyhow, for the knots would draw pretty easy now that the leather was wet. Suddenly an idea struck me. I squeezed myself back to the wall, and leaned against it.

'It's all right, Rube,' said I; 'our cords are as good as off.' 'How's that?' said Rube. 'This wall is made of rough stones, Rube, and there are plenty of sharp edges sticking out through the mud. They will cut through these wet thongs like knives.'

'Hoorah!' shouted Rube at the top of his voice, with a yell that startled the Mexicans from their seats again, and then he commenced thundering out one of the songs the soldiers used to sing on the march. Several Mexicans came running up from the camp to ask if anything was the matter, Rube's yell having reached their ears. They were told it was only those mad Americanos amusing themselves, and with many angry threats of the different sort of yells we should give next day, they sauntered off again.

'That's rather a good thing,' Rube said to me when he stopped making a noise. 'If any sound of the little fight we are going to have here reaches the camp, they will put it down to us shouting for our amusement.'

By this time it had become perfectly dark, and the guard lighted a fire in the middle of the room in which they sat. A pile of wood had been brought in for the purpose, and when the smoke had a little abated, the door was shut and barred. Every three or four minutes one of the men would take a lighted brand and come in to see that we were not near to each other, and that all was secure.

'What time shall we begin, Seth?' Rube asked.

'In another hour or so,' I said; 'by eight. They will be gambling and quarreling round the fire by nine o'clock; and the talk, and the noise of the horses, will prevent them hearing anything here. We must not think of going out for two hours later, and even then they won't be all asleep; but we dare not put it off later, for El Zeres may come back earlier than he said he should, and if he does it's all up with us. Let's arrange our plans for good,' I said, 'and then we can each sit up against a corner and pretend to go to sleep. When I am going to cut my cord I will give a very little cough, and then you do the same when you are free. We had better do that before very long, for you will be a long time before you will get any feeling in your feet. Rub them as hard as you can; but you can't do that till you get the use of your hands. When you are quite ready, snore gently; I'll answer in the same way if I am ready. Then we will keep quiet till the fellow comes in again, and the moment he is gone let us both creep forward: choose a time when the fire is burning low. You creep round your side of the room; I will keep mine, till we meet in the corner where the rifles are piled. We must then open the pans, and shake all the powder out, and, when that is done, each take hold of one by the barrel and hit. Do you quite understand and agree?'

'Quite, Seth. Is there anything else?'

'Yes,' I said; 'you take the door, I will take the corner where the arms are. We must try and keep them from coming within arm's reach to use their knives; but if either of us are hard pressed he must call, and the other must come to him.'

'All right, old hoss, I long to be at work.'

'So do I,' I said. 'And now don't let's have any more talk; shut your eyes, and keep quiet till I cough.'

The men were engaged now in talking over the deeds in which they had been engaged, and so revolting and cold-blooded were the atrocities of which they boasted that I longed for the time when Rube and I should fall upon them. In half an hour I gave the signal. I had picked out a sharp stone in a convenient position, and it was not a minute before I felt the coil of cords loosen with a sudden jerk, and knew that I was free. I found my hands were completely numbed, and it was a long time before I could restore the circulation. It must have been a good half-hour before Rube gave the signal that he had got the cords that bound his ankles loosened, as of course he could not begin at them until he had the free use of his hands. As I had anticipated, the visits of our guards were rather less frequent now that they believed us to be asleep. Fortunately, the din and talk in the next room was now loud and incessant, which enabled Rube to rub, and even stamp his feet a little. In half an hour I heard a snore, which I answered. The moment the next visit was over I crawled to the door, and then, lying pretty nigh on my stomach, crept round to where the rifles were piled.

The fire was burning low, and the guard were sitting so closely round it that the lower part of the room was in black shadow; so that, though I was looking out for Rube, I didn't see him till he was close enough to touch me. It was a delicate job opening all the pans, but we did it without making as much noise as would scare a deer, and then, each taking a rifle by the barrel, we were ready. Pedro was just telling a story of how he had forced an old man to say where his money was hid, by torturing his daughters before his eyes, and how, when he had told his secret, and the money was obtained, he had fastened them up, and set the house alight--a story which was received with shouts of approving laughter. As he finished down came the butt of Rube's rifle on his head with a squelch, while mine did the same on the head of the next man. For an instant there was a pause of astonishment, for no one knew exactly what had happened; then there was a wild yell of surprise and fear, as our rifles came down again with a crashing thud. All leaped to their feet, the man I aimed my next blow at rolling over, and just escaping it. Rube was more lucky, and just got his man as he was rising.

'Hoorah! Seth,' he shouted, 'five down out of eleven.'

We drew back now to our posts as agreed on, and the Mexicans drawing their knives, made a rush forward. They ain't cowards, the Mexicans--I will say that for them; and when these fellows found they were caught like rats in a trap, they fought desperately. They knew there was no mercy to expect from Rube and me. They divided, and three came at each of us. Two went down as if they were shot, and I was just whirling my rifle for another blow, when I heard a crash, and then a shout from Rube,

'Help, Seth!'

I saw at once what had happened. Rube's rifle, as he was making a blow at a man, had struck a beam over his head, and the shock had made it fly from his hands across the room. In another moment the two Mexicans were upon him with their knives. He hit out wildly, but he got a gash across the forehead and another on the arm in a moment. I made two strides across the hut, and the Mexicans who were attacking me, instead of trying to prevent me, made a rush to the corner where their rifles were, which I had left unguarded. It was a fatal mistake. My gun came down crash upon the head of one of Rube's assailants before he knew of my approach, and another minute did for the second. As I turned from him the remaining two Mexicans leveled at Rube, who had rushed across to pick up his gun, and myself, and gave a cry as the flints fell and there was no report. For a minute or two they fought desperately with the guns; but it was no use, and it was soon over, and we stood the masters of the hut, with eleven dead men round us. For they were dead every one, for we examined them. The stocks of our guns had broken with the first blow, and the rest had been given with the iron, and in no case had we to hit twice. I don't say it was anything like Samson and the donkey's jaw-bone you were telling me about, but it war very fair hitting. It was scarcely over when we heard several men come running up outside.

'Is anything the matter, Pedro? We thought we heard a yell.'

'No, nothing,' I said, imitating Pedro's gruff voice, which I felt sure they would not know through the door; 'it's only these mad Americanos yelling.'

The men were apparently quite satisfied with the explanation, for in a minute or two we heard their voices receding, and then all became still. Presently we opened the door and looked out. Many of the fires had begun to burn low, but round others there was still a sound of laughing and singing.

'Another hour,' Rube said, 'and they will all be asleep,'

We threw some more wood on the fire, took some tobacco and cigarette paper from the pocket of one of the Mexicans, and sat down to smoke comfortably. We were both plaguey anxious, and couldn't pretend we warn't, for at any moment that rascal El Zeres might arrive, and then it would be all up with us. At last we agreed that we could not stand it any longer, and made up our minds to go outside and sit down against the wall of the hut till it was safe to make a start, and then if we heard horses coming in the distance we could make a move at once. We each took a hat and cloak, a brace of pistols, and a rifle, and went out. There we sat for another hour, till the camp got quiet enough to make the attempt. Even then we could hear by the talking that many of the men were still awake, but we dared not wait any longer, for we calculated that it must be near eleven o'clock already. We chose a place where the fires had burned lowest, and where everything was quiet, and, crawling along upon the ground, we were soon down among the horses. We had been too long among the Indians to have a bit of fear about getting through these fellows; and, lying on our faces we crawled along, sometimes almost touching them, for they lay very close together, but making no more noise than two big snakes. A quarter of an hour of this and we were through them, and far enough out on the plain to be able to get up on to our feet and break into a long stride. Ten more minutes and we broke into a run: there was no fear now of our steps being heard.

'Done them, by thunder!' Rube said; 'won't El Zeres curse?'

We might have been a mile and a half from the camp, when in the quiet night air we heard the sound of the howl of a dog. We both stopped as if we were shot.

'Thunder!' Rube exclaimed furiously, 'if we haven't forgot the bloodhound.'

I knew what Rube meant, for it was a well-known matter of boast of El Zeres that no one could ever escape him, for that his bloodhound would track them to the end of the world.

'There's only one thing to be done,' I said; 'we must go back and kill that critter.'

'Wait, Seth,' Rube said; 'we don't know where the darned brute is kept. He warn't up at the hut, and we might waste an hour in finding him, and when we did, he ain't a critter to be wiped out like a babby.'

'We must risk it, Rube.' I said. 'It's all up with us if he's once put on our track.' Rube made no answer, and we turned toward the camp.

We hadn't gone twenty yards when Rube said, 'Listen.' I listened, and sure enough I could hear out on the plain ahead a low trampling. There was no need of any more talk. We ran forward as hard as we could go, turning a little out of our course to let the horsemen who were coming pass us.

'In another quarter of an hour they'll know all about it, Rube. It will take them as much more to get ready and put the dog on the track. They'll have some trouble in getting him to take up our scent with all that blood in the room. I should say we may fairly reckon on three-quarters of an hour before, they're well out of the camp.'

'That's about it,' Rube said. 'They will have to tie the dog, so as not to lose him in the darkness. They won't gain on us very fast for the next two hours; we can keep this up for that at a pinch. After that, if we don't strike water, we are done for.'

'We passed a stream yesterday, Rube; how far was it back?'

'About an hour after daylight. Yes, nearly three hours from camp. But we are going faster now than we did then. We ought to do it in two hours.'

"After this we didn't say any more. We wanted all our breath. It was well for us we had both been tramping half our lives, and that our legs had saved our necks more times than once on the prairies. We were both pretty confident we could run sixteen miles in two hours. But we dared not run straight. We knew that if they found we were keeping a line, they would let the dog go their best pace and gallop alongside; so we had to zigzag, sometimes going almost back upon our own track. We did not do this so often as we should have done if we had had more time."

"But how did you know which way to go, Seth," Hubert asked.

"We went by the stars," Seth said. "It was easier than it would have been by day, for when the sun's right overhead, it ain't a very straightforward matter to know how you are going; but there would be no difficulty then to scouts like Rube and me. Well, we had run, maybe, an hour and a quarter when we heard a faint, short bark far behind."

'The brute is on our trail,' Rube said; 'they haven't given us so much start as I looked for. Another half-hour and he will be at our heels sure enough.'

I felt this was true, and felt very bad-like for a bit. In another quarter of an hour the bark was a good bit nearer, and we couldn't go no faster than we were going. All of a sudden I said to Rube, 'Rube, I've heard them dogs lose their smell if they taste blood. Let's try it; it's our only chance. Here, give me a cut in the arm, I can spare it better than you can; you lost a lot to-night from that cut.'

We stopped a minute. I tore off the sleeve of my hunting shirt, and then Rube gave me a bit of a cut on the arm. I let the blood run till the sleeve was soaked and dripping, then Rube tore off a strip from his shirt and bandaged my arm up tight. We rolled the sleeve in a ball and threw it down, then took a turn, made a zigzag or two to puzzle the brute, and then went on our line again. For another ten minutes we could hear the barking get nearer and nearer, and then it stopped all of a sudden. On we went, and it was half an hour again before we heard it, and then it was a long way off.

'I expect we're all right now, Seth,' Rube said.

'I guess we are,' I said; 'but the sooner we strike water the better I shall be pleased.'

It was nigh another half-hour, and we were both pretty nigh done, when we came upon the stream, and the dog couldn't have been more than a mile off. It was a bit of a thing five or six yards wide, and a foot or two deep in the middle.

'Which way?' says Rube. 'Up's our nearest way, so we had better go down.'

'No, no,' says I; 'they're sure to suspect that we shall try the wrong course to throw them off, so let's take the right.'

Without another word up stream we went, as hard as we could run. In a few minutes we heard the dog stop barking, when we might have been half a mile up stream.

'We must get out of this, Rube,' I said. 'Whichever way they try with the dog, they are safe to send horsemen both ways.'

'Which side shall we get out, Seth?'

'It don't matter,' I said; 'it's all a chance which side they take the dog. Let's take our own side.'

Out we got; and we hadn't ran a quarter of a mile before we heard a tramping of horses coming along by the stream. We stopped to listen, for we knew if they had the dog with them, and if he was on our side of the river, we were as good as dead.

'If they take the trail, Seth,' Rube said, 'it's all up with us. Don't let's run any more. We are men enough to shoot the four first who come up, and I only hope one of them may be El Zeres; that'll leave us a pistol each, and we will keep them for ourselves. Better do that, by a long way, than be pulled to pieces with hot pincers.'

'A long way, Rube,' I said. 'That's agreed, then. When I give the word, put the barrel against your eye and fire; that's a pretty safe shot.'

As the Mexicans got to the place where we had got out, we stopped and held our breath. There was no pause--on they went; another minute, and we felt certain they had passed the spot.

'Saved, by thunder!' Rube said; and we turned and went off at a steady trot that we could keep up for hours. 'How long shall we get, do you think, Seth?'

'That all depends how long they follow down stream. They can't tell how far we are ahead. I should think they will go two miles down; then they will cross the stream and come back; and if they don't happen to be on the right side of the stream as they pass where we got out, they will go up another two or three miles, and near as much down, before they strike the trail. We're pretty safe of half an hour's start, and we might get, if we're lucky, near an hour. We ain't safe yet, Rube, by a long way. It's near thirty miles from Pepita's to the camp. We've come sixteen of it good--eighteen I should say; we have got another twelve to the road, and we ain't safe then. No; our only chance is to come across a hacienda and get horses. There are a good many scattered about; but it's so dark we might pass within fifty yards and not see it. There won't be a streak of daylight till four, and it ain't two yet.'

'Not far off, Seth.' By this time we had got our wind again, and quickened up into a fast swing; but our work had told on us, and we couldn't have gone much over seven miles an hour. Several times, as we went on, we could hear a trampling in the dark, and knew that we had scared some horses; but though we had a lasso we had brought with us, we might as well have tried to catch a bird with it. In an hour we heard the dog again, but it was a long way behind. There was nothing for it now but hard running, and we were still seven miles from the road, and even that didn't mean safety. I began to think we were going to lose the race, after all. In another quarter of an hour we stopped suddenly.

'Thunder!' said Rube; 'what's that?' Some animal, that had been lying down, got up just in front of us.

'It's a horse! Your lasso, Rube!' Rube, however, had made a tremendous rush forward, and, before the animal could stretch himself into a gallop, had got close, and grasped him by the mane.

'It's no go,' Rube said, as the horse made a step forward; 'he's an old un, dead lame.'

'Don't leave go, Rube,' I said. 'He'll do for our turn.' He was a miserable old beast, but I felt that he would do as well as the best horse in the world for us. Rube saw my meaning and in a minute we were both astride on his back. He tottered, and I thought he'd have gone down on his head. Kicking weren't of no good; so I out with my knife and gave him a prod, and off we went. It weren't far, some two hundred yards or so, but it was the way I wanted him, right across the line we were going. Then down he tumbled.

'All right,' said I. 'You've done your work, old man; but you mustn't lay here, or they may light upon you and guess what's been up.'

So we lugged him on to his feet, gave him another prod, which sent him limping off; and on we went on our course, sure that we were at last safe, for we had thrown the bloodhound altogether off our trail. For a mile or so we kept right away from our course, for fear that they should keep straight on, and, missing the scent, lead the dog across the trail, and so pick it up again; then we turned and made straight for the road.

'I don't think, Rube,' I said after awhile, 'that we shall strike the road far off where we left it at Pepita's.'

'No, I expect not, Seth. We had better bear a little more to the south, for they will most likely make for Pepita's, and day will soon be breaking now.'

'We'd better not strike the road at all, Rube; likely enough, they will follow it down for a few miles in hopes of picking us up.'

'I hope they will,' Rube said; 'and I expect so. Won't it be a lark, just?'

'What do you mean, Rube?'

'Mean? Why, didn't the Cap tell us to leave San Miguel before daybreak, and to ride to meet him? It warn't likely that he meant us to ride more than ten miles or so; so that he will be within that distance of San Miguel by an hour after daybreak, and will be at Pepita's half an hour later. If them fellows ride on, they are safe to fall into as nice a trap as--'

'Jehoshophat!' said I. 'You're right, Rube. Let's make tracks. It can't be more than another four or five miles to the road, and day will break in half an hour.'

'How strong do you reckon them, Seth?'

'Fifty or sixty,' said I, 'by the regular sound of the horses.'

'That's about what I guessed,' Rube said. 'There are forty of our chaps, and they will be fresh. We'll give 'em goss.'

"We had now long ceased to hear the baying of the dog, which had been most unpleasantly clear when we got off the old hoss that had done us such a good turn. We made sure, too, that we were well ahead, for they would likely wait an hour in trying to pick up the trail again. Daylight came at last; and when it was light enough to see we stopped and took a look from a slight rise, and there, across the plain, we could see the road just where we expected. Nothing was moving upon it, nor, looking back, could we see any sign of the Mexicans. Away to the left, a mile or so, we could see a clump of trees, and something like the roof of a house among them. This, we had no doubt, was Pepita's. About a mile down the road the other way was a biggish wood, through which the road ran."

'Let's make for that wood, Rube, and wait; the Cap will be up in another half-hour, and it ain't likely the Mexicans will be along much before that. They're likely to stop for a drink at Pepita's.'

In another ten minutes we were in shelter in the wood, taking care not to get upon the road, in case the Mexicans should come along with the hound before our men. We hadn't been there twenty minutes before we both heard a trampling of horses; but it was a minute or two more before we could decide which way they were coming. At last, to our great comfort, we found it was the right way. Just before they came up I had an idea I caught a sound from the other way, but I couldn't have sworn to it. We lay till the troop came fairly up, as it might be another party of Mexicans; but it was all right, and we jumped out, with a cheer, into the middle of them. Mighty surprised they were to see us, on foot, and all dust and sweat. Rube's face, too, was tied up; and altogether we didn't look quite ourselves. They all began to talk at once; but I held up my hand urgent, and when they saw it was something particular they shut up, and I said to the Cap: 'Don't ask no questions, Cap; I'll tell you all arterwards. El Zeres with about fifty of his men will be here in about three minutes, I reckon. They've ridden thirty miles, and the beasts ain't fresh; so it's your own fault if one gets away.'

The Cap didn't waste a moment in words. He ordered half his men to ride back two hundred yards, and to charge when they heard his whistle; and he and the rest turned off into the wood, which was very thick, and screened 'em from any one passing. Rube and I, not having horses, were no good for a charge; so we went on in the wood, as near as we could guess, halfway between them, so as to be ready to jump out and join in the skrimmage. It all takes some time to tell, but it didn't take two minutes to do, and in another minute we could hear the Mexicans close. On they came: we knew now that they had passed the Cap, and we clutched our rifles tight and peered out through the leaves. On they came, and we could see El Zeres riding first, with the bloodhound trotting along by the side of his horse. Just as he was opposite we heard a loud, shrill whistle, and the Mexicans halted with a look of uneasiness. They weren't left to wonder long, for in a moment there was a trampling of horses, and down came our fellows on both sides of them. Just before they got up we stepped forward with our rifles up.

'El Zeres!' Rube shouted, and startled as the Mexican was, he looked round. He had just time to see who it was, when Rube's ball hit him in the head, and down he went as dead as a stone. The hound turned and came right at us with a deep growl of rage. I sent a ball through his chest and rolled him over, and just as I did so our fellows came down upon the Mexicans. It was a fierce fight, for the Mexicans were in a trap, and knew that there was no mercy for them. Rube and I sprang out and paid a good many of 'em off for the scare they had given us. We wiped them right out to the last man, losing only six ourselves. I don't know as ever I see a better skrimmage while it lasted. After it was over Rube and I mounted two of their horses, and rode on with the rest of them to San Miguel; but before we started off we told our story to the Cap, and he sent a couple of men back with a dispatch to the general, asking for five hundred men to destroy El Zeres' band at a blow. We stopped at Pepita's, and I never see a girl have a much worse scare than we gave her. She made sure it was El Zeres, and came running out to see if he had caught us; and when she found that she had fallen into the hands of the Rangers, and that we were among them, she was as white as a shirt in a minute. She was plucky enough, though; for as soon as she could get her tongue she cursed us like a wild woman. I expect she made sure we should have shot her for her treachery--and a good many of our bands would have done so right on end--but the Rangers never touched women. However, she warn't to go scot free; so we got fire, and set the house and stable in a blaze.

As we rode off Rube shouted out, 'If you change your mind again about coming with me to Missouri, you just drop me a line, Pepita.'

"I thought, as I looked at her, it was lucky for Rube she hadn't a rifle in her hand; she'd have shot him if she had been hung for it a minute afterward. We rode on to San Miguel, took Colonel Cabra prisoner, with his papers, and sent him back under an escort. At dusk the same day we got on our horses and rode back to where Pepita's house had stood, and where our captain expected the troops he had sent for. In half an hour they came up. They had a couple of hours to rest their horses, and then Rube and I led them straight to the Mexican camp. No doubt they heard us coming when we were close, but made sure it was El Zeres, and so didn't disturb themselves; and it warn't till we had wheeled round and fairly surrounded them that they smelt a rat. But it was too late then, for in another minute we were down upon them, and I don't believe twenty out of the whole lot got away. It was, altogether, one of the most successful businesses in the whole war. And I think that's about all the story."

"Oh, thank you very much, Seth. It is a most exciting story. And what became of Rube?"

"Rube married a year after we got back to the States, and took up a clearing and settled down. It was then I felt lonesome, and made up my mind to go south for awhile. I promised Rube that I would go and settle down by him after a bit, and I've concluded that it's about time to do so. I've saved a few hundred dollars out here, and I am going to start to-morrow morning at daybreak to catch the steamer at Rosario. I shall go up straight from Buenos Ayres to New Orleans, and a steamer will take me up the river in three days to Rube's location. Good-by, all of you. I told your father this afternoon."

There was a hearty leave-taking, and many expressions of regret at his leaving; and after a shake of the hand, and many good wishes, the young Hardys went up to the house, really sorry to part with their Yankee friend.

CHAPTER VIII.
FARM WORK AND AMUSEMENTS.

Although but two months had elapsed since the ground was plowed up and planted, the progress made by the crop of maize and pumpkins was surprising: the former, especially, was now nearly six feet high. This rapid growth was the result of the extreme fertility of the virgin soil, aided by the late abundant supply of water, and the heat of the sun. The maize had given them all a great deal to do; for when it was about six inches high it had to be thinned out so that the plants were nine or ten inches apart. This had been done by the united strength of the party, Mr. Hardy and the boys working for two hours each morning, and as much in the evening. The girls also had assisted, and the peons had worked the whole day, except from eleven to three, when the heat was too great even for them. Many hands make light work, and in consequence the whole ground under maize cultivation was thinned in little over a week. Latterly the maize had grown so fast that the boys declared they could almost see it grow, and at the end of two months after sowing it was all in flower. The maize, or Indian corn, strongly resembles water rushes in appearance, and the feathery blossom also resembles that of the rush. Indian corn forms the main article of food in South America, and in all but the Northern States of North America. It is equally useful and common in India, and in other tropical countries.

Scarcely less is it used in Italy, and other parts of southern Europe. It was first introduced into Europe from the East by the great family of Polenta, who ruled the important town of Ravenna for nearly two hundred years. Ground maize is still called Polenta throughout Italy; and the great family will live in the name of the useful cereal they introduced when all memory of their warlike deeds is lost except to the learned.

One evening when Mr. Hardy, with his wife and children, was strolling down in the cool of the evening to look with pleasure upon the bright green of their healthy and valuable crops, Hubert said:

"Isn't Indian corn, papa, the great yellow heads covered with grain-like beads one sees in corn-dealers' shops in England?"

"Yes, Hubert."

"Well, if that is so, I cannot make out how those long delicate stems can bear the weight. They bend over like corn to every puff of wind. It does not seem possible that they could bear a quarter of the weight of their heavy yellow heads."

"Nor could they, Hubert; but nature has made a wise and very extraordinary provision for this difficulty. All other plants and trees with which I am acquainted have their fruits or seeds where the blossom before grew. In maize it is placed in an entirely different part of the plant. In a very short time you will see--indeed you may see now in most of the plants--the stalk begin to thicken at a foot or eighteen inches from the ground, and in a little time it will burst; and the head of maize, so enveloped in leaves that it looks a mere bunch of them, will come forth. It will for a time grow larger and larger, and then the plant will wither and die down to the place from which the head springs. The part that remains will dry up until the field appears covered with dead stumps, with bunches of dead leaves at the top. Then it is ready for the harvest,"

"What a strange plant, papa! I quite long for the time when the heads will come out. What are you going to plant upon that bit of land you have got ready for sowing now? It is about six acres."

"I mean to plant cotton there, Hubert. I have sent to Buenos Ayres for seeds of what are called Carolina Upland, and I expect them here in a few days."

"But it takes a great deal of labor, does it not, papa?"

"The calculation in the Northern States, Hubert, is that one man can cultivate eight acres of cotton, assisted by his wife and children at certain periods; and that as his labor is not always required, he can with his family cultivate another eight or ten acres of other produce; so that about half of a peon's labor will be required, and in the hoeing and picking time we can all help."

"Is not machinery required to separate the seeds from the cotton?" Charley asked.

"It is not absolutely necessary, Charley, although it is of course economical when the cultivation is carried on upon a large scale. The variety I am going to try is sometimes called 'bowed' Carolina, because it used to be cleaned by placing it upon a number of strings stretched very tight, which were struck with a sort of bow, and the vibration caused the seed to separate from the cotton. I have a drawing of one of these contrivances in a book up at the house, and when the time comes you fellows shall make me one. It will be work for us to do indoors when the weather is too hot to be out. Of course if I find that it succeeds, and pays well, I shall take on more hands, get proper machinery, and extend the cultivation. I intend to plant the rows rather wide apart, so as to use the light plow with the ridge boards between them, instead of hoeing, to save labor."

"How much cotton do they get from an acre?" Mrs. Hardy asked.

"In the Southern States they expect twelve hundred pounds upon new ground--that is, twelve hundred pounds of pods, which make about three hundred of cleaned cotton. When I have got the cotton fairly in the ground I mean to plant an acre or two of tobacco, and the same quantity of sugar cane, as an experiment. But before I do that we must make a garden up at the house: that is a really urgent need."

"Couldn't we grow rice here, papa?"

"No doubt we could, Hubert; but I do not mean to try it. To succeed with rice, we should have to keep the ground on which it grew in a state of swamp, which would be very unhealthy. That is why I do not irrigate the fields oftener than is absolutely necessary. Anything approaching swampy, or even wet lands, in a climate like this, would be almost certain to breed malaria. Besides, we should be eaten alive by mosquitoes. No, I shall certainly not try rice. Other tropical productions I shall some day give a trial to. Ginger, vanilla, and other things would no doubt flourish here. I do not believe that any of them would give an extraordinary rate of profit, for though land is cheap, labor is scarce. Still it would be interesting, and would cause a little variety and amusement in our work, which is always an important point, and no doubt there would be generally some profit, though occasionally we may make a total failure."

Very often at daybreak the girls would go down with their brothers to the river, and watch the waterfowl on its surface; they were so amusing as they dabbled and played in the water, unsuspicious of danger. Their favorites, though, were the beautiful scarlet flamingoes, with their slender legs, and their long, graceful necks, and whose great employment seemed to be to stand quiet in the water, where it was only two or three inches deep, and to preen their glossy red feathers. Over and over again the girls wished that they could get a few waterfowl, especially flamingoes, to tame them, in order that they might swim on the dam pond and come and be fed; and the boys had several talks with each other as to the most practicable way of capturing some of them. At last they thought of making a sort of enclosure of light boughs, with an entrance into which birds could easily pass, but through which they could not easily return, and to scatter grain up to and into the enclosure, to entice the birds to enter. On explaining this plan to Mr. Hardy, he said that he had no doubt that it would succeed in capturing birds, but that when caught it would be impossible to tame full-grown wild-fowl, and that the only plan was to find their nests, and take the eggs or very young birds. This they determined to do; and as the bushes close to the river were too thick to permit an examination from the shore, they started one morning early, and, going down to the river, entered it, and waded along for a considerable distance. They discovered two swans' nests, and several of different descriptions of ducks. In some the birds were sitting upon their eggs, in others the young brood were just hatched, and scuttled away into the bushes with the parent birds upon being disturbed.

Charley and Hubert made no remark at breakfast upon the success of their expedition; but when Charley went two days after to Rosario, he procured from Mr. Percy, who kept a quantity of chickens, two sitting hens. These were placed with their nests in the bullock cart in a hamper; and Mrs. Hardy, who had no idea of the purpose to which they were to be put, was quite pleased, on their arrival at Mount Pleasant, at this addition to the henhouse. Indeed it had been long agreed that they would keep hens as soon as the maize was ripe. The next morning the boys went again, and brought back twenty eggs of various kinds of wild duck, including four swans' eggs--to obtain which they had to shoot the parent birds, which furnished the larder for days--which they placed under the hens in place of their own eggs, and then took the girls in triumph to see this commencement of their tame duck project. The little girls were delighted, and it was an immense amusement to them to go down constantly to see if the eggs were hatched, as of course no one could tell how long they had been sat upon previous to being taken. They had remarked that four of the eggs were much larger than the others, but had no idea that they were swans'. In the course of a few days six of the young ducklings were hatched, and the hens were both so unhappy at their difficulty of continuing to sit while they had the care of their young ones on their mind, that one hen and all the little ones were removed to a distance from the other's nest, and the whole of the eggs were put under the remaining hen. The four swans and five more ducks were safely hatched, when the hen refused to sit longer, and the remaining eggs were lost. Now that the swans were safely hatched, the boys told their sisters what they really were, and their delight was extreme.

In a few days they were all taken down to the dam, and soon found their way into the water, to the great distress of their foster-mother, who was obliged to stand upon the bank calling in vain till the little ones chose to come ashore. A hencoop was soon knocked together from an old box, and this was placed near the dam, and ere long the hens became accustomed to the fancy of their charges for the water, and would walk about picking up insects while the little ones swam about on the pond. Twice a day the girls went down to feed them with grain and bits of boiled pumpkin--for the pumpkins soon began to come into bearing--and the ducklings and cygnets, which last were at present but little larger than the others, would swim rapidly toward them when they saw them, and would feed greedily out of their hands.

It was not for some weeks later that the desire for young flamingoes was gratified. The boys had been out for a ride, and coming upon the river where it was wide, with flat sandy banks, round which the timber grew, they determined to tie up their, horses and enter the stream, to see if they could get some more eggs. With some difficulty they made their way through the bushes, and, getting into the water, waded along until a turn in the river brought them in sight of the flat bank. There were some twenty or thirty flamingoes upon it, for these birds are very gregarious. Some were standing in the water as usual, but the boys could not make out what some of the others were doing. On the flat shore were several heaps of earth, and across them some of the birds were apparently sitting with one leg straddling out each side. So comical was their aspect that the boys burst into a laugh, which so scared the flamingoes that they all took flight instantly. The boys now waded up to the spot, and then got ashore to see what these strange heaps were for. To their great delight they found that they were nests, and upon the top of several of them were eight or nine eggs carefully arranged. The legs of the flamingo are so long that the bird is unable to double them up and sit upon his nest in the usual fashion. The hen bird therefore scrapes together a pile of earth, on the top of which she lays her eggs, and then places herself astride to keep them warm. The boys had an argument whether they should take away two nests entire, or whether they should take a few eggs from each nest; but they decided upon the former plan, in order that each of the young broods might be hatched simultaneously. Upon the boys reaching home with their treasure their sisters' delight was unbounded, and the hens were soon placed upon their new charges, and, both being good sitters, took to them without much difficulty.

When the young broods were hatched the girls were greatly disappointed at the appearance of little grayish fluffy balls, instead of the lovely red things they had expected, and were by no means consoled when their father told them that it would be three or four years before they gained their beautiful color. However, they became great pets, and were very droll, with their long legs, and slender necks, and great curved bills. They became extremely tame, and would, after a time, follow the girls about, and stalk up to the house of their own accord to be fed, their food always being placed in water, as they never feed by picking upon the ground, for which, indeed, the peculiar construction of their beak is entirely unfitted. They were perfectly fearless of the dogs, which, on their part, were too well trained to touch them; and their funny way and their extreme tameness were a source of constant amusement to the whole family.

But we must now retrace our steps. After the important work of getting a certain amount of land under cultivation, the next most urgent business was the formation of a garden. The land inside the enclosure round the house was first plowed up, and then dug by hand, the turf being left in front of the house to serve as a lawn. The rest was planted with seeds brought from England--peas, beans, tomatoes, vegetable marrows, cucumbers, melons, and many others, some of which were natives of warm climates, while others were planted in small patches as an experiment. Fortunately, the well supplied an abundance of water, whose only drawback was that, like most water upon the pampas, it had a strong saline taste, which was, until they had become accustomed to it, very disagreeable to the Hardys. As the well had

been dug close to the house on the highest part of the slope, the water was conducted from the pump by small channels all over the garden; and the growth of the
various vegetables was surprising. But long before these could come into bearing a
welcome supply was afforded by the yams and Indian corn. The yams resemble a
sweet potato; and if the Indian corn is gathered green, and the little corns nibbled
off, boiled, and mixed with a little butter, they exactly resemble the most delicate
and delicious young peas.

The young potatoes, too, had come in, so that they had now an abundance of
vegetables, the only point in which they had before been deficient. Their drink
was the mate, which may be termed the national beverage of Paraguay, Brazil,
and the Argentine Republic. It is made from the leaves of the mate Yule, a plant
which grows in Paraguay and Brazil. The natives generally drink it without sugar
or milk, sucking it up from the vessel in which it is made through a small tube. It is,
however, greatly improved by the addition of sugar and milk, or, better still, cream.
This greatly softens the bitter taste which distinguishes it. None of the party liked
it at first; but as they were assured by those in the country that they would like it
when they became accustomed to it, they persevered, and after a time all came to
prefer it even to tea.

Occasionally one or other of the boys went over to Rosario with the cart, and
Mr. Hardy bought some hundreds of young fruit trees--apple, pear, plum, apricot,
and peach--some of which were planted in the garden at the sides and in rear of the
house, others in the open beyond and round it; a light fence with one wire being
put up to keep the cattle from trespassing. Clumps of young palms, bananas, and
other tropical trees and shrubs were also planted about for the future adornment
of the place. Fences were erected round the cultivated ground, and an enclosure
was made, into which the cattle were driven at night. These fences were easily
and cheaply made. The wire cost little more at Rosario than it would have done in
England, and the chief trouble was bringing the posts, which were made of algaroba
wood, from the town. This wood grows abundantly upon the upper river, and is
there cut down and floated in great rafts down to Rosario. It is a tough wood, which
splits readily, and is therefore admirably suited for posts. It is of a reddish color, and
has a pretty grain when polished. All the furniture was made of it; and this, from
constant rubbing by Sarah and the girls, now shone brightly, and had a very good

effect.

The ceilings were now put to the rooms, which were greatly improved in appearance thereby, and the difference in temperature was very marked. A very short time after the capture of the wild fowls' eggs it was unanimously agreed that chickens were indispensable, and a large hen-house was accordingly built at a short distance from the dam, as it was considered as well not to have any buildings, with the exception of the men's hut, near the house. The hen-house was quickly built, as it was a mere framework covered with felt, with bars across it for the fowls to perch upon.

The floor was made, as that of the house had been, of lime and clay beaten hard; and a small cut was made to the dam, by which water could, at will, be turned over the floor to keep it clean and neat. The next time the cart went to Rosario it brought back fifty fowls, which had only cost a few dollars. Henceforth eggs and omelets became a regular part of the breakfast, and the puddings were notably improved.

The chickens gave very little trouble, as they foraged about for themselves, finding an abundance of insects everywhere, and getting in addition a few pots of Indian corn every morning. Maud and Ethel took it by turns, week about, to take charge of the hen-house; and a great pleasure was it to them to watch the numerous broods of young chickens, and to hunt up the eggs which, in spite of the nests temptingly prepared for them, the hens would frequently persist in laying in nests of their own in the long grass.

The hens had, however, a numerous foe, who were a great trouble to their young mistresses. These were the skunks, an animal of the weasel tribe, but much resembling squirrels in appearance, and possessing a most abominable smell; so much so that the dogs, who would attack almost anything, would run away from them. They were at first exceedingly common, and created terrible depredations among the hens. The girls were in despair, and called in their brothers to their assistance. The boys shot a good many, for the animals were very tame and fearless; but their number was so great that this method of destruction was of slight avail. They then prepared traps of various kinds--some made by an elastic stick bent down, with a noose at the end, placed at a small entrance left purposely in the hen-house, so that, when the skunk was about to enter, he touched a spring, and the stick released, flew into the air carrying the animal with it with the noose round its neck;

other traps let fall a heavy piece of wood, which crushed the invader; and in these ways the skunks were pretty well got rid of, the most unpleasant work being the removal of the body from the trap. This had to be effected by taking hold of it with two pieces of wood, for the odor was so powerful that if the body was touched the smell would remain on the hands for days.

They had now added another species of domestic animal to their stock, but this was the boys' charge. Mr. Hardy, when the pumpkins began to ripen, bought six pigs. They were of little trouble, for although a sty was built for them, they were allowed to wander about as they pleased by day, another wire being added to the fence round the cultivated land, to keep them from trespassing. The crop of pumpkins was enormous; and Mr. Hardy determined that no pigs should be killed for eighteen months, by which time, as these animals increase rapidly, there would be quite a large herd of them.

Although an immense deal of hard work was got through during the four months which followed the completion of the house and the arrival of Mrs. Hardy and her daughters, it must not be supposed that it was not mingled with plenty of relaxation and amusement.

There were few days when one or other of the boys did not go out with his gun for an hour either before sunrise or after sunset, seldom failing to bring home a wild fowl or two of some kind or other. And sometimes of an afternoon they would go out for a ride with their sisters, and have a chase after an ostrich, or a run after the gray foxes, which abounded, and were very destructive among the young lambs. Once or twice during these rides the boys brought a puma to bay; but as they always carried a ball in one of their barrels, with these and their revolvers they soon dispatched their unwelcome visitors. They had contrived an apparatus with straps and a sort of little pocket, in which the muzzle of the gun went, so that it hung from the saddle down in front of their leg; the stock of the gun being secured by a strap against the pommel of the saddle, at the other side of which was their revolver holster. This was an inconvenient way of carrying the gun in some respects, as the strap had to be unfastened to get at it, and the chance of a shot thereby lost; but they considered it preferable to the mode they had at first adopted, of riding with their guns slung behind them. This they gave up, because, with the utmost care, they occasionally got a fall, when galloping, from the armadillo holes, and the shock was greatly increased from the weight of the gun, besides the risk, to any one riding near, of the gun exploding. When riding quietly, and upon the lookout for game, they carried the gun in readiness upon their arms.

It was after one of these rides, when Hubert had brought down with a bullet a swan which was making for his bed in the river, that Maud said at tea:

"I wish we could shoot too; it would be a great amusement, and I should enjoy my rides a good deal more if I knew that I could take a shot in case a lion or a deer came out."

"Well, girls," Mr. Hardy said, "I had always intended that you should learn to shoot. We have had so much to do since you came here that I did not think of it, and I had besides intended to wait until one of you expressed a desire to learn. I brought out three light rook-shooting rifles on purpose for you and your mamma, and you can begin to-morrow morning if you like."

"Oh, thank you, papa, thank you very, very much; that will be nice!" both the girls exclaimed, clapping their hands in their excitement.

"And what do you say, mamma?" Mr. Hardy asked.

"No, thank you," Mrs. Hardy said; "I have plenty to do, and, with a husband and two sons and two daughters to defend me, I do not consider that it is essential. But I think that it will be a nice amusement for the girls."

And so next morning, and nearly every morning afterward, the girls practiced with the light rifle at a mark, until in time their hands became so steady that at short distances of sixty or seventy yards they could beat their brothers, who were both really good shots. This was principally owing to the fact that the charge of powder used in these rifles was so small that there was scarcely any recoil to disturb the aim. It was some time before they could manage to hit anything flying; but they were very proud one evening when, having been out late with the boys, a fat goose came along overhead, and the girls firing simultaneously, he fell with both bullets in his body. After this they, too, carried their rifles out with them during their rides.

Any one who had known Maud and Ethel Hardy at home would have scarcely recognized them now in the sunburnt-looking lassies, who sat upon their horses as if they had never known any other seat in their lives. Their dress, too, would have been most curious to English eyes. They wore wide straw hats, with a white scarf wound round the top to keep off the heat. Their dresses were very short, and made of brown holland, with a garibaldi of blue-colored flannel. They wore red flannel knickerbockers, and gaiters coming up above the knee, of a very soft, flexible leather, made of deer's skin. These gaiters were an absolute necessity, for the place literally swarmed with snakes, and they constantly found them in the garden when going out to gather vegetables. Most of these snakes were harmless; but as some of them were very deadly, the protection of the gaiters was quite necessary. The girls did not like them at first, especially as their, brothers could not help joking them a little, and Hubert said that they reminded him of two yellow-legged partridges. However, they soon became accustomed to them, and felt so much more comfortable about snakes afterward that they would not have given them up upon any account. The boys always wore high boots for the same reason, and had no fear whatever of the snakes; but Mr. Hardy insisted that each of them should always carry in a small inner pocket of their coats a phial of spirits of ammonia, a small surgical knife, and a piece of whipcord; the same articles being always kept in readiness at the house. His instructions were, that in case of a bite they should first suck the wound, then tie the whipcord round the limb above the place bitten, and that they should then cut deeply into the wound crossways, open it as much as possible, and pour in some spirits of ammonia; that they should then pour the rest of the ammonia into their water-bottle, which they always carried slung over their shoulders, and should drink it off. If these directions were instantly and thoroughly carried out, Mr. Hardy had little fear that the bite, even of the deadliest snake, would prove fatal. In addition he ordered that in case of their being near home they should, upon their arrival, be made to drink raw spirits until they could not stand, and that, if they were some distance away from home, and were together, the one bitten should lie down while the other galloped at full speed to take back a bottle of brandy, and order assistance to be sent. This remedy is well known throughout India. Any one bitten by a poisonous snake is made to drink spirits, which he is able to do without being affected by them, to an extraordinary extent; a man who at ordinary times could scarcely take a strong tumbler of spirits and water, being able, when bitten, to drink a bottle of pure brandy without being in the least affected by it. When the spirit does at last begin to take effect, and the patient shows signs of drunkenness, he is considered to be safe, the poison of the spirit having overcome the poison of the snake.

CHAPTER IX.
NEIGHBORLY VISITS AND ADVICE.

It must not be supposed that the Hardys, during the whole of this time, were leading a perfectly solitary life. Upon the contrary, they had a great deal of sociable companionship. Within a range of ten miles there were no less than four estancias owned by Englishmen, besides that of their first friend Mr. Percy. A ride of twenty miles is thought nothing of out on the pampas. The estate immediately to the rear of their own was owned by Senor Jaqueras, a native. The tract upon the east of his property was owned by three young Englishmen, whose names were Herries, Cooper, and Farquhar. They had all been in the army, but had sold out, and agreed to come out and settle together.

The southwestern corner of their property came down to the river exactly opposite the part where the north-eastern corner of Mount Pleasant touched it: their house was situated about four miles from the Hardys. To the west of Senor Jaqueras, the estate was owned by two Scotchmen, brothers of the name of Jamieson: their estancia was nine miles distant. In the rear of the estate of Senor Jaqueras, and next to that of Mr. Percy, were the properties of Messrs. Williams and Markham: they were both about ten miles from Mount Pleasant. These gentlemen had all ridden over to call upon the newcomers within a very few days of Mr. Hardy's first arrival, and had offered any help in their power.

The Hardys were much pleased with their visitors, who were all young men, with the frank, hearty manner natural to men free from the restraints of civilized life. The visits had been returned in a short time, and then for awhile all communication with the more distant visitors had ceased, for the Hardys were too busy to spare time upon distant rides. One or other of the party at Canterbury, as the three Englishmen had called their estancia, very frequently dropped in for a talk, and Mr. Hardy and the boys often rode over there when work was done, Canterbury was also a young settlement--only four or five months, indeed, older than Mount Pleasant--so that its owners, like themselves, had their hands full of work; but sometimes, when they knew that the Hardys were particularly hard at work, one or two of them would come over at daybreak and give their assistance. During the final week's work, especially just before Mrs. Hardy's arrival, all three came over and lent their aid, as did the Jamiesons.

As soon as Mrs. Hardy had arrived all their neighbors came over to call, and a very friendly intercourse was quickly established between them. As there was no spare bedroom at Mount Pleasant, some hammocks were made, and hooks were put into the sitting-room walls, so that the hammocks could be slung at night and taken down in the morning. The English party always rode back to Canterbury, as the distance was so short, and the Jamiesons generally did the same; but Messrs. Percy, Williams, and Markham usually came over in the afternoon, and rode back again next morning.

When the press of work was over the boys and their sisters often cantered over to Canterbury to tea, and sometimes, but more seldom, to the Jamiesons' estancia. The light-hearted young Englishmen were naturally more to their fancy than the quiet and thoughtful Scotchmen. The latter were, however, greatly esteemed by Mr. and Mrs. Hardy, who perceived in them a fund of quiet good sense and earnestness.

Upon Sunday morning Mr. Hardy had service, and to this the whole of their friends generally came. It was held early, so that the Jamiesons and the Englishmen could ride back to their homes before the heat of the day, the other three remaining to dine, and returning in the cool of the evening. Canterbury was entirely a sheep and cattle farm. The owners had five thousand sheep, and some hundreds of cattle; but they had comparatively a good deal of time upon their hands, as stock and sheep farming does not require so much personal care and supervision as must be bestowed upon agricultural farms. The Jamiesons, on the contrary, were entirely occupied in tillage: they had no sheep, and only a few head of cattle.

Mr. Hardy was remarking upon this one day to Mr. Percy, who replied, "Ah, the poor fellows are very unfortunate. They brought out a fair capital, and had as large a stock of sheep and cattle as the Canterbury party have. About six months, however, before you arrived--yes, it's just a year now--the Indians swept down upon them, and carried off every animal they had. They attacked the house, but the Jamiesons defended themselves well; and the Indians were anxious to get off with their booty, and so they beat a retreat. Pursuit was hopeless; every horse had been driven off, and they had to walk six miles to the next hacienda to give the news; and long before a party could be got together the Indians were beyond the possibility of pursuit. Two or three hundred sheep and a dozen or two of the bullocks found their way back, and these and their land was all that remained to the Jamiesons of their capital, for they had invested all they had in their stock. However, they looked affairs manfully in the face, sold their animals, bought a couple of plows and draught bullocks, hired a peon or two, and set to work with a will. They will get on but slowly for a time; but I have no doubt that they will do well in the course of a few years. Men with their pluck and perseverance are certain to get on. That puts me in mind, Hardy, of a matter upon which I had intended to speak to you. We are just getting now to the time of the year when Indian attacks are most likely to take place. Sometimes they are quiet for a year or two, then they are very trouble-some again. Five or six years ago, just after I first came out, we had terrible times with them. Vast numbers of cattle were driven off: the sheep they less seldom take, because they cannot travel so fast, but they do drive them off sometimes. A good many shepherds were killed, and two or three estancias captured and burned, and the inmates murdered. You are now the furthest settler, and consequently the most exposed. Your estancia is strong and well built, and you are all well armed and good shots. You are, I think, in that respect safe, except from sudden surprise. The dogs are sure to give an alarm; still I should sleep with everything in readiness."

"Thank you, Percy; I shall take your advice. I expected it from what I had heard when I bought the place; but from hearing nothing of Indians all this time, I had almost forgotten it. I will prepare for defense without the loss of a day. The house has only one vulnerable point--the doors and shutters. I will measure them this af-ternoon, and will get you to take over a letter and forward it to Rosario by the first opportunity, for some sheets of thin iron to cover them with."

Mr. Percy promised to forward the letter the very next day by a bullock-cart he was sending in, and also that the same cart should bring them back. He said that if a conveyance were sent over in two days' time for them they would be in readiness at his place.

This conversation caused Mr. Hardy great uneasiness. It was a possibility he had been quite prepared for; but he could not feel that the danger was really at hand without an anxious feeling. His thousand sheep had cost him twelve hundred and fifty dollars, and his cattle as much more. The lambing season had come and gone, and the flock of sheep had doubled in number. The cattle, too, had greatly increased, and the sheep were nearly ready for shearing. Altogether the value of the stock was over five thousand dollars. The loss would not be absolute ruin, as he had still three thousand dollars of his original capital in the bank at Buenos Ayres; but it would be a very serious loss.

Mr. Hardy had been alone with Mr. Percy when the conversation took place; but he determined at once to take the boys into his entire confidence. He therefore called to them to come out for a stroll down to the dam, and told them word for word what Mr. Percy had related to him.

Charley's eyes brightened at the thought of the excitement of a fight with Indians, for which when in England, eighteen months before, he had longed; and his fingers tightened upon his gun as he said, "All right, papa, let them come." Hubert's face grew a little paler, for he was not naturally of so plucky or pugnacious a disposition as his brother. However, he only said, "Well, papa, if they do come we shall all do our best."

"I am sure you will, my boy," said his father kindly. "But there is no fear if it comes to fighting. We three with our arms can thrash a hundred of them. What I am thinking of is our cattle, and not ourselves. We will take good care against a sudden surprise; and it's more than a whole tribe could do to take Mount Pleasant if we are prepared."

"Do you mean to tell mamma and the girls, papa?"

"I mean to tell them that it is necessary for a time to be on their guard, that the girls are on no account to venture to ride out alone, and that they must not stir out of the enclosure even as far as the hen-house, without first of all going up to the top of the lookout to see that all is clear. We must see that, in future, the sheep and cattle and horses are all driven at night into their wire enclosures--we have not been very particular about the cattle lately--and that the gates are fastened and padlocked at night. It will puzzle them to get them out. Our own three horses I will have in future kept within our own enclosure, so that they may be always at hand, night or day. I bought them with a special eye to Indians; they are all remarkably fast; and whether we run away or pursue, can be relied on. And now, boys, come up to the house, and I will open the mysterious box."

The box of which Mr. Hardy spoke was a long case, which had never been opened since their arrival. No entreaties of his children could induce Mr. Hardy to say what were its contents, and the young ones had often wondered and puzzled over what they could be. It had come, therefore, to be known in the family as the mysterious box.

With greatly excited curiosity the boys now walked toward the house; but there was a slight delay, for as they approached Maud and Ethel came running to meet them.

"Is anything the matter with the dam, papa? We have been watching you having such a long talk with the boys. What is it all about?"

Mr. Hardy now told them as much as he thought proper of the state of things, and gave them their instructions. The girls, who had no idea there was any real danger, and who had besides an unlimited confidence in their father and brothers, were disposed to look upon It as fun, and Mr. Hardy had to speak quite seriously to be sure that his orders would be strictly attended to. The boys then informed them that the mysterious box was to be opened, and the whole party went up to the house.

The box had been placed in the storeroom on the upper floor of the tower, and the boys took up screwdrivers and hammers to open it. The latter tools were not necessary, as the case was very carefully screwed up; and when the top was taken off it was found that there was an inside case of tin soldered up. As the boys were cutting through this they expressed their opinion that, from the extreme care taken, the contents must be very valuable. Still Mr. Hardy would give no clew; and when the case was finally opened, the astonishment of all was unbounded to find that it contained four dozen large rockets and a dozen blue-lights. One dozen of these rockets were ordinary signal rockets, but the rest were covered with strong tin cases.

"Fireworks!" they all exclaimed in intense surprise. "What have you brought fireworks all this way for, papa?"

"I will tell you, my dears. I knew that the Indians of the pampas were horse Indians, and the idea struck me that as they could never have seen rockets, they would be horribly scared at night by them. rockets, you know, are used in war; and even if the riders are not frightened, it is quite certain that the horses would be horribly alarmed by one or two of these rushing fiery things charging into their midst. I therefore had them specially made for me by a pyrotechnist in London. One dozen, as you see, are ordinary rockets of the largest size; they contain colored balls, which will give out a most brilliant light. One of them thrown into the air, even where we believe any Indians to be, will light up the plain, and give us a fair view of them. The other three dozen are loaded with crackers. As you see, I have had a strong case of tin placed over the ordinary case; and one of them striking a man will certainly knock him off his horse, and probably kill him. The roar, the rush, the train of fire, and finally the explosion and the volley of crackers in their midst would be enough to frighten their horses altogether beyond control. What do you think of my idea?"

"Capital, capital!" they all cried.

"But how, papa," Hubert asked, "will you manage to make your rockets go straight at the Indians? All rockets I ever saw went straight up into the air."

"Yes, Hubert, because they were pointed up. A rocket goes whichever way it is pointed. Rockets in war are fired through a tube, or from a trough. We will use the trough. Set to at once, boys, and make a trough about four feet long, without ends. It must stand on legs high enough to raise it above the level of the wall round the top of the tower. Let there be two legs on the front end, and one leg behind; and this leg behind must have a hinge, so that, when it stands upright, it will be six or eight inches higher than the front, in case we want to fire at anything close at hand. When we want to elevate the head of the rocket to fire at anything at a distance, we pull the hind leg back, so that that end is lower than the front. Put a spike at the end of the leg, to let it have a firm hold on the floor."

Charley thought a moment, and then said: "I think, papa, it would be firmer, and more easily managed, if we made two legs behind, with another one sliding up and down between them, and with holes in it so that it can be pegged up and down as we like."

"That would be certainly better, Charley. Put your idea down upon paper, and let me see exactly what you mean before you begin."

Charley did so, and Mr. Hardy pronounced it to be excellent; and by night the trough was finished, and placed in position at the top of the lookout.

Mr. Hardy, in the course of the evening, explained to his wife that it was possible the Indians might venture to make a dash to carry off some of the cattle, and that, therefore, he had ordered the girls to be on the lookout, and to adopt every precaution upon moving out. To them he made an addition to his former instructions, namely, that not only should they look out before leaving the enclosure, but that, if one went out, the other should go up to the top of the tower every quarter of an hour to see that everything was still clear, and that if both were out, Sarah should do the same. The boys needed no instructions to load their revolving carbines, and the pistols and a double-barreled gun were handed over both to Lopez and Terence, with instructions to carry them always with them. Lopez required no orders on this score. He knew what Indians were, and had a perfect horror of them. Their friends at Canterbury were also put upon their guard, as their estates were also very much exposed. Three days passed over, and then the light iron plates arrived for the door and window shutters. Before they were nailed on large holes were cut in them for firing through, corresponding slits being cut in the woodwork. When they were fastened in their places all felt that Mount Pleasant could defy any number of assailants.

Orders were given to Terence that in case of the dogs giving the alarm at night, the occupants of the hut were to retire at once to the house; to which he replied characteristically:

"Sure, your honor, I suppose I may stop for a bit and pepper the blackguards till they get close to me."

"Not at all, Terence; you are to retire at once to the house. When we are once all together we shall be able to decide, according to the number of the enemy, as to whether we shall sally out and pepper them, or stand upon the defensive."

And so, every one having received their instructions in case of emergency, things went on pretty much as before.

CHAPTER X.
THE LOST CATTLE.

A fortnight passed without the slightest incident or alarm. The rules which Mr. Hardy had laid down were strictly observed. The sheep and cattle were carefully secured at night; two or three of the native dogs were fastened up, down at the fold; one of the mastiffs was kept at the men's hut, while the other's kennel was placed by the house; the retrievers, as usual, sleeping indoors. A flagstaff was erected upon the lookout, with a red flag in readiness to be run up to summon those who might be away on the plain, and a gun was kept loaded to call attention to the signal. The boys, when they went out for their rides, carried their carbines instead of their guns. The girls fulfilled the duties of lookouts, going up every half-hour from daybreak to dusk; and the call of "Sister Anne, do you see horsemen?" was invariably answered in the negative. One day, however, Mr. Hardy had ridden over to Canterbury to arrange with his friends about hiring shearers from Rosario for the united flocks. The boys and Terence were in the fields plowing, at a distance of half a mile from the house, when they were startled by the sound of a gun. Looking round, they saw both the girls standing upon the tower: Maud had just fired the gun, and Ethel was pulling up the flag.

"Be jabers! and the Indians have come at last!" Terence exclaimed, and they all three started at a run. Maud turned round and waved her hand to them, and then she and Ethel continued looking over the plain. At this moment they were joined on the tower by Mrs. Hardy and Sarah.

"It is all right," Charley, who was of an unexcitable temperament, said. "The Indians must be a long way off, or the girls would be waving to us to make haste. Take it easy; we shall want to keep our hands steady."

So they broke from the headlong speed at which they had started into a steady trot, which in five minutes brought them up to the house.

"What is it?" they exclaimed as they gained the top of the tower.

"Oh, dear, oh, dear!" Ethel said. "They have got all the animals."

"And I fear they have killed Gomez and Pedro," Mrs. Hardy added.

It was too evidently true. At a distance of six miles the boys could see a dark mass rapidly retreating, and numerous single specks could be seen hovering round them. Two miles from the house a single horseman was galloping wildly. The girls had already made him out to be Lopez.

The boys and Terence stood speechless with dismay. The Irishman was the first to find his tongue,

"Och, the thundering villains!" he exclaimed; "the heathen thieves! And to think that not one of us was there to give them a bating."

"What will papa say?" Hubert ejaculated.

Charley said nothing, but looked frowningly, with tightly closed lips, after the distant mass, while his hands closed upon his carbine. "How was it, Maud?" he asked at length.

"I was downstairs," Maud said, "when Ethel, who had just gone up, called down, 'Come up, Maud, quickly; I think that something's the matter.' I ran up the steps, and I saw our animals a long way off, nearly four miles, and I saw a black mass of something going along fast toward them from the left. They were rather nearer to us than the cattle were, and were in one of the slopes of the ground, so that they would not have been seen by any one with the cattle; then, as they got quite near the animals, I saw a sudden stir. The beasts began to gallop away, and three black specks--who, I suppose, were the men--separated themselves from them and went off sideways. One seemed to get a start of the other two. These were cut off by the black mass, and I did not see anything more of them. Lopez got away; and though some of the others rode after him for about a mile, they could not overtake him. Directly I saw what it was, I caught up the gun and fired, and Ethel ran up the flag. That's all I saw."

Ethel confirmed her sister's account, merely adding that, seeing the two bodies in the distance, one going very fast toward the other, she suspected that something was wrong, and so called at once to Maud.

The animals were now quite out of sight, and the whole party went down to meet Lopez, who was just riding up to the enclosure. He was very pale, and his horse was covered with foam.

"Are the peons killed, Lopez?" was Mrs. Hardy's first question.

"I do not know, signora; but I should think so. The Indians caught them; I heard a scream," and the man shuddered. "Santa Virgine" --and he crossed himself piously--"what an escape! I will burn twenty pounds of candles upon your altar."

"How was it that you were surprised, Lopez?" Charley asked. "You were so particularly ordered to keep a good lookout."

"Well, Signor Charles, I was keeping a good lookout, and it is lucky that I was. I was further away than I ought to have been--I know that, for the signor told me not to go far; but I knew that the rise that I took them to was the highest in that direction, and that I could see for miles away into the Indian country. So I got out there, and Pedro and Gomez had got the sheep and cattle all well together, and there was no fear of them straying, for the grass there is very good. So the men lay down for their siesta, and I was standing by my horse looking over the campo. Some of the beasts seemed uneasy, and I thought that there must be a lion somewhere about. So I got on my horse, and just as I did so I heard a noise; and looking behind, where I had never dreamed of them, I saw a lot of Indians coming up at full gallop from the hollow. The cattle went off at the same instant; and I gave a shout to the men, and stuck my spurs into Carlos. It was a near touch of it, and they gave me a hard chase for the first mile; but my horse was fresher than theirs, and they gave it up."

"How many Indians were there?" Charley asked.

"I don't know, Signor Charles. It was only those in front that I caught sight of, and I never looked round after I started. Some of them had firearms, for eight or ten of them fired after me as I made off, and the arrow, fell all round me."

"What do you think, girls, about the number?"

The girls were silent, and then Ethel said: "They were all in a lump, Charley. One could not see them separately."

"The lump seemed to be about the size that our cattle do when they are close together at the same distance. Don't you think so, Ethel?" Maud said.

"Yes," Ethel thought that they were.

"Then there must be from a hundred to a hundred and fifty of them," Charley said.

"I wonder what papa will do! One of us had better ride off at once and fetch him."

"I will go," Hubert said, moving away to saddle his horse.

"Stop, Hubert," Charley said; "I think you had better take Lopez's horse. I don't know what papa may make up his mind to do, and it is better to have your horse quite fresh."

Hubert agreed at once, and was mounting, when Maud said: "Wait a moment, Hubert, I will run up to the lookout. I may see papa; it is nearly time for him to be home."

Hubert paused while Maud ran up to the house, and in a minute appeared at the top of the tower. She stood for a moment looking across the stream toward Canterbury, and then held up her hand. "I can see him," she called out. "He is a long way off, but he is coming."

Hubert was about to alight again, when Mrs. Hardy said: "You had better ride to meet your papa, Hubert. He will be very much alarmed when he sees the flag, and it will be a great satisfaction to him to know that we at least are all safe."

Hubert at once galloped off, while Maud continued to watch her father. He was about two miles distant, and was riding quietly. Then for a little while she lost sight of him. As he came up on the next rise she saw him suddenly stop his horse. She guessed that he was gazing at the flagstaff, for there was not a breath of wind, and the flag drooped straight down by the pole, so that it was difficult to distinguish it at a distance. Then she was sure that he made it out, for he came on at a furious gallop; and as he came nearer she could see that he had taken his gun from its place and was carrying it across his arm in readiness for instant action. In a few minutes Hubert met him, and after a short pause the two rode together back to the house at a canter.

Mr. Hardy paused at the men's hut to give Lopez a hearty rating for his disobedience of orders in going so far out upon the plain. Then he came up to the house. "This is a bad affair, my dear," he said cheerfully; "but as long as we are all safe we can thank God that it's no worse. We shall get some of our beasts back yet, or I am mistaken. Ethel, run down to Terence, and tell him to drive the bullocks that are down with the plows into their enclosure, and to fasten the gate after them. Maud, give all the horses a feed of Indian corn and some water. Boys, tell Sarah to put some cold meat and bread into your hunting-bags. Load the spare chambers of your carbines, and see that your water-gourds are full."

Mr. Hardy then retired with his wife--who had been looking on anxiously while these orders were being given--into their own room, where they remained about ten minutes. When they came back into the sitting-room Mrs. Hardy was pale, but composed, and the children could see that she had been crying.

"Your mamma and I have been talking the matter over, boys, and I have told her that I must do my best to get some, at least, of our animals back. I shall take you bath with me. It is unfortunate that two of our friends at Canterbury have ridden over early this morning to Mr. Percy's, and will not be back until late to-night. Had they been at home, they would, I know, have joined us. I thought at first of sending over for Mr. Farquhar, who is at home, but I do not like losing the time. I shall send Lopez over with a note, asking him to come and sleep here to-night. We shall not be back till to-morrow. There is no fear of another alarm to-day; still I shall be more comfortable in knowing that you have some one with you. Do not go beyond the enclosure, girls, until we return. Terence, too, is to remain inside, and can sleep in the house to-night; so also can Lopez. You will therefore be well protected. Let us have something to eat, and then in ten minutes we will be in the saddle. Charley, fetch down three blue-lights, two signal rockets, and two of the tin rockets. Maud, fill our pocket-flasks with brandy. Hubert, you boys will each take your carbine and a revolver; I will carry my long rifle, and the other two Colts." In ten minutes they were ready to mount, and after a final embrace, and many a "Be sure and take care of yourselves" from their mother and sisters, they started off across the plain at a long, steady gallop.

"They have got just an hour's start, boys," Mr. Hardy said. "Your mother said that it was exactly half an hour from the first alarm to my arrival, and I was in the house a minute or two under that time. It is about half-past twelve now."

"It is very fortunate, papa, that we had our horses safe up at the house."

"Yes, boys. If we had been obliged to wait until tomorrow morning before starting, our chance of coming up would have been very slight. As it is, we shall be up with them in three or four hours. The sheep cannot go really fast more than twelve or fifteen miles, especially with their heavy fleeces on."

Half an hour's riding took them to the scene of the attack. As they neared it they saw two figures lying upon the grass. There was no occasion to go near: the stiff and distorted attitudes were sufficient to show that they were dead.

Mr. Hardy purposely avoided riding close to them, knowing that the shocking sight of men who have met with a violent death is apt to shake the nerves of any one unaccustomed to such a sight, however brave he may be.

"They are evidently dead, poor fellows!" he said. "It is no use our stopping."

Charley looked at the bodies with a fierce frown upon his face, and muttered to himself. "We'll pay them out for you, the cowardly scoundrels."

Hubert did not even glance toward them. He was a tender-hearted boy and he felt his face grow pale and a strange feeling of sickness come over him, even at the momentary glance which he had at first taken at the rigid figures.

"I suppose you do not mean to attack them until night, papa?" Charley asked.

"Well, boys, I have been thinking the matter over, and I have come to the conclusion that it will be better to do so directly we get up to them."

"And do you think, papa, that we three will be able to thrash the lot of them? They must be a poor, miserable set of cowards."

"No, Charley; I do not think that we shall be able to thrash the lot, as you say; but with our weapons, we shall be able to give them a terrible lesson. If we attack at night they will soon find out how few are our numbers, and having no particular dread of our weapons, may rush at us, and overpower us in spite of them. Another thing, boys, is, I want to give them a lesson. They must know that they shan't come and murder and steal on our place with impunity."

Scarcely another word was exchanged for the next hour. At a long, steady gallop they swept along. There was no difficulty in following the track, for the long grass was trampled in a wide swath. Several times, too, exclamations of rage burst from the boys as they came across a dead sheep, evidently speared by the savages because he could not keep up with the others. After passing several of them, Mr. Hardy called to the boys to halt, while he leaped off his horse by the side of one of the sheep, and put his hand against its body and into its mouth.

"It's quite dead; isn't it, papa?" Hubert said.

"Quite, Hubert; I never thought it was alive." And Mr. Hardy leaped upon his horse again. "I wanted to see how warm the body was. If we try again an hour's ride ahead, we shall be able to judge, by the increased heat of the body, as to how much we have gained on the Indians, and whether they are far ahead. You see, boys, when I was young man, I was out many times in Texas against the Comanches and Apaches, who are a very different enemy from these cowardly Indians here. One had to keep one's eyes open there, for they were every bit as brave as we were. Don't push on so fast, Charley. Spare your horse; you will want all he's got in him before you have done. I think that we must be gaining upon them very fast now. You see the dead sheep lie every hundred yards or so, instead of every quarter of a mile. The Indians know well enough that it would take a whole day out on the edge of the settlements to collect a dozen men for pursuit, and would have no idea that three men would set off alone; so I expect that they will now have slackened their pace a little, to give the sheep breathing time."

After another ten minutes' ride Mr. Hardy again alighted, and found a very perceptible increase of warmth in the bodies of the sheep. "I do not think that they can have been dead much more than a quarter of an hour. Keep a sharp lookout ahead, boys; we may see them at the top of the next rise."

Not a word was spoken for the next few minutes. Two or three slight swells were crossed without any sign of the enemy; and then, upon breasting a rather higher rise than usual, they saw a mass of moving beings in the distance.

"Halt!" Mr. Hardy shouted, and the boys instantly drew rein. "Jump off, boys. Only our heads have shown against the sky. They can hardly have noticed them. There, hold my horse; loosen the saddle-girths of yours too, and let them breathe freely. Take the bridles out of their mouths. It seemed to me, by the glimpse I got of our enemies, that they were just stopping. I am going on to make sure of it."

So saying Mr. Hardy again went forward a short distance, going on his hands and knees as he came on to the crest of the rise, in order that his head might not show above the long grass. When he reached it he saw at once that his first impression had been correct. At a distance of a little over a mile a mass of animals were collected, and round them were scattered a number of horses, while figures of men were moving among them.

"It is as I thought, boys," he said when he rejoined his sons. "They have stopped for awhile. The animals must all be completely done up; they cannot have come less than thirty miles, and will require three or four hours' rest, at the least, before they are fit to travel again. One hour will do for our horses. Rinse their mouths out with a little water, and let them graze if they are disposed: in half an hour we will give them each a double handful of Indian corn."

Having attended to their horses, which they hobbled to prevent their straying, Mr. Hardy and the boys sat down and made a slight meal. None of them felt very hungry, the excitement of the approaching attack having driven away the keen appetite that they would have otherwise gained from their ride; but Mr. Hardy begged the boys to endeavor to eat something, as they would be sure to feel the want of food later.

The meal over, Mr. Hardy lit his favorite pipe, while the boys went cautiously up the hill to reconnoiter. There was no change; most of the animals were lying down, and there was little sign of movement. Two or three Indians, however, were standing motionless and rigid by their horses' sides, evidently acting as sentries. The boys thought that hour the longest that they had ever passed. At last, however, their father looked at his watch, shook the ashes out of his pipe and put it in his pocket. "Now, boys, it is five minutes to the hour. Examine your carbines and revolvers, see that everything is in order, and that there is no hitch. Tighten the saddle-girths and examine the buckles. See that your ammunition and spare carbine chambers are ready at hand."

In another five minutes the party were in their saddles.

"Now, boys, my last words. Don't ride ahead or lag behind: regulate your pace by mine. Look out for armadillo holes--they are more dangerous than the Indians. Remember my orders: on no account use the second chamber of your carbines unless in case of great urgency. Change the chambers directly you have emptied them, but don't fire a shot until the spare ones are charged again. Now, boys, hurrah for old England!"

"Hurrah!" the boys both shouted as they started at a canter up the rise. As they caught sight of the Indians everything was quiet as before; but in another moment they saw the men on watch throw themselves on to their horses' backs, figures leaped up from the grass and ran toward their horses, and in little over a minute the whole were in motion.

"Surely they are not going to run away from three men!" Charley said in a disgusted tone.

"They won't run far, Charley," Mr. Hardy said quietly. "By the time that we are halfway to them they will see that we can have no one with us, and then they will come on quickly enough."

It was as Mr. Hardy said. Keen as had been the watch kept by the Indians, in spite of their belief that no pursuing force could be sent after them, it was some little time before they could get the weary animals on their legs and in motion; and even at the easy canter at which Mr. Hardy approached, he had neared them to within half a mile before they were fairly off. A small party only continued to drive the animals, and the rest of the Indians, wheeling sharp round, and uttering a wild war-cry, came back at full gallop toward the whites.

"Halt, boys-steady, dismount: take up your positions quietly. Don't fire till I give you the word. I shall try my rifle first."

The well-trained horses, accustomed to their masters firing from their backs, stood as steady as if carved in stone, their heads turned inquiringly toward the yelling throng of horsemen who were approaching. Mr. Hardy and the boys had both dismounted, so that the horses were between them and the Indians, the saddles serving as rests for their firearms.

"Five hundred yards, Charley?" his father asked quietly.

"A little over, papa; nearly six, I should say."

Mr. Hardy waited another ten seconds, and then his rifle cracked; and a yell of astonishment and rage broke from the Indians, as one of their chiefs, conspicuous from an old dragoon helmet, taken probably in some skirmish with the soldiers, fell from his horse.

"Hurrah!" Charley cried. "Shall we fire now, papa?"

"No, Charley," Mr. Hardy said as he reloaded his rifle; "wait till they are four hundred yards off, then fire slowly. Count ten between each shot, and take as steady an aim as possible. Now! Well done, two more of the scoundrels down. Steady, Hubert, you missed that time: there, that's better"

The Indians yelled with rage and astonishment as man after man dropped before the steady and, to them, mysterious fire which was kept up upon them. Still they did not abate the rapidity of their charge.

"Done, papa," Charley said as the two boys simultaneously fired their last shot, when the leading Indians were about two hundred and fifty yards distant.

"Change your chambers and mount," Mr. Hardy said as he again took aim with his rifle.

The enemy was not more than a hundred and fifty yards distant, when they leaped into their saddles and started at a gallop.

"Steady, boys, keep your horses well in hand. Never mind their balls; they could no more hit a man at this distance from the back of a horse than they could fly. There is no chance of their catching us; there won't be many horses faster than ours, and ours are a good deal fresher. Keep a good lookout for holes."

Both pursuers and pursued were now going over the ground at a tremendous pace. The Indians had ceased firing, for most of those who had guns had discharged them as Mr. Hardy and his sons had mounted, and it was impossible to load at the speed at which they were going.

During the first mile of the chase Mr. Hardy had looked round several times, and had said each time, "We are holding our own, boys; they are a good hundred yards behind; keep your horses in hand."

At the end of another mile his face brightened as he looked round. "All right, boys, they are tailing off fast. Three-quarters of them have stopped already. There are not above a score of the best mounted anywhere near us. Another mile and we will give them a lesson."

The mile was soon traversed, and Mr. Hardy saw that only about twelve Indians had maintained their distance.

"Now is the time, boys. When I say halt, draw up and jump off, but take very steady aim always at the nearest. Don't throw away a shot. They are only a hundred yards off, and the revolvers will tell. Don't try to use the second chamber; there is no time for that. Use your pistols when you have emptied your carbines. Halt!"

Not five seconds elapsed after the word was spoken before Charley's carbine rang out. Then came the sharp cracks of the carbines and pistols in close succession. The Indians hesitated at the tremendous fire which was opened upon them, then halted. The delay was fatal to them. In little over half a minute the eighteen shots had been fired. Five Indians lay upon the plain; another, evidently a chief, had been carried off across the saddle of one of his followers, who had leaped off when he saw him fall; and two others were evidently wounded, and had difficulty in keeping their seats.

"Now, boys, change your chambers, and take a shot or two after them," Mr.

Hardy said as he again reloaded his rifle.

The boys, however, found by the time they were ready that the flying Indians were beyond any fair chance of hitting; but their father took a long and steady aim with his deadly rifle, and upon its report a horse and man went down. But the rider was in an instant upon his feet again, soon caught one of the riderless horses which had galloped off with its companions, and followed his comrades.

"Well done, boys," Mr. Hardy said, with a hearty pat on their shoulders. "You have done gallantly for a first fight, and I feel proud of you."

Both boys colored with pleasure.

"How many have we killed?"

"I think seven fell at our first attack, papa, and six here, counting the one they carried off, besides wounded."

"Thirteen. It is enough to make them heartily wish themselves back. Now let us give the horses ten minutes' rest, and then we will stir them up again. We must not lose time; it will be sunset in another three-quarters of an hour."

Half an hour's riding again brought them up to the Indians, who had stopped within a mile of their former halting-place.

"The moon will be up by one o'clock, boys, and they mean to remain where they are till then. Do you see that hollow that runs just this side of where they are? No doubt there is a small stream there."

This time the Indians made no move to retreat further. They knew now that their assailants were only three in number. They were armed, indeed, with weapons which, in their terrible rapidity of fire, were altogether beyond anything they had hitherto seen; but in the darkness these would be of no avail against a sudden rush.

But if the Indians did not run away neither did they, as before, attack their assailants. Their horses had been placed in the middle of the cattle, with a few Indians standing by them to keep them quiet. The rest of the Indians were not to be seen, but Mr. Hardy guessed that they were lying down in the long grass, or were concealed among the animals.

"The rascals have got a clever chief among them, boys. Except those half-dozen heads we see over the horses' backs, there is nothing to see of them. They know that if we go close they can pick us off with their guns and bows and arrows, without giving us a single fair shot at them. Don't go any nearer, boys; no doubt there are many of their best shots hidden in the grass."

"We could scatter the cattle with a rocket, papa."

"Yes, we could, Hubert, but we should gain nothing by it; they have got men by their horses, and would soon get the herd together again. No, we will keep that for the night. Halloo! to the right, boys, for your lives."

Not a moment too soon did Mr. Hardy perceive the danger. The chief of the Indians, expecting another attack, had ordered twenty of his best mounted men to separate themselves from the main body, and to hide themselves in a dip of the ground near the place where the first attack had taken place. They were to allow the whites to pass, and were then to follow quietly, and fall suddenly upon them.

Complete success had attended the maneuver; and it was fortunate that the party had no firearms, these having been distributed among the main body with the cattle, for they were within forty yards of Mr. Hardy before they were seen. It was, in fact, a repetition of the maneuver which had proved so successful in their attack upon the cattle.

They were not immediately in the rear of Mr. Hardy, but rather to the left. As Mr. Hardy and his sons turned to fly, a number of Indians sprang upon their feet from among the grass, and discharged a volley of guns and arrows at them. Fortunately the distance was considerable. One of their arrows, however, struck Mr. Hardy's horse in the shoulder, while another stuck in the rider's arm. Another went through the calf of Hubert's leg, and stuck in the flap of the saddle.

There was no time for word or complaint. They buried their spurs in their horses' sides, and the gallant animals, feeling that the occasion was urgent, seemed almost to fly. In a mile they were able to break into a steady gallop, the enemy being now seventy or eighty yards behind. Mr. Hardy had already pulled the arrow from his arm, and Hubert now extracted his. As he stooped to do so his father, who had not noticed that he was wounded, saw what he was doing.

"Hurt much, old man?"

"Not much," Hubert said; but it did hurt a good deal nevertheless.

"I don't want to tire our horses any more, boys," Mr. Hardy said; "I shall try and stop those rascals with one of my revolvers."

So saying, he drew one of his pistols from his holster, and turning round in his saddle, took a steady aim and fired.

At the same instant, however, his horse trod in a hole and fell, Mr. Hardy being thrown over its head with tremendous force. The boys reined their horses hard in, and Hubert gave a loud cry as he saw his father remain stiff and unmoved on the ground. The Indians set up a wild yell of triumph.

"Steady, Hubert. Jump off. Pick up papa's pistol. Arrange the horses in a triangle round him. That's right. Now don't throw away a shot."

The nearest Indian was scarcely thirty yards off when Charley's bullet crashed into his brain. The three immediately following him fell in rapid succession, another chief's arm sank useless to his side, while the horse of another fell, shot through the brain.

Both the boys were pale, but their hands were as steady as iron. They felt as if, with their father lying insensible under their protection, they could not miss.

So terrible was the destruction which the continued fire wrought among the leaders that the others instinctively checked the speed of their horses as they approached the little group, from which fire and balls seemed to stream, and began to discharge arrows at the boys, hanging on the other side of their horses, so that by their foes they could not be seen, a favorite maneuver with the Indians. As the boys fired their last barrels they drew their revolvers from the holsters, and, taking aim as the Indians showed a head or an arm under their horses' necks or over their backs, their twelve barrels added to the Indians scattered over the ground.

"Now, Hubert, give me the two last revolvers, and put the two fresh chambers into the carbines."

Seeing only one of their foes on the defense, the Indians again made a rush forward. Charley shot the two first with a revolver, but the others charged up, and he stooped a moment to avoid a spear, rising a little on one side, and discharging with both hands his pistols at the Indians, who were now close. "Quick, Hubert," he said, as he shot with his last barrel an Indian who had just driven his spear into the heart of Mr. Hardy's horse.

The animal fell dead as it stood, and the Indians with a yell charged at the opening, but as they did so Hubert slipped a carbine into his brother's hand, and the two again poured in the deadly fire which had so checked the Indians' advance.

The continuation of the fire appalled the Indians, and the seven that survived turned and fled.

"I will load, Hubert," Charley said, trying to speak steadily. "See to papa at once. Empty one of the water-gourds upon his face and head."

Hubert looked down with a cold shudder. Neither of the boys had dared to think during that brief fight. They had had many falls before on the soft turf of the pampas, but no hurt had resulted, and both were more frightened at the insensibility of their father than at the Indian horde which were so short a distance away, and which would no doubt return in a few minutes in overwhelming force.

Great, then, was Hubert's delight, when upon looking round he saw that Mr. Hardy had raised himself with his arms.

"What has happened?" he said in a confused manner.

"Are you hurt, papa?" Hubert asked, with tears of joy running down his face; "you frightened us both so dreadfully. Please drink a little water, and I will pour a little over your face."

Mr. Hardy drank some water, and Hubert dashed some more in his face. "That will do, Hubert," he said with a smile; "you will drown me. There, I am all right now. I was stunned, I suppose. There you are," and he got up on to his feet; "you see I am not hurt. And now, where are the Indians?"

"There, papa," said the boys with pardonable triumph, as they pointed to thirteen dead Indians.

Their father could not speak. He grasped their hands warmly. He saw how great the danger must have been, and how gallantly his boys must have borne themselves.

"The Indians may be back in a few minutes, papa. Your horse is dead, but there is one of the Indians' standing by his dead master. Let us catch him and shift the saddle." The animal, when they approached it, made no move to take flight, and they saw that his master's foot, as he fell, had become entangled in the lasso, and the well-trained beast had stood without moving. In three minutes the saddles were transferred, and the party again ready for fight or flight.

"What next, papa?"

"We turned to the right, and rather toward home, when we started; so the Indian halting-place is to the southeast of us, is it not?"

"Yes, papa; as near as may be," Charley said, making out the points with some difficulty on the pocket compass, one of which they each carried, as the danger of being lost upon the pathless pampas is very great.

"We had ridden about two miles when I got my fall, so we are a mile to the west of their camp. We will ride now a couple of miles due north. The Indians are sure to send out a scout to see whether we have returned home, and our track will lead them to believe that we have. It is dusk now. We shall get three hours' rest before we have to move."

It was perfectly dark before they reached their halting-place. The saddles were again loosened, a little Indian corn, moistened with water, given to the horses, and another slight meal taken by themselves. The boys, by Mr. Hardy's orders, though sorely against their own wishes, then lay down to get a couple of hours' sleep; while Mr. Hardy went back about a hundred yards along the trail they had made on coming, and then turned aside and sat down at a distance of a few yards to watch, in case any Indian should have followed up their trail.

Here he sat for over two hours, and then returned to the boys. Charley he found fast asleep. The pain of Hubert's wound had kept him awake. Mr. Hardy poured some water over the bandage, and then, waking Charley, gave them instructions as to the part they were to play.

Both of them felt rather uncomfortable when they heard that they were to be separated from their father. They raised no objections, however, and promised to obey his instructions to the letter. They then mounted their horses--Hubert having to be lifted up, for his leg was now very stiff and sore--and then began to retrace their steps, keeping a hundred yards or so to the west of the track by which they had come. They rode in single file, and they had taken the precaution of fastening a piece of tape round their horses' nostrils and mouth, to prevent their snorting should they approach any of their own species. The night was dark, but the stars shone out clear and bright. At starting Mr. Hardy had opened his watch, and had felt by the hands that it was ten o'clock. After some time he felt again.

It was just half an hour from the time of their starting.

"Now, boys, we are somewhere close to the place of your fight. In another ten minutes we must separate."

At the end of that time they again closed up.

"Now, boys, you see that bright star. That is nearly due east of us; go on as nearly as you can guess for ten minutes, at a walk, as before. You will then be within a mile of the enemy. Then get off your horses. Mind, on no account whatever are you to leave their bridles, but stand with one hand on the saddle, ready to throw yourself into it. Keep two blue-lights, and give me one. Don't speak a word, but listen as if your lives depended upon detecting a sound, as indeed they do. You are to remain there until you see that I have fairly succeeded and then you are to dash in behind the cattle and fire off your revolvers, and shout so as to quicken their pace as much as possible. I do not think there is the least fear of the Indians following, the rockets will scare them too much. When you have chased the herd for about two miles, draw aside half a mile on their side, and then listen for the Indians passing in pursuit of the cattle; wait ten minutes, and then blow your dog-whistle--a sharp, short note. If you hear Indians following you, or think there is danger, blow twice, and go still further to the right. God bless you, boys. I don't think there is much fear of your falling upon any scouts; they have been too badly cut up to-day, and must look upon our guns as witches. I need not say keep together, and, if attacked, light a blue-light and throw it down; ride a short way out of its circle of light, and I will come straight to you through everything. Don't be nervous about me. There is not the least danger."

In another minute the boys lost sight of their father, and turning their horses proceeded in the direction he had ordered. Every now and then they stopped to listen, but not a sound could they hear. Their own horses' hoofs made no noise as they fell upon the soft turf.

At the end of the ten minutes, just as Charley was thinking of stopping, they heard a sound which caused them to halt simultaneously. It was the low baa of a sheep, and seemed to come from directly ahead of them. Charley now alighted, and Hubert brought his horse up beside him, keeping his place, however, in the saddle, but leaning forward on the neck of his horse, for he felt that if he got off he should be unable to regain his seat hurriedly in case of alarm.

"About a mile off, I should say, by the sound," Charley whispered; "and just in the direction we expected."

The spot Charley had chosen for the halt was a slight hollow, running east and west; so that, even had the moon been up, they would not have been visible except to any one in the line of the hollow.

Here, their carbines cocked and ready for instant use, they remained standing for what appeared to them ages, listening with the most intense earnestness for any sound which might tell of the failure or success of their father's enterprise.

Mr. Hardy had ridden on for, as nearly as he could tell, two miles, so that he was now to the southwest of the enemy; then, turning west, he kept along for another mile, when he judged that he was, as nearly as possible, a mile in their direct rear. He now advanced with the greatest caution, every faculty absorbed in the sense of listening. He was soon rewarded by the sound of the baaing of the sheep; and dismounting and leading his horse, he gradually approached the spot. At last, on ascending a slight rise, he fancied that he could make out a black mass, at a distance of a quarter of a mile. Of this, however, he was not certain; but he was sure, from an occasional sound, that the herd was exactly in this direction, and at about that distance. He now left his horse, taking the precaution of tying all four legs, to prevent his starting off at the sound of the rockets. He next set to work to cut some turf, with which he formed a narrow sloping bank, with a hollow for the rocket to rest in--calculating the exact distance, and the angle required. During this operation he stopped every minute or two and listened with his ear on the ground; but except a faint stamping noise from the distant cattle all was quiet.

All being prepared, Mr. Hardy took the signal rocket, and placing it at a much higher angle than that intended for the others, struck a match and applied it to the touch-paper. In a moment afterward there was a loud roar, and the rocket soared up, with its train of brilliant sparks behind it, and burst almost over the Indian camp. Five or six balls of an intense white light broke from it, and gradually fell toward the ground, lighting tip the whole surrounding plain.

A yell of astonishment and fear broke from the Indians, and in a moment another rocket rushed out. Mr. Hardy watched its fiery way with anxiety, and saw with delight that its direction was true. Describing a slight curve, it rushed full at the black mass, struck something, turned abruptly, and then exploded with a loud report, followed instantly by a cracking noise, like a straggling fusillade of musketry. It had scarcely ceased before the third followed it, greeted, like its predecessors, with a yell from the Indians.

Its success was equal to that of its predecessors, and Mr. Hardy was delighted by the sound of a dull, heavy noise, like distant thunder, and knew, that the success was complete, and that he had stampeded the cattle.

He now ran to his horse, which was trembling in every limb and struggling wildly to escape, soothed it by patting it, loosed its bonds, sprang into the saddle, and went off at full gallop in the direction by which he had come. He had not ridden very far before he heard, in the still night air, the repeated sound of firearms, and knew that the boys were upon the trail of the cattle. Mr. Hardy had little fear of the Indians pursuing them; he felt sure that the slaughter of the day by the new and mysterious firearms, together with the effect of the rockets, would have too much terrified and cowed them for them to think of anything but flight. He was, however, much alarmed when, after a quarter of a hour's riding, he heard a single sharp whistle at about a few hundred yards' distance.

"Hurrah! papa," the boys said as he rode up to them. "They have gone by at a tremendous rush--sheep and cattle and all. We started the moment we saw your first rocket, and got up just as they rushed past, and we joined in behind and fired, and yelled till we were hoarse. I don't think they will stop again to-night."

"Did you see or hear anything of the Indians, boys?"

"Nothing, papa. When the first rocket burst we saw several dark figures leap up from the grass--where they had been, no doubt, scouting--and run toward the camp but that was all. What are we to do now?"

"Ride on straight for home. We need not trouble about the animals; they won't stop till they are back. We must go easily, for our horses have done a very long day's work already. They have been between fifty and sixty miles. I think that we had better ride on for another hour. By that time the moon will be up, and we shall be able to see for miles across the plain. Then we will halt till daybreak--it will only be three hours--and the horses will be able to carry us in at a canter afterward."

And so it was done. In an hour the moon was fairly up, and, choosing a rise whence a clear view could be obtained, the horses were allowed to feed, and Mr. Hardy and Hubert lay down to sleep, Charley taking the post of sentry, with orders to wake the others at daybreak.

The day was just dawning when he aroused them. "Wake up, papa. There are some figures coming over the plain."

Mr. Hardy and Hubert were on their feet in an instant. "Where, Charley?"

"From the north, papa. They must have passed us in their pursuit of the cattle, and are now returning--empty-handed, anyhow; for there are only seven or eight of them, and they are driving nothing before them."

By this time all three were in the saddle again.

"Shall we attack them, papa?"

"No, boys; we have given them quite a severe lesson enough. At the same time, we will move a little across, so that we can get a good sight of them as they pass, and make sure that they have got nothing with them."

"They are coming exactly this way, papa."

"Yes, I see, Hubert; they are no doubt riding back upon their trail. They will turn off quickly enough when they see us."

But the newcomers did not do so, continuing straight forward.

"Get your carbines ready, boys; but don't fire till I tell you. They must belong to some other party, and cannot know what has happened. No doubt they take us for Indians."

"I don't think they are Indians at all," Hubert said as the figures rapidly approached.

"Don't you, Hubert? We shall soon see. Halloo!"

"Halloo! hurrah!" came back to them; and in another five minutes they were shaking hands heartily with their three friends from Canterbury, the Jamiesons, and two or three other neighboring settlers.

They told them that Farquhar, as soon as Lopez brought news of the attack, had sent mounted men off to all the other settlements, begging them to meet that night at Mount Pleasant. By nine o'clock they had assembled, and, after a consultation, had agreed that the Indians would be satisfied with their present booty, and that therefore no guard would be necessary at their own estancias.

A good feed and four hours' rest had been given to their horses, and when the moon rose they had started. Two hours after leaving they had seen a dark mass approaching, and had prepared for an encounter; but it had turned out to be the animals, who were going toward home at a steady pace. There seemed, they said, to be a good many horses among them.

Assured by this that some encounter or other had taken place with the Indians, they had ridden on with much anxiety, and were greatly relieved at finding Mr. Hardy and his boys safe.

The whole party now proceeded at a rapid pace toward home, which they reached in four hours' riding. As they came in sight of the watch-tower Mr. Herries separated himself from the others, and rode thirty or forty yards away to the left, returning to the others. This he repeated three times, greatly to Mr. Hardy's surprise.

"What are you doing, Herries?" he asked.

"I am letting them know you are all well. We agreed upon that signal before we started. They would be able to notice one separate himself from the rest in that way as far as they could see us, and long before they could make out any other sort of signal."

In a short time three black spots could be seen upon the plain in the distance. These the boys very shortly pronounced to be Mrs. Hardy and the girls.

When they approached the rest of the party fell back, to allow Mr. Hardy and his sons to ride forward and have the pleasure of the first meeting to themselves. Needless is it to tell with what a feeling of delight and thankfulness Mrs. Hardy, Maud, and Ethel received them. After the first congratulations the girls observed that Mr. Hardy had his arm bound up with a handkerchief.

"Are you hurt, papa?" they exclaimed anxiously.

"Nothing to speak of--only an arrow in my arm. Old Hubert has got the worst of it: he has had one through the calf of his leg."

"Poor old Hubert!" they cried. And Hubert had some difficulty in persuading the girls that he could wait on very fairly till he reached home without his being bandaged or otherwise touched.

"And how did it all happen?" Mrs. Hardy asked.

"I will tell you all about it when we have had breakfast, my dear," her husband said. "I have told our friends nothing about it yet, for it is a long story, and one telling will do for it. I suppose the animals have got back? How many are missing?"

"Lopez came in from counting them just as we started," Mrs. Hardy said. "He says there are only four or five cattle missing, and about a couple of hundred sheep; and, do you know, in addition to our own horses, there are a hundred and twenty-three Indian horses?"

"Hurrah!" the boys shouted delightedly, "That is a triumph; isn't it, papa?"

"It is indeed, boys; and explains readily enough how it was that there was not the slightest attempt at pursuit. The Indian horses evidently broke their lariats and joined in the stampede. I suppose Lopez has driven them all into the enclosure?"

"Oh, yes, papa. They went in by themselves with our own animals, and Terence shut the gate at once."

In another quarter of an hour they reached the house, received by Sarah and Terence--the latter being almost beside himself with joy at his master's safe return, and with vexation when he heard that there had been a fight, and that he had not been able to take part in it.

Orders had been given to Sarah to prepare breakfast the instant the returning party had been seen, and their signal of "all safe" been made out. It was now ready; but before sitting down to it Mr. Hardy begged all present to join in a short thanksgiving to God for their preservation from extreme peril.

All knelt, and as they followed Mr. Hardy's words, they were sure, from the emotion with which he spoke, that the peril, of the particulars of which they were at present ignorant, had been indeed a most imminent one.

This duty performed, all fell to with great heartiness to breakfast; and when that was over Mr. Hardy related the whole story. Very greatly were Mrs. Hardy and the girls amazed at the thoughts of the great peril through which their father and the boys had passed, and at the account of the defense by the boys when their father was lying insensible. Mrs. Hardy could not restrain herself from sobbing in her husband's arms at the thought of his fearful danger, while the girls cried sore and kissed their brothers, and all their friends crowded round them and wrung their hands warmly; while Terence sought relief by going out into the garden, dancing a sort of jig, and giving vent to a series of wild war-whoops.

It was some time before all were sufficiently calm to listen to the remainder of the story, which was received with renewed congratulations.

When it was all over a council was held, and it was agreed that there was no chance whatever of the Indians returning to renew the contest, as they would be helpless on foot; but that if by a spy they found out that their horses were there, they might endeavor to recover them. It was therefore agreed that they should be driven over at once to Mr. Percy's, there to remain until a purchaser was obtained for them. In the afternoon the party dispersed, with many thanks from the Hardys for their prompt assistance.

CHAPTER XI.
QUIET TIMES.

After a storm comes a calm:" a saying true in the case of the Hardys, as in that of most others. All their neighbors agreed that after the very severe loss of the Indians, and the capture of the whole of their horses, there was no chance whatever of another attack, at any rate for many months. After that it was possible, and indeed probable, that they would endeavor to take vengeance for their disastrous defeat; but that at present they would be too crippled and disheartened to think of it.

The settlers were now, therefore, able to give their whole attention to the farm. The first operation was the sheep-shearing. Four men had been hired to do the shearing at Canterbury, and then to come over to Mount Pleasant. Charley rode over to their neighbors' with Mrs. Hardy and his sisters, Mr. Hardy and Hubert remaining at home--the latter laid up with the wound in his leg.

It was an amusing sight to see three or four hundred sheep driven into an enclosure, and then dragged out by the shearers. These men were paid according to the number shorn, and were very expert, a good hand getting through a hundred a day. They were rather rough, though, in their work, and the girls soon went away from the shearing-place with a feeling of pity and disgust, for the shearers often cut the sheep badly. Each man had a pot of tar by his side, with which he smeared over any wound. A certain sum was stopped from their pay for each sheep upon which they made a cut of over a certain length; but although this made them careful to a certain extent, they still wounded a great many of the poor creatures.

A much more exciting amusement was seeing the branding of the cattle, which took place after the shearing was over. The animals were let out, one by one, from their enclosure, and, as they passed along a sort of lane formed of hurdles, they were lassoed and thrown on to the ground. The hot branding-iron was then clapped against their shoulder, and was received by a roar of rage and pain. The lasso was then loosened, and the animal went off at a gallop to join his companions on the plain. Some caution was required in this process, for sometimes the animals, upon being released, would charge their tormenters, who then had to make a hasty leap over the hurdles; Terence, who stood behind them, being in readiness to thrust a goad against the animals' rear, and this always had the effect of turning them. For a few days after this the cattle were rather wild, but they soon forgot their fright and pain, and returned to their usual ways.

Mr. Hardy had by this time been long enough in the country to feel sure of his position. He therefore determined to embark the rest of his capital in agricultural operations. He engaged ten native peons, and set-to to extend the land under tillage. The watercourses from the dam were deepened and lengthened, and side channels cut, so that the work of irrigation could be effectually carried on over the whole of the low-lying land, the water being sufficient for the purpose for nearly ten months in the year. Four plows were kept steadily at work, and the ground was sown with alfalfa or lucern as fast as it was got into condition. Patches of Indian corn, pumpkins, and other vegetables were also planted. Mr. Hardy resolved that until the country beyond him became so settled that there could be little danger from Indian incursions, he would not increase his stock of sheep and cattle, but would each year sell off the increase.

He also decided upon entering extensively upon dairy operations. He had already ascertained that a ready sale could be obtained, among the European residents of Rosario and Buenos Ayres, of any amount of butter and fresh cheese that he could produce, and that European prices would be readily given for them. Up to the present time the butter made had been obtained from the milk of two cows only, but he now determined to try the experiment upon a large scale.

A dairy was first to be made. This was partially cut out of the side of the slope, and lined with sun-baked bricks. Against the walls, which projected above the ground, earth was piled, to make them of a very considerable thickness. Strong beams were placed across the roof; over these rafters was nailed felt, whitewashed upon both sides to keep out insects. Upon this was placed a considerable thickness of rushes, and, over all, puddled clay was spread a foot deep. Ventilation was given by a wide chimney rising behind it, and light entered by two windows in front. The whole of the interior was whitewashed.

In this way a dairy was obtained which, from the thickness of its walls, was cool enough for the purpose during the hottest weather. Preparations were now made for breaking in the cows to be milked. A sort of lane was made of two strong fences of iron wire. This lane was of the shape of a funnel, narrowing at one end to little more than the width of a cow. At the end of this was a gate, and attached to the gate a light trough filled with fresh alfalfa.

Half a dozen cows which had recently calved were now separated from the herd, and driven into the wide end of the enclosure. One by one they approached the narrow end, and when one had reached the extremity, and had begun to devour the alfalfa, of which they are very fond, a bar was let down behind her, so that she could now neither advance, retreat, nor turn round.

One of the boys now began cautiously and quietly to milk her, and the cows in few cases offered any resistance. One or two animals were, however, very obstreperous, but were speedily subdued by having their legs firmly fastened to the posts behind. In a few days all were reconciled to the process, and ere long would come in night and morning to be milked, with as much regularity as English cows would have done.

The wives of the peons were now taught to milk; and more and more cows were gradually added to the number, until in six months there were fifty cows in full milk. Maud and Ethel had now no longer anything to do with the house, Mrs. Hardy undertaking the entire management of that department, while the girls had charge of the fowl-house and dairy.

The milk was made partly into butter, partly into fresh cheese. These were sent off once a week to catch the steamer for Buenos Ayres. Mr. Hardy had a light cart made for one horse, and by this conveyance the butter--starting as soon as the sun went down--arrived in Rosario in time for the early boat to the capital. It was sent in large baskets made of rushes, and packed in many layers of cool, fresh leaves; so that it arrived at Buenos Ayres, forty hours after leaving Mount Pleasant, perfectly fresh and good. The skim milk was given to the pigs, who had already increased to quite a numerous colony.

Although they had been planted less than a year, the fruit trees round the house had thriven in a surprising manner, and already bore a crop of fruit more than sufficient for the utmost wants of the household. Peaches and nectarines, apricots and plums, appeared at every meal, either fresh, stewed, or in puddings, and afforded a very pleasant change and addition to their diet. As Maud said one day, they would have been perfectly happy had it not been for the frogs.

These animals were a very great nuisance. They literally swarmed. Do what they would, the Hardys could not get rid of them. If they would but have kept out of the house, no one would have minded them; indeed, as they destroyed a good many insects, they would have been welcome visitors in the garden; but this was just what they would not do. The door always stood open, and they evidently considered that as an invitation to walk in. There they would hide behind boxes, or get under beds, and into water-jugs and baths, and, in fact, into every possible corner, They would even get into boots; and these had always to be shaken before being put on, in case frogs or insects should have taken up their abode there.

It used at first to be quite a matter of difficulty to know what to do with the frogs after they were caught; but after a time a covered basket was kept outside the door, and into this the frogs were popped, and taken once a day and emptied into the stream. At first they had got into the well, and had proved a great nuisance; and they were only got rid of by nearly emptying the well out with buckets, and by then building a wall round its mouth, with a tightly-fitting lid.

Insects of all kinds were indeed a great pest, scorpions being by no means uncommon, while large centipedes occasionally intruded into the house. These creatures were a great trouble to the girls in their dairy, for the frogs and toads would climb up the walls, and fall squash into the milk-pans. The only way that they could be at all kept out was by having the door sawn asunder three feet from the ground, so that the lower half could be shut while the girls were engaged inside. However, in spite of the utmost pains, the little ones would crawl in through crevices, or leap in at the window; and at last the girls had to get wicker-work covers made for all the pans; and as the natives are very skillful at this work, they were thus enabled to keep the milk clean. Almost as great a trouble as the frogs were the brocachas, who committed terrible havoc in the garden and among the crops. They are about the size, and have somewhat the appearance of hares, and burrow in immense quantities in the pampas. The only way to get rid of them was by puffing the fumes of burning sulphur down into their holes; and it was quite a part of the boys' regular work to go out with the machine for the purpose, and to suffocate these troublesome creatures. Their holes, however, are not so dangerous to horsemen as are those of the armadillos, as the ground is always bare in their neighborhood.

The armadillos are of three or four species, all of them small. The peludo is about a foot in length, and has hair sticking out between his scales. The muletas are smaller. Both are excellent eating; but the girls were some time before they could bring themselves to touch them. The matajo, in addition to the protection of his I scales, is able to roll himself into a ball at the approach of danger, and, clothed in his impervious armor, is proof against any attacks except those of man. These animals are so common that the plain is in many cases quite honeycombed with them.

The girls had a great scare the first time they came upon an iguana, thinking that it was a crocodile. These great lizards are about five feet long, and are ferocious-looking, but very harmless unless attacked. Then they will defend themselves, and can inflict a sharp blow with their tails, or a severe bite with their teeth. They are very common, and the Indians eat them, and say that the meat is excellent; but the young Hardys could never be persuaded to taste it. Thus matters proceeded for some time without any noteworthy incident. Their circle of acquaintances grew little by little. Several neighboring plots had been taken up; and although the new settlers had little time for making visits, still the very fact of their presence near gave a feeling of companionship and security. Very frequently young men would arrive with letters of introduction, and would stay a few days with them while they inspected the country.

Their household, too, had received an increase. A young Englishman named Fitzgerald, the son of some very old friend of the Hardys, had written expressing a very strong desire to come out, and asking their advice in the matter. Several letters had been exchanged, and at length, at Mr. Fitzgerald's earnest request, Mr. Hardy agreed to receive his son for a year, to learn the business of a pampas farmer, before he embarked upon his own account. A small room was accordingly cleared out for him, and Mr. Hardy never had any reason to regret having received him. He was a pleasant, light-hearted young fellow of about twenty years of age.

One change, however, had taken place which deserves mention. Sarah one day came to her mistress, and with much blushing and hesitation said that Terence

Kelly had asked her to marry him.

Mrs. Hardy had long suspected that an attachment had sprung up between the Irishman and her servant, so she only smiled and said, "Well, Sarah, and what did you say to Terence? The year you agreed to stop with us is over, so you are at liberty to do as you like, you know."

"Oh, ma'am, but I don't want to leave you. That is just what I told Terence. 'If master and mistress are willing that I shall marry you and stay on with them as before, I won't say no, Terence; but if they say that they would not take a married servant, then Terence, we must stay as we are.'"

"I have no objection at all, Sarah, and I think I can answer for Mr. Hardy having none. Terence is a very good, steady fellow, and I know that Mr. Hardy has a high opinion of him; so you could not make a marriage which would please us more. We should be very sorry to Jose you, but we could not in any case have opposed you marrying whom you liked, and now we shall have the satisfaction of keeping you here with us."

And so it was settled, and a fortnight afterward Terence and Sarah had two days' holiday, and went down to Buenos Ayres, where there was an English church, and came back again man and wife. After that each went back to work as usual, and the only change was, that Terence now took his meals and lived in the house instead of down in the men's huts. By this time they had begun to find out which of the crops peculiar to warm countries would pay, and which would not, or rather-- for they all paid more or less--which was the most suitable.

The cotton crop had proved a success; the field had in time been covered with cotton plants, which had burst first into a bright yellow blossom, and had then been covered with many balls of white fluff. The picking the cotton had been looked upon at first as great fun, although it had proved hard work before it was finished.

Its weight had rather exceeded Mr. Hardy's anticipation. The process of cleaning the cotton from the pods and seeds had proved a long and troublesome operation, and had taken an immense time. Judging by the progress that they at first made with it, they really began to despair of ever finishing it, but with practice they became more adroit. Still it was found to be too great a labor during the heat of the day, although carried on within doors. It had been a dirty work too; the light particles of fluff had got everywhere, and at the end of a couple of hours' work the party had looked like a family of bakers. Indeed, before more than a quarter of the quantity raised was cleaned they were heartily sick of the job, and the remainder was sold in the pod to an Englishman who had brought out machinery, and was attempting to raise cotton near Buenos Ayres. Although the profits had been considerable, it was unanimously determined that the experiment should not be repeated, at any rate for the present.

Mr. Hardy had not at first carried out his idea of planting a couple of acres with tobacco and sugar-cane, the ground having been required for other purposes. He had not, however abandoned the idea; and about two months before the marriage of Terence and Sarah he had planted some tobacco, which was, upon their return from Buenos Ayres, ready to be picked.

The culture of tobacco requires considerable care. The ground is first prepared with great care, and is well and thoroughly manured; but this was not required in the present case, as the rich virgin soil needed no artificial aid. It is then dug in beds something like asparagus beds, about two feet wide, with a deep trench between each. The seeds are raised in a seed-bed, and when nine or ten inches high they are taken up and carefully transplanted into the beds, two rows being placed in each, and the plants being a foot apart.

There are various methods of cultivation, but this was the one adopted by Mr. Hardy. The plants grew rapidly, the ground between them being occasionally hoed, and kept free from weeds. When they were four feet high the tops were nipped off, and any leaves which showed signs of disease were removed. Each stem had from eight to ten leaves. When the leaves began to turn rather yellow, Mr. Hardy announced that the time for cutting had arrived, and one morning all hands were mustered to the work. It consisted merely in cutting the stems at a level with the earth, and laying the plants down gently upon the ground. By breakfast-time the two acres were cleared. They were left all day to dry in the sun, and a little before sunset they were taken up, and carried up to one of the store-sheds, which had been cleared and prepared for the purpose. Here they were placed in a heap on the ground, covered over with raw hides and mats, and left for three days to heat. After this they were uncovered, and hung up on laths from the roof, close to each other, and yet sufficiently far apart to allow the air to circulate between them. Here they remained until they were quite dry, and were then taken down, a damp covering being chosen for the operation, as otherwise the dry leaves would have crumbled to dust. They were again laid in a heap, and covered up to allow them to heat once more, This second heating required some days to accomplish, and this operation required great attention, as the tobacco would have been worthless if the plants had heated too much.

In ten days the operation was complete. The leaves were then stripped off, the upper leaves were placed by themselves, as also the middle and the lower leaves; the higher ones being of the finest quality. They were then tied in bundles of twelve leaves each, and were packed in layers in barrels, a great pressure being applied with a weighted lever, to press them down into an almost solid mass. In all they filled three barrels, the smallest of which, containing sixty pounds of the finest tobacco, Mr. Hardy kept for his own use and that of his friends; the rest he sold at Buenos Ayres at a profitable rate. The venture, like that of the cotton, had proved a success, but the trouble and care required had been very great, and Mr. Hardy determined in future to plant only sufficient for his own use and that of the men employed upon the estate.

The next experiment which was perfected was that with the sugar-cane. In this, far more than in the others, Mrs. Hardy and the girls took a lively interest. Sugar had been one of the few articles of consumption which had cost money, and it had been used in considerable quantities for converting the fruit into fine puddings and preserves. It was not contemplated to make sugar for sale, but only for the supply of the house: two acres, therefore, was the extent of the plantation. Mr. Hardy procured the cuttings from a friend who had a small sugar plantation near Buenos Ayres.

The cultivation of sugar is simple. The land having been got in perfect order, deep furrows were plowed at a distance of five feet apart. In these the cuttings, which are pieces of the upper part of the cane, containing two or three knots, were laid at a distance of three feet apart. The plow was then taken along by the side of the furrow, so as to fill it up again and cover the cuttings. In sugar plantations the rows of canes are close together, but Mr. Hardy had chosen this distance, as it enabled his horse-hoe to work between them, and thus keep the ground turned up and free from weeds, without the expense of hard labor. In a short time the shoots appeared above the soil. In four months they had gained the height of fourteen feet, and their glossy stems showed that they were ready to cut.

"Now, Clara," Mr. Hardy said, "this is your manufacture, you know, and we are only to work under your superintendence. The canes are ready to cut: how do you intend to crush the juice out? because that is really an important question."

The young Hardys looked aghast at each other, for in the pressure of other matters the question of apparatus for the sugar manufacture had been quite forgotten.

"Have you really no idea how to do it, Frank?"

"No, really I have not, my dear. We have certainly no wood on the place which would make the rollers; besides, it would be rather a difficult business."

Mrs. Hardy thought for a minute, and then said, "I should think that the mangle would do it."

There was a general exclamation of "Capital, mamma!" and then a burst of laughter at the idea of making sugar with a mangle. The mangle in question was part of a patent washing apparatus which Mr. Hardy had brought with him from England, and consisted of two strong iron rollers, kept together by strong springs, and turning with a handle.

"I do think that the mangle would do, Clara," Mr. Hardy said, "and we are all much obliged to you for the idea. I had thought of the great washing copper for boiling the sugar, but the mangle altogether escaped me. We will begin to-morrow. Please get all the tubs scrubbed out and scalded, and put out in the sun to dry."

"How long will it take, papa?"

"Some days, Ethel; we must only cut the canes as fast as the boiler can boil the juice down."

The next day the work began. The canes were cut at a level with the ground, the tops were taken off, and the canes cut into lengths of three feet. They were then packed on a bullock cart and taken up to the house. They were next passed through the mangle, which succeeded admirably, the juice flowing out in streams into the tub placed below to receive it. When all the canes had been passed through the mangle, the screws were tightened to increase the pressure, and they were again passed through; by which time, although the juice was not so thoroughly extracted as it would have been by a more powerful machine, the quantity that remained was not important. As the tub was filled the contents were taken to the great copper, under which a fire was then lighted. The crushing of the canes was continued until the copper was nearly full, when Mr. Hardy ordered the cutting of the canes to be discontinued for the day. The fire under the copper was fed with the crushed canes, which burned very freely. Mr. Hardy now added a small quantity of lime and some sheep's blood, which last ingredient caused many exclamations of horror from Mrs. Hardy and the young ones. The blood, however, Mr. Hardy informed them, was necessary to clarify the sugar, as the albumen contained in the blood would rise to the surface, bringing the impurities with it. The fire was continued until the thermometer showed that the syrup was within a few degrees of boiling, and the surface was covered with a thick, dark-colored scum. The fire was then removed, and the liquor allowed to cool, the family now going about other work, as so large a quantity of liquor would not be really cold until the next day.

The following morning the tap at the bottom of the boiler was turned, and the syrup came out bright and clear--about the color of sherry wine. The scum descended unbroken on the surface of the liquor; and when the copper was nearly empty the tap was closed, and the scum and what little liquor remained was taken out. The bright syrup was now again poured into the boiler, the fire re-lighted, and the syrup was kept boiling, to evaporate the water and condense the syrup down to the point at which it would crystallize. It required many hours' boiling to effect this, any scum which rose to the surface being carefully taken off with a skimmer. At last it was found that the syrup on the skimmer began to crystallize, and Mr. Hardy pronounced it to be fit to draw off into the large washing tubs to crystallize. A fresh batch of canes was now crushed, and so the process was repeated until all the canes were cut. It took a fortnight altogether, but only five days of this were actually oc-cupied in cutting and crushing the canes. As the sugar crystallized it was taken out-a dark, pulpy-looking mass, at which the young Hardys looked very doubtfully-and was placed in a large sugar hogshead, which had been procured for the purpose. In the bottom of this eight large holes were bored, and these were stopped up with pieces of plantain stalk. Through the porous substance of these stalks the molasses or treacle slowly drained off. As the wet sugar was placed in the cask, layers of slices of plantain stems were laid upon it, as the spongy substance draws the dark color-ing matter out from the sugar. The plantain grows freely in South America, and Mr. Hardy had planted a number of this graceful tree near his house; but these had not been advanced enough to cut, and he had therefore procured a sufficient quantity from a friend at Rosario. It was three months before the drainage of the molasses quite ceased; and the Hardys were greatly pleased, on emptying the hogshead and removing the plantain stems, to find that their sugar was dry, and of a very fairly light color. The sugar-canes did not require planting again, as they will grow for many years from the same roots; and although the canes from old stools, as they are called, produce less sugar than those of the first year's planting, the juice is clearer, and requires far less trouble to prepare and refine. Before another year came round the boys made a pair of wooden rollers of eighteen inches in diameter. These were covered with strips of hoop iron, nailed lengthways upon them at short intervals from each other, thereby obtaining a better grip upon the canes, and preventing the wood from being bruised and grooved. These rollers were worked by a horse mill, which Mr. Hardy had ordered from England. It was made for five horses, and did a great deal of useful work, grinding the Indian corn into fine flour for home consumption and for sale to neighboring settlers, and into coarse meal, and pulping the pumpkins and roots for the pigs and other animals.

Mr. Hardy also tried many other experiments, as the climate is suited to almost every kind of plant and vegetable. Among them was the cultivation of ginger, of the vanilla bean, of flax, hemp, and coffee. In all of them he obtained more or less success; but the difficulty of obtaining labor, and the necessity of devoting more and more attention to the increasing flocks, herds, and irrigated land, prevented him from carrying them out on a large scale. However, they served the purpose for which he principally undertook them--of giving objects of interest and amusement to his children.

CHAPTER XII.
A STEADY HAND.

It was now more than eighteen months since the Hardys had been fairly established at Mount Pleasant. A stranger who had passed along at the time the house was first finished would certainly fail to recognize it now. Then it was a bare, uninviting structure, looking, as has been said, like a small dissenting chapel built on the top of a gentle rise, without tree or shelter of any kind. Now it appeared to rise from a mass of bright green foliage, so rapidly had the trees grown, especially the bananas and other tropical shrubs planted upon each side of the house. At the foot of the slope were some sixty or seventy acres of cultivated ground, while to the right were three or four large and strong wire enclosures, in which the milch cows, the cattle, the sheep, and the pigs were severally driven at night.

Everything was prospering beyond Mr. Hardy's most sanguine expectations. More and more land was monthly being broken up and irrigated. Large profits had been realized by buying lean cattle during the dry season, fattening them upon alfalfa, and sending them down to Rosario for sale. The pigs had multiplied astonishingly; and the profits from the dairy were increasing daily, as more cows were constantly added. The produce of Mount Pleasant was so valued at both Rosario and Buenos Ayres that the demand, at most remunerative prices, far exceeded the supply.

Additions had been made to the number of peons, and the farm presented quite an animated appearance.

The two years which had elapsed since the Hardys left England had effected a considerable change in their appearance. Charley was now eighteen--a squarely-built, sturdy young fellow. From his life of exposure in the open air he looked older than he was. He had a strong idea that he was now becoming a man; and Ethel had one day detected him examining his cheeks very closely in the glass, to see if there were any signs of whiskers. It was a debated question in his own mind whether a beard would or would not be becoming to him. Hubert was nearly seventeen: he was taller and slighter than his brother, but was younger both in appearance and manners. He had all the restlessness of a boy, and lacked somewhat of Charley's steady perseverance.

The elder brother was essentially of a practical disposition. He took a lively interest in the affairs of the farm, and gave his whole mind to it. If he went out shooting he did so to get game for the table. He enjoyed the sport, and entered heartily into it, but he did so in a business sort of way.

Hubert was a far more imaginative boy. He stuck to the work of the farm as conscientiously as his brother did, but his attention was by no means of the same concentrated kind. A new butterfly, an uncommon insect, would be irresistible to him; and not unfrequently, when he went out with his gun to procure some game which Mr. Hardy had wanted upon the arrival of some unexpected visitor, he would come back in a high state of triumph with some curious little bird, which he had shot after a long chase, the requirements of the household being altogether forgotten.

Maud was fifteen. Her constant out-of-door exercise had made her as nimble and active as a young fawn. She loved to be out and about, and her two hours of lessons with her mamma in the afternoon were a grievous penance to her.

Ethel wanted three months of fourteen, and looked under twelve. She was quite the home-bird of the family, and liked nothing better than taking her work and sitting by the hour, quietly talking to her mother.

The time was now again approaching when the Indian forays were to be expected. It was still a month earlier than the attack of the year before, and Mr. Hardy, with the increased number of his men, had not the least fear of any successful assault upon Mount Pleasant; but he resolved, when the time came, to take every possible precaution against attacks upon the animals. He ordered that the iron gates of the enclosures should be padlocked at night, and that some of the native dogs should be chained there as sentinels. He looked forward with some little anxiety to the Indian moon, as it is called, because, when he had ridden out with Lopez and two of their Canterbury friends to the scene of the encounter a few days after it had taken place, they found that the Indians had fled so precipitately upon the loss of their horses that they had not even buried the bodies of their friends, and that, short as the time had been, the foxes had left nothing but a few bones remaining of these. From the moccasins, however, and from other relics of the Indians strewn about, Lopez had pronounced at once that two tribes had been engaged in the fray: the one, inhabitants of the pampas--a people which, although ready to murder any solitary whites, seldom attack a prepared foe; and the other, of Indians from the west, of a far more warlike and courageous character. The former tribe, Lopez affirmed--and the natives of the country agreed with him--would not of themselves have been likely to attempt a fresh attack upon antagonists who had proved themselves so formidable, but the latter would be almost certain to make some desperate attempt to wipe off the disgrace of their defeat. Under these circumstances, although perfectly confident of their power to beat off any attack, it was resolved that every precaution should be taken when the time approached.

Late one afternoon, however, Mr. Fitzgerald had gone out for a ride with Mr. Hardy. Charley had gone down to the dam with his gun on his shoulder, and Hubert had ridden to a pool in the river at some distance off, where he had the day before observed a wild duck, which he believed to be a new sort. The cattle and flocks had just been driven in by Lopez and two mounted peons at an earlier hour than usual, as Mr. Hardy had that morning given orders that the animals were all to be in their enclosures before dusk. The laborers in the fields below were still at work plowing. Ethel was in the sitting-room working with Mrs. Hardy, while Maud was in the garden picking some fruit for tea.

Presently the occupants of the parlor were startled by a sharp cry from Maud, and in another instant she flew into the room, rushed at a bound to the fireplace, snatched down her light rifle from its hooks over the mantel, and crying, "Quick, Ethel, your rifle!" was gone again in an instant.

Mrs. Hardy and Ethel sprang to their feet, too surprised for the moment to do anything, and then Mrs. Hardy repeated Maud's words, "Quick, Ethel, your rifle!"

Ethel seized it, and with her mother ran to the door. Then they saw a sight which brought a scream from both their lips. Mrs. Hardy fell on her knees and covered her eyes, while Ethel, after a moment's pause, grasped the rifle, which had nearly fallen from her hands, and ran forward, though her limbs trembled so that they could scarcely carry her on.

The sight was indeed a terrible one. At a distance of two hundred yards Hubert was riding for his life. His hat was off, his gun was gone, his face was deadly pale. Behind him rode three Indians. The nearest one was immediately behind him, at a distance of scarce two horses' length; the other two were close to their leader. All were evidently gaining upon him.

Maud had thrown the gate open, and stood by the post with the barrel of her rifle resting on one of the wires. "Steady, Ethel, steady," she said in a hard, strange voice, as her sister joined her; "Hubert's life depends upon your aim. Wait till I fire, and take the man on the right. Aim at his chest."

The sound of Maud's steady voice acted like magic upon her sister; the mist which had swum before her eyes cleared off; her limbs ceased to tremble, and her hand grew steady. Hubert was now within a hundred yards, but the leading Indian was scarce a horse's length behind. He had his tomahawk already in his hand, in readiness for the fatal blow. Another twenty yards and he whirled it round his head with a yell of exultation.

"Stoop, Hubert, stoop!" Maud cried in a loud, clear voice; and mechanically, with the wild war-whoop behind ringing in his ears, Hubert bent forward on to the horse's mane. He could feel the breath of the Indian's horse against his legs, and his heart seemed to stand still.

Maud and her rifle might have been taken for a statue, so immovable and rigid did she stand; and then as the Indian's arm went back for the blow, crack, and without a word or a cry the Indian fell back, struck with the deadly little bullet in the center of the forehead.

Not so silently did Ethel's bullet do its work. A wild cry followed the report: for an instant the Indian reeled in his saddle, and then, steadying himself, turned his horse sharp round, and with his companion galloped off.

Hubert, as his horse passed through the gate and drew up, almost fell from his seat; and it was with the greatest difficulty that he staggered toward Maud, who had gone off in a dead faint as she saw him ride on alone.

Ethel had sat down on the ground, and was crying passionately, and Terence came running down from the house with a gun in his hand, pouring out Irish threats and ejaculations after the Indians. These were changed into a shout of triumph as

Charley stepped from behind the henhouse, as they passed at a short distance, and at the discharge of his double barrels the unwounded Indian fell heavily from his horse.

Anxious as he was to assist his young mistresses, for Hubert was far too shaken to attempt to lift Maud from the ground, Terence stood riveted to the spot watching the remaining Indian. Twice he reeled in the saddle, and twice recovered himself, but the third time, when he was distant nearly half a mile, he suddenly fell off to the ground.

"I thought the murdering thief had got it," muttered Terence to himself, as he ran down to raise Maud, and with the assistance of Sarah to carry her up to the house, against the doorway of which Mrs. Hardy was still leaning, too agitated to trust herself to walk.

Hubert, now somewhat recovered, endeavored to pacify Ethel, and the two walked slowly up toward the house. In a minute or two Charley came running up, and the peons were seen hurrying toward them. After a silent shake of the hand to his brother, and a short "Thank God!" Charley, with his accustomed energy, took the command.

"Hubert, do you and Terence get all the arms loaded at once. Lopez, tell the peons to hurry up the plow oxen, shut them in the enclosure, and padlock all the gates. I will warn you if there's any danger. Then bring all the men and women up here. I am going to run up the danger flag. Papa is out somewhere on the plains." So saying, and taking his Colt's carbine, he ran up the stairs.

In a moment afterward his voice was heard again. "Hubert, Terence, bring all the guns that are loaded up here at once--quick, quick!" and then he shouted loudly in Spanish, "Come in all; come in for your lives!" In another minute they joined him on the tower with Mr. Hardy's long rifle, Hubert's carbine, and their double-barreled shotguns, into each of which Terence dropped a bullet upon the top of the shot. Hubert could scarcely help giving a cry. At a distance of a quarter of a mile Mr. Hardy and Fitzgerald were coming along, pursued by at least a dozen Indians, who were thirty or forty yards in their rear. They were approaching from behind the house, and would have to make a sweep to get round to the entrance, which was on the right, on the side facing the dam. This would evidently give their pursuers a slight advantage.

"They hold their own," Charley said after a minute's silence; "there is no fear. Lopez!" he shouted, "run and see that the outside as well as the inside gates are open."

It has been already said that a low wire fence had been placed at a distance of a hundred yards beyond the inner enclosure, to protect the young trees from the animals. It was composed of two wires, only a foot apart, and was almost hidden by the long grass. It had a low gate, corresponding in position to the inner one. Charley's quick eye saw at once the importance of the position.

"I think you might use the long rifle now," Hubert said; "it might stop them if they feel that they are in reach of our guns."

"No, no," Charley said, "I don't want to stop them; don't show the end of a gun above the wall." Then he was silent until his father was within three hundred yards. He then shouted at the top of his voice, "Mind the outside fence, mind the outside fence!"

Mr. Hardy raised a hand to show that he heard, and as he approached, Charley shouted again, "Sweep well round the fence, well round it, for them to try and cut you off."

Charley could see that Mr. Hardy heard, for he turned his horse's head so as to go rather wide of the corner of the fence. "Now, Hubert and Terence, get ready; we shall have them directly."

Mr. Hardy and his companion galloped past, with the Indians still fifty yards behind them. Keeping twenty yards from the corner of the fence, the fugitives wheeled round to the right, and the Indians, with a cry of exultation, turned to the right also to cut them off. The low treacherous wire was unnoticed, and in another moment men and horses were rolling in a confused mass upon the ground.

"Now," Charley said, "every barrel we have;" and from the top of the tower a rain of lead poured down upon the bewildered Indians. The horses, frightened and wounded, kicked and struggled dreadfully, and did almost as much harm to their masters as the deadly bullets of the whites; and when the fire ceased not more than half of them regained their seats and galloped off, leaving the rest, men and horses, in a ghastly heap. Seeing them in full retreat, the occupants of the tower descended to receive Mr. Hardy and Fitzgerald, Terence much delighted at having at last had his share in a skirmish.

"Well done, boys! Very well planned, Charley!" Mr. Hardy said as he reined in his horse. "That was a near escape."

"Not as near a one as Hubert has had, by a long way, papa."

"Indeed!" Mr. Hardy said anxiously. "Let me hear all about it."

"We have not heard ourselves yet," Charley answered. "It occurred only a few minutes before your own. The girls behaved splendidly; but they are rather upset now. If you will go up to the house to them, I will be up directly, but there are a few things to see about first. Lopez," he went on, "carry out what I told you before: get the men in from the plows and see all secured. Tell them to hurry, for it will be dark soon. Kill a couple of sheep and bring them up to the house; we shall be a large party, and it may be wanted. Then let the peons all have supper. Come up to the house in an hour for instructions. See yourself that the dogs are fastened down by the cattle. Terence, take your place on the lookout, and fire a gun if you see any one moving."

Having seen that his various orders were obeyed, Charley went up to the house. He found the whole party assembled in the sitting-room. Maud and Ethel had quite recovered, although both looked pale. Mrs. Hardy, absorbed in her attention to them, had fortunately heard nothing of her husband's danger until the firing from above, followed by a shout of triumph, told her that any danger there was had been defeated.

"Now, papa," Charley said, "you give us your account first."

"I have not much to tell, Charley. Fitzgerald and I had ridden out some distance--five miles, I should say--when the dogs stopped at a thicket and put out a lion. Fitzgerald and I both fired with our left-hand barrels, which were loaded with ball. The beast fell, and we got off to skin him. Dash barked furiously, and we saw a couple of dozen Indians coming up close to us. We stopped a moment to give them our barrels with duck-shot, and then jumped into our saddles and rode for it. Unfortunately, we had been foolish enough to go out without our revolvers. They pressed us hard, but I was never in fear of their actually catching us; my only alarm was that one of us might repeat my disaster of the armadillo hole. So I only tried to hold my own thirty or forty yards ahead. I made sure that one or other of you would see us coming, and I should have shouted loudly enough, I can tell you, to warn you as I came up. Besides, I knew that at the worst the arms were hanging above the fireplace, and that we only wanted time to run in, catch them up, and get to the door, to be able to defend the house till you could help us. And now, what is your story, Charley?"

"I have even less than you, papa. I was down at the dam, and then I went into the henhouse, and I was just thinking that I could make a better arrangement for the nests, when I heard an Indian war-yell between me and the house. It was followed almost directly by two cracks which I knew were the girls' rifles. I rushed to the door and looked out, and I saw two Indians coming along at full gallop. By the direction they were taking, they would pass only a little way from the henhouse; so I stepped back till I heard they were opposite, and then, going out, I gave both barrels to the nearest to me, and stopped his galloping about pretty effectually. When I reached the place I saw that Hubert had had a narrow squeak of it, for Maud had fainted, and Ethel was in a great state of cry. But I had no time to ask many questions, for I ran up to hoist the danger flag, and then saw you and Fitzgerald coming along with the Indians after you. Now, Hubert, let's hear your story."

"Well, papa, you know I said yesterday that I was sure that I had seen a new duck, and this afternoon I rode out to the pools, in hopes that he might still be there. I left my horse and crept on very cautiously through the reeds till I got sight of the water. Sure enough, there was the duck, rather on the other side. I waited for a long half-hour, and at last he came over rather nearer. He dived at my first barrel, but as he came up I gave him my second. Flirt went in and brought him out. He was new, sure enough--two blue feathers under the eye--"

"Bother the duck, Hubert," Charley put in. "We don't care for his blue feathers; we want to hear about the Indians."

"Well, I am coming to the Indians," Hubert said; "but it was a new duck, for all that; and if you like it, I will show it you. There!" And he took it out of his pocket and laid it on the table. No one appeared to have the slightest interest in it, or to pay any attention to it. So Hubert went on: "Well, after looking at the duck, I put it into my pocket, and went out from the bushes to my horse. As I got to him I heard a yell, which nearly made me tumble down, it startled me so; and not a hundred yards away, and riding to cut me off from home, were thirty or forty Indians. I was not long, as you may guess, climbing into my saddle, and bolted like a shot. I could not make straight for home, but had to make a sweep to get round them. I was better mounted than all of them, except three; but they kept gradually gaining on me, while all the rest in turn gave up the chase; and, like papa, I had left my revolver behind. Black Tom did his best, and I encouraged him to the utmost; but I began to think that it was all up with me, for I was convinced that they would catch me before I could get in. When I was little more than three hundred yards from the gate I saw Maud come dashing down with her rifle toward the gate, and a little afterward Ethel came too. The Indians kept getting nearer and nearer, and I expected every moment to feel the tomahawk. I could not think why the girls did not fire, but I supposed that they did not feel sure enough of their aim: and I had the consolation that the Indian nearest could not be going to strike, or they would risk a shot. On I went: the Indian was so close that I could feel his horse's breath, and the idea came across my mind that the brute was trying to catch hold of the calf of my leg. At a hundred yards I could see Maud's face quite plain, and then I felt certain I was saved. She looked as steady as if she had been taking aim at a mark, and the thought flashed across me of how last week she had hit a small stone on a post, at eighty yards, first shot, when Charley and I had missed it half a dozen times each. Then there was a frightful yell, almost in my ear. Then I heard Maud cry out, 'Stoop, Hubert, stoop!' I was stooping before, but my head went down to the horse's mane, I can tell you.' And then there was the crack of the two rifles, and a yell of pain. I could not look round, but I felt that the horse behind me had stopped, and that I was safe. That's my story, papa."

A few more questions elicited from Mrs. Hardy all that she knew of it, and then the warmest commendations were bestowed upon the girls. Ethel, however, generously disclaimed all praise, as she said that she should have done nothing at all had it not been for Maud's steadiness and coolness.

"And now let us have our tea," Mr. Hardy said; "and then we can talk over our measures for to-night."

"Do you think that they will attack us, papa?" Ethel asked.

"Yes, Ethel, I think that most likely they will. As we came across the plain I noticed several other parties quite in the distance. There must be a very strong body out altogether, and probably they have resolved upon vengeance for their last year's defeat. They had better have left it alone, for they have no more chance of taking this house, with us all upon our guard, than they have of flying. There is one advantage in it--they will get such a lesson that I do think we shall be perfectly free from Indian attacks for the future."

After tea Lopez came up for orders. "You will place," Mr. Hardy said, "two peons at each corner of the outside fence. One of us will come round every half-hour to see that all is right. Their instructions are that in case they hear any movement one is to come up to us immediately with the news, and the other is to go round to tell the other sentries to do the same. All this is to be done in perfect silence. I do not want them to know that we are ready for their reception. Bring some fresh straw up and lay it down here on the floor: the women can sleep here."

"What shall I do about your own horses, signor?" Lopez asked.

Mr. Hardy thought a moment. "I think you had better send them down to the enclosure with the others; they might be driven off if they are left up here, and I do not see that we can require them."

"But what about the cattle, papa?" Charley asked.

"It would be a serious loss if they were driven off, especially the milch cows. If you like, I will go down with Terence, and we can take up our station among them. It would be a strong post, for the Indians of course could not attack us on horseback; and with my carbine, and Terence's gun, and a brace of revolvers, I think we could beat them off easily enough, especially as you would cover us with your guns."

"I had thought of that plan, Charley; but it would be dangerous, and would cause us up here great anxiety, I imagine, too, that as no doubt their great object is vengeance, they will attack us first here, or they may make an effort upon the cattle at the same time that they attack here. They will not begin with the animals. They will find it a very difficult business to break down the fence, which they must do to drive them out; and while they are about it we shall not be idle, depend upon it."

The preparations were soon made and it was agreed that Mr. Hardy and Hubert should go the rounds alternately with Charley and Fitzgerald. As a usual thing, the Indian attacks take place in the last hour or two of darkness. Mr. Hardy thought, however, that an exception would be made in the present case, in order that they might get as far as possible away before any pursuit took place. The wives of the peons lay down to sleep on the straw which had been thrown down for them. The men sat outside the door, smoking their cigarettes and talking in low whispers. Mrs. Hardy was in her room; Ethel kept her company, Maud dividing her time between them and the top of the tower, where Mr. Hardy, Fitzgerald, and the boys were assembled in the intervals between going their rounds.

At about ten o'clock there was a sharp bark from one of the dogs fastened up by the fold, followed up by a general barking of all the dogs on the establishment.

"There they are," Mr. Hardy said. "Charley, bring the mastiffs inside, and order them, and the retrievers too, to be quiet. We do not want any noise up here, to tell the Indians that we are on the watch. Now, Fitzgerald, you go to the sentries behind the house, and I will go to those in front, to tell them to fall back at once."

This mission was, however, unnecessary, for the eight peons all arrived in a minute or two, having fled from their posts at the first barking of the dogs, and without obeying their orders to send round to each other to give notice of their retreat.

Mr. Hardy was very angry with them, but they were in such abject fear of the Indians that they paid little heed to their master's words, but went and huddled themselves together upon the straw in the sitting-room, remaining there without movement until all was over. Terence was now recalled from the gate, which had been his post.

"Did you hear anything, Terence?"

"Sure, your honor, and I thought I heard a dull sound like a lot of horses galloping in the distance. I should say that there were a great many of them. It seemed to get a little louder, and then it stopped."

"That was before the dogs began to bark, Terence?"

"About five minutes before, your honor."

"Yes. I have no doubt that they all dismounted to make the attack on foot. How quiet everything is!"

The general barking of the dogs had now ceased: sometimes one or another gave a suspicious yelping bark, but between these no sound whatever was audible. The door was now closed and barred; candles were lighted and placed in every room, thick cloths having been hung up before the loopholes in the shutters, to prevent a ray of light from escaping; and the windows themselves were opened. Mr. Fitzgerald, the boys, and Maud took their station on the tower, Mr. Hardy remaining with his wife and Ethel, while Terence and Lopez kept watch in the other apartments. The arrangements for the defense were that Mr. Fitzgerald, Lopez, and

Terence should defend the lower part of the house. There were in all six double-barreled guns--two to each of them; and three of the peons more courageous than the others offered to load the guns as they were discharged.

Mr. Hardy and the boys had their place on the tower, from which they commanded the whole garden. They had the long rifle, the carbines, and four revolvers. Mrs. Hardy and the girls took their place in the upper room of the tower, where there was a light. Their rifles were ready in case of necessity, but their principal duty was to load the spare chambers of the carbines and pistols as fast as they were emptied, the agreement being that the girls should go up by turns to take the loaded ones and bring down the empties. Sarah's place was her kitchen, where she could hear all that was going on below, and she was to call up the ladder in case aid was required. And so, all being in readiness, they calmly awaited the attack.

CHAPTER XIII.
THE INDIAN ATTACK.

For nearly half an hour the occupants of the tower remained without hearing the smallest sound. Then there was a slight jarring noise.

"They are getting over the fence," Mr. Hardy whispered. "Go down now every one to his station. Keep the dogs quiet, and mind, let no one fire until I give the signal."

Over and over again the clinking noise was repeated. Cautious as the Indians were, it was impossible even for them to get over that strange and difficult obstacle without touching the wires with their arms. Occasionally Mr. Hardy and the boys fancied that they could see dark objects stealing toward the house through the gloom; otherwise all was still.

"Boys," Mr. Hardy said, "I have changed my mind. There will be numbers at the doors and windows, whom we cannot get at from here. Steal quietly downstairs, and take your position each at a window. Then, when the signal is given, fire both your revolvers. Don't throw away a shot. Darken all the rooms except the kitchen. You will see better to take aim through the loopholes; it will be quite light outside. When you have emptied your revolvers, come straight up here, leaving them for the girls to load as you pass."

Without a word the boys slipped away. Mr. Hardy then placed on a round shelf nailed to the flagstaff, at about eight feet from the ground, a blue-light, fitting into a socket on the shelf. The shelf was made just so large that it threw a shadow over the top of the tower, so that those standing there were in comparative darkness, while everything around was in bright light. There, with a match in his hand to light the blue-light, he awaited the signal.

It was a long time coming--so long that the pause grew painful, and every one in the house longed for the bursting of the coming storm. At last it came. A wild, long, savage yell from hundreds of throats rose on the still night air, and, confident as they were in their position, there was not one of the garrison but felt his blood grow cold at the appalling ferocity of the cry. Simultaneously there was a tremendous rush at the doors and windows, which tried the strength of frame and bar. Then, as they stood firm, came a rain of blows with hatchet and tomahawk.

Then came a momentary pause of astonishment. The weapons, instead of splintering the wood, merely made deep dents, or glided off harmlessly. Then the blows redoubled, and then a bright light suddenly lit up the whole scene. As it did so, from every loophole a stream of fire poured out, repeated again and again. The guns, heavily loaded with buckshot, told with terrible effect upon the crowded mass of Indians around the windows, and the discharge of the four barrels from each of the three windows of the room at the back of the house, by Fitzgerald, Lopez, and Terence, for awhile cleared the assailants from that quarter. After the first yell of astonishment and rage, a perfect quiet succeeded to the din which had raged there, broken only by the ring of the ramrods, as the three men and their assistants hastily reloaded their guns, and then hurried to the front of the house, where their presence was urgently required.

Knowing the tremendous rush there would be at the door, Charley and Hubert had posted themselves at its two loopholes, leaving the windows to take care of themselves for the present. The first rush was so tremendous that the door trembled on its posts, massive as it was; and the boys, thinking that it would come in, threw the weight of their bodies against it. Then with the failure of the first rush came the storm of blows; and the boys stood with their pistols leveled through the holes, waiting for the light which was to enable them to see their foes.

As it came they fired together, and two Indians fell. Again and again they fired, until not an Indian remained standing opposite the fatal door. Then each took a window, for there was one at each side of the door, and these they held, rushing occasionally into the rooms on either side to check the assailants there.

In this fight Sarah had certainly the honor of first blood. She was a courageous woman, and was determined to do her best in defense of the house. As an appropriate weapon, she had placed the end of the spit in the fire, and at the moment of the attack it was white-hot. Seeing the shutter bend with the pressure of the Indians against it, she seized the spit, and plunged it through the loophole with all her force. A fearful yell followed, which rose even above the tremendous din around.

There was a lull so profound after the discharge of the last barrels of the boys' revolvers as to be almost startling. Running upstairs, they fitted fresh chambers to their weapons, left the empty ones with their sisters, and joined their father.

"That's right, boys; the attack is beaten off for the present. Now take your carbines. There is a band of Indians down by the animals. I heard their war-whoops when the others began, but the light hardly reaches so far. Now look out, I am going to send up a rocket over them. The cows are the most important; so, Charley, you direct all your shots at any party there. Hubert, divide yours among the rest."

In another moment the rocket flew up into the air, and as the bright light burst out a group of Indians could be seen at the gateway of each of the enclosures. As the brilliant light broke over them they scattered with a cry of astonishment. Before the light faded the twelve barrels had been fired among them.

As the rocket burst Mr. Hardy had gazed eagerly over the country, and fancied that he could see a dark mass at a distance of half a mile. This he guessed to be the Indians' horses.

By this time the blue-light was burning low, and Mr. Hardy, stretching his hand up, lit another at its blaze, and planted the fresh one down upon it. As he did so a whizzing of numerous arrows showed that they were watched. One went through his coat, fortunately without touching him; another went right through his arm; and a third laid Charley's cheek open from the lip to the ear.

"Keep your heads below the wall, boys," their father shouted. "Are you hurt, Charley?"

"Not seriously, papa, but it hurts awfully;" and Charley stamped with rage and pain.

"What has become of the Indians round the house?" Hubert asked. "They are making no fresh attack."

"No," Mr. Hardy said; "they have had enough of it. They are only wondering how they are to get away. You see the fence is exposed all round to our fire, for the trees don't go within twenty yards of it. They are neither in front nor behind the house, for it is pretty open in both directions, and we should see them. They are not at this side of the house, so they must be standing close to the wall between the windows, and must be crowded among the trees and shrubs at the other end. There is no window there, so they are safe as long as they stay quiet."

"No, papa," Hubert said eagerly; "don't you remember we left two loopholes in each room, when we built it, on purpose, only putting in pieces of wood and filling up the cracks with clay to keep out the wind?"

"Of course we did, Hubert. I remember all about it now. Run down and tell them to be ready to pull the wood out and to fire through when they hear the next rocket go off. I am going to send another light rocket over in the direction where I saw the horses; and directly I get the line I will send off cracker-rocket after cracker-rocket as quickly as I can at them. What with the fire from below among them, and the fright they will get when they see the horses attacked, they are sure to make a rush for it."

In a minute Hubert came back with the word that the men below were ready. In a moment a rocket soared far away to behind the house; and just as its light broke over the plains another one swept over in the direction of a dark mass of animals, seen plainly enough in the distance.

A cry of dismay burst from the Indians, rising in yet wilder alarm as three shots were fired from the wall of the house into their crowded mass. Again and again was the discharge repeated, and with a yell of dismay a wild rush was made for the fence. Then the boys with their carbines, and Mr. Hardy with the revolvers, opened upon them, every shot telling in the dense mass who struggled to surmount the fatal railings.

Frenzied with the danger, dozens attempted to climb them, and, strong as were the wires and posts, there was a cracking sound, and the whole side fell. In another minute, of the struggling mass there remained only some twenty motionless forms. Three or four more rockets were sent off in the direction where the horses had been seen, and then another signal rocket, whose light enabled them to see that the black mass was broken up, and that the whole plain was covered with scattered figures of men and animals, all flying at the top of their speed.

"Thank God, it is all over, and we are safe!" Mr. Hardy said solemnly. "Never again will an Indian attack be made upon Mount Pleasant. It is all over now, my dear," he said to Mrs. Hardy as he went down the stairs; "they are off all over the country, and it will take them hours to get their horses together again. Two of us have got scratched with arrows, but no real harm is done. Charley's is only a flesh wound. Don't be frightened," he added quickly, as Mrs. Hardy turned pale and the girls gave a cry at the appearance of Charley's face, which was certainly alarming. "A little warm water and a bandage will put it all right."

"Do you think it will leave a scar?" Charley asked rather dolorously.

"Well, Charley, I should not be surprised if it does; but it won't spoil your beauty long, your whiskers will cover it: besides, a scar won in honorable conflict is always admired by ladies, you know. Now let us go downstairs; my arm, too, wants bandaging, for it is beginning to smart amazingly; and I am sure we all must want something to eat."

The supper was eaten hurriedly, and then all but Terence, who, as a measure of precaution, was stationed as watchman on the tower, were glad to lie down for a few hours' sleep. At daybreak they were up and moving.

Mr. Hardy requested that neither his wife nor daughters should go outside the house until the dead Indians were removed and buried, as the sight could not but be a most shocking one. Two of the peons were ordered to put in the oxen and bring up two carts, and the rest of the men set about the unpleasant duty of examining and collecting the slain.

These were even more numerous than Mr. Hardy had anticipated, and showed how thickly they must have been clustered round the door and windows. The guns had been loaded with buckshot; two bullets he dropped down each barrel in addition; and the discharge of these had been most destructive, more especially those fired through the loopholes at the end of the house. There no less than sixteen bodies were found, while around the door and windows were thirteen others. All these were dead. The guns, having been discharged through loopholes breast-high, had taken effect upon the head and body.

At the fence were fourteen. Of these twelve were dead, another still breathed, but was evidently dying, while one had only a broken leg. Unquestionably several others had been wounded, but had managed to make off. The bullets of revolvers, unless striking a mortal point, disable a wounded man much less than the balls of heavier caliber. It was evidently useless to remove the Indian who was dying; all that could be done for him was to give him a little water, and to place a bundle of grass so as to raise his head. Half an hour later he was dead. The other wounded man was carried carefully down to one of the sheds, where a bed of hay was prepared for him. Two more wounded men were found down by the cattle enclosures, and these also Mr. Hardy considered likely to recover. They were taken up and laid by their comrade. Three dead bodies were found here. These were all taken in the bullock carts to a spot distant nearly half a mile from the house.

Here, by the united labor of the peons, a large grave was dug, six feet wide, as much deep, and twelve yards long. In this they were laid side by side, two deep; the earth was filled in, and the turf replaced. At Hubert's suggestion, two young palm trees were taken out of the garden and placed one at each end, and a wire fence was erected all round, to keep off the animals.

It was a sad task; and although they had been killed in an attack in which, had they been victorious, they would have shown no mercy, still Mr. Hardy and his sons were deeply grieved at having caused the destruction of so many lives.

It was late in the afternoon before all was done, and the party returned to the house with lightened hearts, that the painful task was finished. Here things had nearly resumed their ordinary aspect. Terence had washed away the stains of blood; and save that many of the young trees had been broken down, and that one side of the fence was leveled, no one would have imagined that a sanguinary contest had taken place there so lately.

Mr. Hardy stopped on the way to examine the wounded men. He had acquired a slight knowledge of rough surgery in his early life upon the prairies, and he discovered the bullet at a short distance under the skin in the broken leg. Making signs to the man that he was going to do him good, and calling in Fitzgerald and Lopez to hold the Indian if necessary, he took out his knife, cut down to the bullet, and with some trouble succeeded in extracting it. The Indian never flinched or groaned, although the pain must have been very great while the operation was being performed. Mr. Hardy then carefully bandaged the limb, and directed that cold water should be poured over it from time to time, to allay the inflammation. Another of the Indians had his ankle-joint broken: this was also carefully bandaged. The third had a bullet wound near the hip, and with this Mr. Hardy could do nothing. His recovery or death would depend entirely upon nature.

It may here be mentioned at once that all three of the Indians eventually recovered, although two of them were slightly lamed for life. All that care and attention could do for them was done; and when they were in a fit condition to travel their horses and a supply of provisions were given to them. The Indians had maintained during the whole time the stolid apathy of their race. They had expressed no thanks for the kindness bestowed upon them. Only when their horses were presented to them, and bows and arrows placed in their hands, with an intimation that they were free to go, did their countenances change.

Up to that time it is probable that they believed that they were only being kept to be solemnly put to death. Their faces lit up, and without a word they sprang on to the horses' backs, and dashed over the plains.

Ere they had gone three hundred yards they halted, and came back at equal speed, stopping abruptly before the surprised and rather startled group. "Good man," the eldest of them said, pointing to Mr. Hardy. "Good," he repeated, motioning to the boys. "Good misses," and he included Mrs. Hardy and the girls; and then the three turned-and never slackened their speed as long as they were in sight.

The Indians of the South American pampas and sierras are a very inferior race to the noble-looking Comanches and Apaches of the North American prairies. They are generally short, wiry men, with long black hair. They have flat faces, with high cheek bones. Their complexion is a dark copper color, and they are generally extremely ugly.

In the course of the morning after the fight Mr. Cooper rode over from Canterbury, and was greatly surprised to hear of the attack. The Indians had not been seen or heard of at his estate, and he was ignorant of anything having taken place until his arrival.

For the next few days there was quite a levee of visitors, who came over to hear of the particulars, and to offer their congratulations. All the outlying settlers were particularly pleased, as it was considered certain that the Indians would not visit that neighborhood again for some time.

Shortly afterward the government sales for the land beyond Mount Pleasant took place. Mr. Hardy went over to Rosario to attend them, and bought the plot of four square leagues immediately adjoining his own, giving the same price that he had paid for Mount Pleasant. The properties on each side of this were purchased by the two Edwards, and by an Englishman who had lately arrived in the colony. His name was Mercer: he was accompanied by his wife and two young children, and his wife's brother, whose name was Parkinson. Mr. Hardy had made their acquaintance at Rosario, and pronounced them to be a very pleasant family. They had brought out a considerable capital, and were coming in a week with a strong force to erect their house. Mr. Hardy had promised them every assistance, and had invited Mrs. Mercer to take up her abode at Mount Pleasant with her children, until the frame house which they had brought out could be erected--an invitation which had been gladly accepted.

There was great pleasure at the thought of another lady in the neighborhood; and Mrs. Hardy was especially pleased for the girls' sake, as she thought that a little female society would be of very great advantage to them.

The plots of land next to the Mercers and Edwards were bought, the one by three or four Germans working as a company together, the other by Don Martinez, an enterprising young Spaniard; so that the Hardys began to be in quite an inhabited country. It is true that most of the houses would be six miles off; but that is close, on the pampas. There was a talk, too, of the native overseer of the land between Canterbury and the Jamiesons selling his ground in plots of a mile square. This would make the country comparatively thickly populated. Indeed, with the exception of Mr. Mercer, who had taken up a four-league plot, the other new settlers had in no case purchased more than a square league. The settlements would therefore be pretty thick together.

In a few days Mrs. Mercer arrived with her children. The boys gave up their room to her--they themselves, with Mr. Fitzgerald and four peons, accompanying Mr. Mercer and the party he had brought with him, to assist in erecting his house, and in putting up a strong wire fence, similar to their own, for defense. This operation was finished in a week; and Mrs. Mercer, to the regret of Mrs. Hardy and the girls, then joined her husband. The house had been built near the northeast corner of the property. It was therefore little more than six miles distant from Mount Pleasant, and a constant interchange of visits was arranged to take place.

Shortly afterward Mr. Hardy suggested that the time had now come for improving the house, and laid before his assembled family his plans for so doing, which were received with great applause.

The new portion was to stand in front of the old, and was to consist of a wide entrance-hall, with a large dining and drawing-room upon either side. Upon the floor above were to be four bedrooms. The old sitting-room was to be made into the kitchen, and was to be lighted by a skylight in the roof. The present kitchen was to become a laundry, the windows of that and the bedroom opposite being placed in the side walls, instead of being in front. The new portion was to be made of properly baked bricks, and was to be surrounded by a wide veranda. Of the present bedrooms, two were to be used as spare rooms, one of the others being devoted to two additional indoor servants whom it was now proposed to keep.

It was arranged that the carts should at once commence going backward and forward to Rosario, to fetch coal for the brickmaking, tiles, wood, etc., and that an experienced brickmaker should be engaged, all the hands at the farm being fully occupied. It would take a month or six weeks, it was calculated, before all would be ready to begin building; and then Mrs. Hardy and the girls were to start for a long promised visit to their friends the Thompsons, near Buenos Ayres, so as to be away during the mess and confusion of the building. An engagement was made on the following week with two Italian women at Rosario, the one as a cook, the other as general servant, Sarah undertaking the management of the dairy during her mistress' absence.

CHAPTER XIV.
TERRIBLE NEWS.

Another two years passed over, bringing increased prosperity to the Hardys. No renewal of the Indian attacks had occurred, and in consequence an increased flow of emigration had taken place in their neighborhood. Settlers were now established upon all the lots for many miles upon either side of Mount Pleasant; and even beyond the twelve miles which the estate stretched to the south the lots had been sold. Mr. Hardy considered that all danger of the flocks and herds being driven off had now ceased, and had therefore added considerably to their numbers, and had determined to allow them to increase without further sales until they had attained to the extent of the supporting power of the immense estate.

Two hundred acres of irrigated land were under cultivation; the dairy contained the produce of a hundred cows; and altogether Mount Pleasant was considered one of the finest and most profitable estancias in the province.

The house was now worthy of the estate; the inside fence had been removed fifty yards further off, and the vegetable garden to a greater distance, the includes space being laid out entirely as a pleasure garden.

Beautiful tropical trees and shrubs, gorgeous patches of flowers, and green turf surrounded the front and sides; while behind was a luxuriant and most productive orchard.

The young Hardys had for come time given up doing any personal labor, and were incessantly occupied in the supervision of the estate and of the numerous hands employed: for them a long range of adobe huts had been built at some little distance in the rear of the enclosure.

Maud and Ethel had during this period devoted much more time to their studies, and the time was approaching when Mrs. Hardy was to return with them to England, in order that they might pass a year in London under the instruction of the best masters. Maud was now seventeen, and could fairly claim to be looked upon as a young woman. Ethel still looked very much younger than her real age: any one, indeed, would have guessed that there was at least three years' difference between the sisters. In point of acquirements, however, she was quite her equal, her much greater perseverance more than making up for her sister's quickness.

A year previously Mr. Hardy had, at one of his visits to Buenos Ayres, purchased a piano, saying nothing of what he had done upon his return; and the delight of the girls and their mother, when the instrument arrived in a bullock cart, was unbounded. From that time the girls practiced almost incessantly; indeed, as Charley remarked, it was as bad as living in the house with a whole boarding-school of girls.

After this Mount Pleasant, which had always been considered as the most hospitable and pleasant estancia in the district, became more than ever popular, and many were the impromptu dances got up. Sometimes there were more formal affairs, and all the ladies within twenty miles would come in. These were more numerous than would have been expected. The Jamiesons were doing well, and in turn going for a visit to their native country, had brought out two bright young Scotchwomen as their wives.

Mrs. Mercer was sure to be there, and four or five other English ladies from nearer or more distant estancias. Some ten or twelve native ladies, wives or daughters of native proprietors, would also come in, and the dancing would be kept up until a very late hour. Then the ladies would lie down for a short time, all the beds being given up to them, and a number of shake-downs improvised; while the gentlemen would sit and smoke for an hour or two, and then, as day broke, go down for a bathe in the river. These parties were looked upon by all as most enjoyable affairs; and as eatables of all sorts were provided by the estate itself, they were a very slight expense, and were of frequent occurrence. Only one thing Mr. Hardy bargained for--no wines or other expensive liquors were to be drunk. He was doing well--far, indeed, beyond his utmost expectation--but at the same time he did not consider himself justified in spending money upon luxuries.

Tea, therefore, and cooling drinks made from fruits, after the custom of the country, were provided in abundance for the dancers; but wine was not produced. With this proviso, Mr. Hardy had no objection to his young people having their dances frequently; and in a country where all were living in a rough way, and wine was an unknown luxury, no one missed it. In other respects the supper tables might have been admired at an English ball. Of substantials there was abundance--turkeys and fowls, wild duck and other game. The sweets were represented by trifle, creams, and blanc-manges; while there was a superb show of fruit--apricots, peaches, nectarines, pineapples, melons, and grapes. Among them were vases of gorgeous flowers, most of them tropical in character, but with them were many old English friends, of which Mr. Hardy had procured seeds.

Their neighbors at Canterbury were still their most intimate friends: they were shortly, however, to lose one of them. Mr. Cooper had heard six months before of the death of his two elder brothers in rapid succession, and he was now heir to his father's property, which was very extensive. It had been supposed that he would at once return to England, and he was continually talking of doing so; but he had, under one excuse or other, put off his departure from time to time. He was very frequently over at Mount Pleasant and was generally a companion of the boys upon their excursions.

"I think Cooper is almost as much here as he is at Canterbury," Charley said, laughing, one day.

Mrs. Hardy happened to glance at Maud, and noticed a bright flush of color on her cheeks. She made no remark at the time, but spoke to Mr. Hardy about it at night.

"You see, my dear," she concluded, "we are still considering Maud as a child, but other people may look upon her as a woman."

"I am sorry for this," Mr. Hardy said after a pause, "We ought to have foreseen the possibility of such a thing. Now that it is mentioned, I wonder we did not do so before. Mr. Cooper has been here so much that the thing would have certainly struck us, had we not, as you say, looked upon Maud as a child. Against Mr. Cooper I have nothing to say. We both like him extremely. His principles are good, and he would, in point of money, be of course an excellent match for our little girl. At the same time, I cannot permit anything like an engagement. Mr. Cooper has seen no other ladies for so long a time that it is natural enough he should fall in love with

Maud. Maud, on the other hand, has only seen the fifteen or twenty men who came here; she knows nothing of the world and is altogether inexperienced. They are both going to England, and may not improbably meet people whom they may like very much better, and may look upon this love-making in the pampas as a folly. At the end of another two years, when Maud is nineteen, if Mr. Cooper renew the acquaintance in England, and both parties agree, I shall of course offer no objection, and indeed should rejoice much at a match which would promise well for her happiness."

Mrs. Hardy thoroughly agreed with her husband, and so the matter rested for a short time.

It was well that Mr. Hardy had been warned by his wife, for a week after this Mr. Cooper met him alone when he was out riding, and after some introduction, expressed to him that he had long felt that he had loved his daughter, but had waited until she was seventeen before expressing his wishes. He said that he had delayed his departure for England on this account alone, and now asked permission to pay his addresses to her, adding that he hoped that he was not altogether indifferent to her.

Mr. Hardy heard him quietly to the end.

"I can hardly say that I am unprepared for what you say, Mr. Cooper, although I had never thought of such a thing until two days since. Then your long delay here, and your frequent visits to our house, opened the eyes of Mrs. Hardy and myself. To yourself, personally, I can entertain no objection. Still, when I remember that you are only twenty-six, and that for the last four years you have seen no one with whom you could possibly fall in love, with the exception of my daughter, I can hardly think that you have had sufficient opportunity to know your own mind. When you return to England you will meet young ladies very much prettier and very much more accomplished than my Maud, and you may regret the haste which led you to form an engagement out here."

"You shake your head, as is natural that you should do; but I repeat, you cannot at present know your own mind. If this is true of you, it is still more true of my daughter. She is very young, and knows nothing whatever of the world. Next month she proceeds to England with her mother, and for the next two years she will be engaged upon finishing her education. At the end of that time I shall myself return to England, and we shall then enter into society. If at that time you are still of the same way of thinking, and choose to renew our acquaintance, I shall be very happy, in the event of Maud accepting you, to give my consent. But I must insist that there shall be no engagement, no love-making, no understanding of any sort or kind, before you start. I put it to your honor as a gentleman, that you will make no effort to meet her alone, and that you will say nothing whatever to her, to lead her to believe that you are in love with her. Only when you say good-by to her, you may say that I have told you that as the next two years are to be passed in study, to make up for past deficiencies, I do not wish her to enter at all into society, but that at the end of that time you hope to renew the acquaintance."

Mr. Cooper endeavored in vain to alter Mr. Hardy's determination, and was at last obliged to give the required promise.

Mr. and Mrs. Hardy were not surprised when, two or three days after this, Mr. Cooper rode up and said that he had come to say good-by, that he had received letters urging him to return at once, and had therefore made up his mind to start by the next mail from Buenos Ayres.

The young Hardys were all surprised at this sudden determination, but there was little time to discuss it, as Mr. Cooper had to start the same night for Rosario.

Very warm and earnest were the adieus; and the color, which had rather left Maud's face, returned with redoubled force as he held her hand, and said very earnestly the words Mr. Hardy had permitted him to use.

Then he leaped into his saddle and galloped off, waving his hand, as he crossed the river, to the group which were still standing in the veranda watching him.

For a few days after this Maud was unusually quiet and subdued, but her natural spirits speedily recovered themselves, and she was soon as lively and gay as ever.

About a fortnight after the departure of Mr. Cooper an event took place which for awhile threatened to upset all the plans which they had formed for the future.

One or other of the girls were in the habit of frequently going over to stay for a day or two with Mrs. Mercer.

One evening Hubert rode over with Ethel, and Mrs. Mercer persuaded the latter to stay for the night; Hubert declining to do so, as he had arranged with Charley to go over early to Canterbury to assist at the branding of the cattle at that station.

In the morning they had taken their coffee, and were preparing for a start, when, just as they were mounting their horses, one of the men drew their attention to a man running at full speed toward the house from the direction of Mr. Mercer's.

"What can be the matter?" Charley said. "What a strange thing that a messenger should come over on foot instead of on horseback!"

"Let's ride and meet him, Charley," Hubert said; and putting spurs to their horses, they galloped toward the approaching figure.

As they came close to him he stumbled and fell, and lay upon the ground, exhausted and unable to rise.

The boys sprang from their horses with a feeling of vague uneasiness and alarm.

"What is the matter?" they asked. The peon was too exhausted to reply for a moment or two; then he gasped out, "Los Indies! the Indians!"

The boys gave a simultaneous cry of dread.

"What has happened? Tell us quick, man; are they attacking the estancia?" The man shook his head.

"Estancia burnt. All killed but me," he said.

The news was too sudden and terrible for the boys to speak. They stood white and motionless with horror. "All killed! Oh, Ethel, Ethel!" Charley groaned.

Hubert burst into tears. "What will mamma do?"

"Come, Hubert," Charley said, dashing away the tears from his eyes, "do not let us waste a moment. All hope may not be over. The Indians seldom kill women, but carry them away, and she may be alive yet. If she is, we will rescue her, if we go right across America. Come, man, jump up behind me on my horse."

The peon obeyed the order, and in five minutes they reached the gate. Here they dismounted.

"Let us walk up to the house, Hubert, so as not to excite suspicion. We must call papa out and tell him first, so that he may break it to mamma. If she learn it suddenly, it may kill her."

Mr. Hardy had just taken his coffee, and was standing at the door, looking with a pleased eye upon the signs of comfort and prosperity around him. There was no need, therefore, for them to approach nearer. As Mr. Hardy looked round upon hearing the gate shut, Charley beckoned to him to come down to them. For a moment he seemed puzzled, and looked round to see if the signal was directed to himself. Seeing that no one else was near him, he again looked at the boys, and Charley earnestly repeated the gesture.

Mr. Hardy, feeling that something strange was happening, ran down the steps and hurried toward them.

By the time he reached them, he had no need to ask questions. Hubert was leaning upon the gate, crying as if his heart would break; Charley stood with his hand on his lips, as if to check the sobs from breaking out, while the tears streamed down his cheeks.

"Ethel?" Mr. Hardy asked.

Charley nodded, and then said, with a great effort, "The Indians have burned the estancia; one of the men has escaped and brought the news. We know nothing more. Perhaps she is carried off, not killed."

Mr. Hardy staggered under the sudden blow. "Carried off!" he murmured to himself. "It is worse than death."

"Yes, papa" Charley said, anxious to give his father's thoughts a new turn. "But we will rescue her, if she is alive, wherever they may take her."

"We will, Charley; we will, my boys," Mr. Hardy said earnestly, and rousing himself at the thought. "I must go up and break it to your mother; though how I shall do so, I know not. Do you give what orders you like for collecting our friends. First, though, let us question this man. When was it?"

"Last night, signor, at eleven o'clock. I had just lain down in my hut, and I noticed that there were still lights downstairs at the house, when, all of a sudden, I heard a yell as of a thousand fiends, and I knew the Indians were upon us. I knew that it was too late to fly, but I threw myself out of the window, and lay flat by the wall, as the Indians burst in. There were eight of us, and I closed my ears to shut out the sound of the others' cries. Up at the house, too, I could hear screams and some pistol shots, and then more screams and cries. The Indians were all round, everywhere, and I dreaded lest one of them should stumble up against me. Then a sudden glare shot up, and I knew they were firing the house. The light would have shown me clearly enough, had I remained where I was; so I crawled on my stomach till I came to some potato ground a few yards off. As I lay between the rows, the plants covered me completely. In another minute or two the men's huts were set fire to, and then I could hear a great tramping, as of horses and cattle going away in the distance. They had not all gone, for I could hear voices all night, and Indians were moving about everywhere, in search of any one who might have escaped. They came close to me several times, and I feared that they would tread on me. After a time all became quiet; but I dared not move till daylight. Then, looking about carefully, I could see no one, and I jumped up, and never stopped running until you met me."

Mr. Hardy now went up to the house to break the sad tidings to his wife. Charley ordered eight peons to saddle horses instantly, and while they were doing so he wrote on eight leaves of his pocketbook: "The Mercers' house destroyed last night by Indians; the Mercers killed or carried off. My sister Ethel with them. For God's sake, join us to recover them. Meet at Mercer's as soon as possible. Send this note round to all neighbors."

One of these slips of paper was given to each peon, and they were told to ride for their lives in different directions, for that Miss Ethel was carried off by the Indians.

This was the first intimation of the tidings that had arrived, and a perfect chorus of lamentation arose from the women, and of execrations of rage from the men. Just at this moment Terence came running down from the house. "Is it true, Mister Charles? Sarah says that the mistress and Miss Maud are gone quite out of their minds, and that Miss Ethel has been killed by the Indians!"

"Killed or carried away, Terence; we do not know where to yet"

Terence was a warm-hearted fellow, and he set up a yell of lamentation which drowned the sobs and curses of the natives.

"Hush, Terence," Charley said. "We shall have time to cry for her afterward; we must be doing now."

"I will, Mister Charles; but you will let me go with you to search for her. Won't you, now, Mister Charles?"

"Yes, Terence; I will take you with us, and leave Lopez in charge. Send him here."

Lopez was close. He, too, was really affected at the loss of his young mistress; for Ethel, by her unvarying sweetness of temper, was a favorite with every one.

"Lopez, you will remain here in charge. We may be away two days--we may be away twenty. I know I can trust you to look after the place just as if we were here."

The capitaz bowed with his hand on his heart. Even the peasants of South America preserve the grand manner and graceful carriage of their Spanish ancestors. "And now, Lopez, do you know of any of the Gauchos in this part of the country who have ever lived with the Indians, and know their country at all?"

"Martinez, one of the shepherds at Canterbury, Signor Charles, was with them for seven months; and Perez, one of Signor Jamieson's men, was longer still."

Charles at once wrote notes asking that Perez and Martinez might accompany the expedition, and dispatched them by mounted peons.

"And now, Lopez, what amount of charqui have we in store?"

"A good stock, signor; enough for fifty men for a fortnight."

Charqui is meat dried in the sun. In hot climates meat cannot be kept for many hours in its natural state. When a bullock is killed, therefore, all the meat which is not required for immediate use is cut up into thin strips, and hung up in the sun to dry. After this process it is hard and strong, and by no means palatable; but it will keep for many months, and is the general food of the people. In large establishments it is usual to kill several animals at once, so as to lay in sufficient store of charqui to last for some time.

"Terence, go up to the house and see what biscuit there is. Lopez, get our horses saddled, and one for Terence--a good one--and give them a feed of maize. Now, Hubert, let us go up to the house, and get our carbines and pistols."

Mr. Hardy came out to meet them as they approached. "How are mamma and Maud, papa?"

"More quiet and composed now, boys. They have both gone to lie down. Maud wanted sadly to go with us, but she gave way directly. I pointed out to her that her duty was to remain here by her mother's side. And now, Charley, what arrangements have you made?"

Charley told his father what he had done.

"That is right. And now we will be off at once. Give Terence orders to bring on the meat and biscuit in an hour's time. Let him load a couple of horses, and bring a man with him to bring them back."

"Shall we bring any rockets, papa?"

"It is not likely that they will be of any use, Hubert; but we may as well take three or four of each sort. Roll up a poncho, boys, and fasten it on your saddles. Put plenty of ammunition in your bags; see your brandy flasks are full, and put out half a dozen bottles to go with Terence. There are six pounds of tobacco in the storeroom; let him bring them all. Hubert, take our water-skins; and look in the storeroom-- there are three or four spare skins; give them to Terence, some of our friends may not have thought of bringing theirs, and the country may, for aught we know, be badly watered. And tell him to bring a dozen colored blankets with him."

In a few minutes all these things were attended to, and then, just as they were going out of the house, Sarah came up, her face swollen with crying.

"Won't you take a cup of tea and just something to eat, sir? You've had nothing yet, and you will want it. It is all ready in the dining-room."

"Thank you, Sarah. You are right. Come, boys, try and make a good breakfast. We must keep up our hearts, you know, and we will bring our little woman back ere long."

Mr. Hardy spoke more cheerfully, and the boys soon, too, felt their spirits rising a little. The bustle of making preparations, the prospect of the perilous adventure before them, and the thought that they should assuredly, sooner or later, come up with the Indians, all combined to give them hope. Mr. Hardy had little fear of finding the body of his child under the ruins of the Mercers' house. The Indians never deliberately kill white women, always carrying them off; and Mr. Hardy felt confident that, unless Ethel had been accidentally killed in the assault, this was the fate which had befallen her.

A hasty meal was swallowed, and then, just as they were starting, Mrs. Hardy and Maud came out to say "Good-by," and an affecting scene occurred. Mr. Hardy and the boys kept up as well as they could, in order to inspire the mother and sister with hope during their absence, and with many promises to bring their missing one back they galloped off.

They were scarcely out of the gate, when they saw their two friends from Canterbury coming along at full gallop. Both were armed to the teeth, and evidently prepared for an expedition, They wrung the hands of Mr. Hardy and his sons.

"We ordered our horses the moment we got your note, and ate our breakfasts as they were being got ready. We made a lot of copies of your note, and sent off half a dozen men in various directions with them. Then we came on at once. Of course most of the others cannot arrive for some time yet, but we were too anxious to hear all about it to delay, and we thought that we might catch you before you started, to aid you in your first search. Have you any more certain news than you sent us?"

"None," Mr. Hardy said, and then repeated the relation of the survivor.

There was a pause when he had finished, and then Mr. Herries said:

"Well, Mr. Hardy, I need not tell you, if our dear little Ethel is alive, we will follow you till we find her, if we are a year about it."

"Thanks, thanks," Mr. Hardy said earnestly. "I feel a conviction that we shall yet recover her."

During this conversation they had been galloping rapidly toward the scene of the catastrophe, and, absorbed in their thoughts, not another word was spoken until they gained the first rise, from which they had been accustomed to see the pleasant house of the Mercers. An exclamation of rage and sorrow burst from them all, as only a portion of the chimney and a charred post or two showed where it had stood. The huts of the peons had also disappeared; the young trees and shrubs round the house were scorched up and burned by the heat to which they had been exposed, or had been broken off from the spirit of wanton mischief.

With clinched teeth, and faces pale with rage and anxiety, the party rode on past the site of the huts, scattered round which were the bodies of several of the murdered peons. They halted not until they drew rein, and leaped off in front of the house itself.

It had been built entirely of wood, and only the stumps of the corner posts remained erect. The sun had so thoroughly dried the boards of which it was constructed that it had burned like so much tinder, and the quantity of ashes that remained was very small. Here and there, however, were uneven heaps; and in perfect silence, but with a sensation of overpowering dread, Mr. Hardy and his friends tied up their horses, and proceeded to examine these heaps, to see if they were formed by the remains of human beings.

Very carefully they turned them over, and as they did so their knowledge of the arrangements of the different rooms helped them to identify the various articles. Here was a bed, there a box of closely-packed linen, of which only the outer part was burned, the interior bursting into flames as they turned it over; here was the storeroom, with its heaps of half-burned flour where the sacks had stood.

In half an hour they were able to say with tolerable certainty that no human beings had been burned, for the bodies could not have been wholly consumed in such a speedy conflagration.

"Perhaps they have all been taken prisoners," Hubert suggested, as with a sigh of relief they concluded their search, and turned from the spot.

Mr. Hardy shook his head. He was too well acquainted with the habits of the Indians to think such a thing possible. Just at this moment Dash, who had followed them unnoticed during their ride, and who had been ranging about uneasily while they had been occupied by the search, set up a piteous howling. All started and looked round. The dog was standing by the edge of the ditch which had been dug outside the fence. His head was raised high in air, and he was giving vent to prolonged and mournful howls.

All felt that the terrible secret was there. The boys turned ghastly pale, and they felt that not for worlds could they approach to examine the dreadful mystery.

Mr. Hardy was almost as much affected.

Mr. Herries looked at his friend, and then said gravely to Mr. Hardy, "Do you wait here, Mr. Hardy; we will go on."

As the friends left them the boys turned away, and leaning against their horses, covered their eyes with their hands. They dared not look round. Mr. Hardy stood still for a minute, but the agony of suspense was too great for him. He started off at a run, came up to his friends, and with them hurried on to the fence.

Not as yet could they see into the ditch. At ordinary times the fence would have been an awkward place to climb over; now they hardly knew how they scrambled over, and stood by the side of the ditch. They looked down, and Mr. Hardy gave a short, gasping cry, and caught at the fence for support.

Huddled together in the ditch was a pile of dead bodies, and among them peeped out a piece of a female dress. Anxious to relieve their friend's agonizing suspense, the young men leaped down into the ditch, and began removing the upper bodies from the ghastly pile.

First were the two men employed in the house; then came Mr. Mercer; then the two children and an old woman-servant; below them were the bodies of Mrs. Mercer and her brother. There were no more. Ethel was not among them.

When first he had heard of the massacre Mr. Hardy had said, "Better dead than carried off," but the relief to his feelings was so great as the last body was turned over, and that it was evident that the child was not there, that he would have fallen had not Mr. Herries hastened to climb up and support him, at the same time crying out to the boys, "She is not here."

Charley and Hubert turned toward each other, and burst into tears of thankfulness and joy. The suspense had been almost too much for them, and Hubert felt so sick and faint that he was forced to lie down for awhile, while Charley went forward to the others. He was terribly shocked at the discovery of the murder of the entire party, as they had cherished the hope that Mrs. Mercer at least would have been carried off. As, however, she had been murdered, while it was pretty evident that Ethel had been spared, or her body would have been found with the others, it was supposed that poor Mrs. Mercer had been shot accidentally, perhaps in the endeavor to save her children.

The bodies were now taken from the ditch, and laid side by side until the other settlers should arrive. It was not long before they began to assemble, riding up in little groups of twos and threes. Rage and indignation were upon all their faces at the sight of the devastated house, and their feelings were redoubled when they found that the whole of the family, who were so justly liked and esteemed, were dead. The Edwards and the Jamiesons were among the earliest arrivals, bringing the Gaucho Martinez with them. Perez, too, shortly after arrived from Canterbury, he having been out on the farm when his master left.

Although all these events have taken some time to relate, it was still early in the day. The news had arrived at six, and the messengers were sent off half an hour later. The Hardys had set out before eight, and had reached the scene of the catastrophe in half an hour. it was nine o'clock when the bodies were found, and half an hour after this friends began to assemble. By ten o'clock a dozen more had arrived, and several more could be seen in the distance coming along at full gallop to the spot.

"I think," Mr. Hardy said, "that we had better employ ourselves, until the others arrive, in burying the remains of our poor friends."

There was a general murmur of assent, and all separated to look for tools. Two or three spades were found thrown down in the garden, where a party had been at work the other day. And then all looked to Mr. Hardy.

"I think," he said, "we cannot do better than lay them where their house stood. The place will never be the site of another habitation. Any one who may buy the property would choose another place for his house than the scene of this awful tragedy. The gate once locked, the fence will keep out animals for very many years."

A grave was accordingly dug in the center of the space once occupied by the house. In this the bodies of Mr. Mercer and his family were laid. And Mr. Hardy having solemnly pronounced such parts of the burial service as he remembered over them, all standing by bareheaded, and stern with suppressed sorrow, the earth was filled in over the spot where a father, mother, brother, and two children lay together. Another grave was at the same time dug near, and in this the bodies of the three servants whose remains had been found with the others were laid.

By this time it was eleven o'clock, and the number of those present had reached twenty. The greater portion of them were English, but there were also three Germans, a Frenchman, and four Gauchos, all accustomed to Indian warfare.

"How long do you think it will be before all who intend to come can join us?" Mr. Hardy asked.

There was a pause; then one of the Jamiesons said:

"Judging by the time your message reached us, you must have set off before seven. Most of us, on the receipt of the message, forwarded it by fresh messengers on further; but of course some delay occurred in so doing, especially as many of us may probably have been out on the plains when the message arrived. The persons to whom we sent might also have been out. Our friends who would be likely to obey the summons at once all live within fifteen miles or so. That makes thirty miles, going and returning. Allowing for the loss of time I have mentioned, we should allow five hours. That would bring it on to twelve o'clock."

There was a general murmur of assent.

"In that case," Mr. Hardy said, "I propose that we eat a meal as hearty as we can before starting. Charley, tell Terence to bring the horses with the provisions here."

The animals were now brought up, and Mr. Hardy found that, in addition to the charqui and biscuit, Mrs. Hardy had sent a large supply of cold meat which happened to be in the larder, some bread, a large stock of tea and sugar, a kettle, and some tin mugs.

The cold meat and bread afforded an ample meal, which was much needed by those who had come away without breakfast.

By twelve o'clock six more had arrived, the last comer being Mr. Percy. Each newcomer was filled with rage and horror upon hearing of the awful tragedy which had been enacted.

At twelve o'clock exactly Mr. Hardy rose to his feet. "My friends," he said, "I thank you all for so promptly answering to my summons. I need say no words to excite your indignation at the massacre that has taken place here. You know, too, that my child has been carried away. I intend, with my sons and my friends from Canterbury, going in search of her into the Indian country. My first object is to secure her, my second to avenge my murdered friends. A heavy lesson, too, given the Indians in their own country, will teach them that they cannot with impunity commit their depredations upon us. Unless such a lesson is given, a life on the plains will become so dangerous that we must give up our settlements. At the same time, I do not conceal from you that the expedition is a most dangerous one. We are entering a country of which we know nothing. The Indians are extremely numerous, and are daily becoming better armed. The time we may be away is altogether vague; for if it is a year I do not return until I have found my child. I know that there is not a man here who would not gladly help to rescue Ethel--not one who does not long to avenge our murdered friends. At the same time, some of you have ties, wives and children, whom you may not consider yourselves justified in leaving, even upon an occasion like this. Some of you, I know, will accompany me; but if any one feels any doubts, from the reasons I have stated--if any one considers that he has no right to run this tremendous risk--let him say so at once, and I shall respect his feelings, and my friendship and good-will will in no way be diminished."

As Mr. Hardy ceased, his eye wandered round the circle of stalwart-looking figures around him, and rested upon the Jamiesons. No one answered for a moment, and then the elder of the brothers spoke:

"Mr. Hardy, it was right and kind of you to say that any who might elect to stay behind would not forfeit your respect and esteem, but I for one say that he would deservedly forfeit his own. We have all known and esteemed the Mercers. We have all known, and I may say, loved you and your family. From you we have one and all received very great kindness and the warmest hospitality. We all know and love the dear child who has been carried away; and I say that he who stays behind is unworthy of the name of a man. For myself and brother, I say that if we fall in this expedition--if we never set eyes upon our wives again--we shall die satisfied that we have only done our duty. We are with you to the death."

A loud and general cheer broke from the whole party as the usually quiet Scotchman thus energetically expressed himself. And each man in turn came up to Mr. Hardy and grasped his hand, saying, "Yours till death."

Mr. Hardy was too much affected to reply for a short time; then he briefly but heartily expressed his thanks. After which he went on: "Now to business. I have here about three hundred pounds of charqui. Let every man take ten pounds, as nearly as he can guess. There are also two pounds of biscuit a man. The tea, sugar, and tobacco, the kettle, and eighty pounds of meat, I will put on to a spare horse, which Terence will lead. If it is well packed, the animal will be able to travel as quickly as we can."

There was a general muster round the provisions. Each man took his allotted share. The remainder was packed in two bundles, and secured firmly upon either side of the spare horse; the tobacco, sugar, and tea being enveloped in a hide, and placed securely between them, and the kettle placed at the top of all. Then, mounting their horses, the troop sallied out; and, as Mr. Hardy watched them start, he felt that in fair fight by day they could hold their own against ten times their number of Indians.

Each man, with the exception of the young Hardys, who had their Colt's carbines, had a long rifle; in addition to which all had pistols--most of them having revolvers, the use of which, since the Hardys had first tried them with such deadly effect upon the pampas, had become very general among the English settlers. Nearly all were young, with the deep sunburned hue gained by exposure on the plains. Every man had his poncho--a sort of native blanket, used either as a cloak or for sleeping in at will--rolled up before him on his saddle. It would have been difficult to find a more serviceable-looking set of men; and the expression of their faces, as they took their last look at the grave of the Mercers, boded very ill for any Indian who might fall into their clutches.

CHAPTER XV.
THE PAMPAS ON FIRE.

The party started at a canter--the pace which they knew their horses would be able to keep up for the longest time--breaking every half-hour or so into a walk for ten minutes, to give them breathing time. All were well mounted on strong, serviceable animals; but these had not in all cases been bought specially for speed, as had those of the Hardys. It was evident that the chase would be a long one. The Indians had twelve hours' start; they were much lighter men than the whites, and carried less additional weight. Their horses, therefore, could travel as fast and as far as those of their pursuers. The sheep would, it is true, be an encumbrance; the cattle could scarcely be termed so; and it was probable that the first day they would make a journey of fifty or sixty miles, traveling at a moderate pace only, as they would know that no instant pursuit could take place. Indeed their strength, which the peon had estimated at five hundred men, would render them to a certain extent careless, as upon an open plain the charge of this number of men would sweep away any force which could be collected short of obtaining a strong body of troops from Rosario.

For the next two days it was probable that they would make as long and speedy journeys as the animals could accomplish. After that, being well in their own country, they would cease to travel rapidly, as no pursuit had ever been attempted in former instances.

There was no difficulty in following the track. Mr. Mercer had possessed nearly a thousand cattle and five thousand sheep, and the ground was trampled, in a broad, unmistakable line. Once or twice Mr. Hardy consulted his compass. The trail ran southwest by west.

There was not much talking. The whole party were too impressed with the terrible scene they had witnessed, and the tremendously hazardous nature of the enterprise they had undertaken, to indulge in general conversation. Gradually, however, the steady, rapid motion, the sense of strength and reliance in themselves and each other, lessened the somber expression, and a general talk began, mostly upon Indian fights, in which most of the older settlers had at one time or other taken a part.

Mr. Hardy took a part in and encouraged this conversation. He knew how necessary, in an expedition of this sort, it was to keep up the spirits of all engaged; and he endeavored, therefore, to shake off his own heavy weight of care, and to give animation and life to them all.

The spirits of the younger men rose rapidly, and insensibly the pace was increased, until Mr. Hardy, as leader of the party, was compelled to recall to them the necessity of saving their animals, many of which had already come from ten to fifteen miles before arriving at the rendezvous at the Mercers'.

After three hours' steady riding they arrived at the banks of a small stream. There Mr. Hardy called a halt, for the purpose of resting the animals.

"I think," he said, "that we must have done twenty-five miles. We will give them an hour's rest, and then do another fifteen. Some of them have already done forty, and it will not do to knock them up the first day."

Girths were loosened, and the horses were at work cropping the sweet grass near the water's edge. The whole party threw themselves down on a sloping bank, pipes were taken out and lit, and the probable direction of the chase discussed.

In a short time Charley rose, and saying, "I will see if I can get anything better than dried meat for supper," exchanged his rifle for Mr. Hardy's double-barreled gun, which was carried by Terence, and whistling for the retriever, strolled off up the stream. In ten minutes the double-barrels were heard at a short distance, and a quarter of an hour afterward again, but this time faintly. Ten minutes before the hour was up he appeared, wiping the perspiration from his face, with seven and a half brace of plump duck.

"They were all killed in four shots," he said, as he threw them down. "They were asleep in the pools, and I let fly right into the middle of them before they heard me."

There was a general feeling of satisfaction at the sight of the birds, which were tied in couples, and fastened on the horses.

In two minutes more they were again in the saddles, Hubert saying to his father as they started, "There is one satisfaction, papa, we can't miss the way. We have only to ride far enough, and we must overtake them."

Mr. Hardy shook his head. He knew enough of Indian warfare to be certain that every artifice and maneuver would have to be looked for and baffled; for even when believing themselves safe from pursuit, Indians never neglect to take every possible precaution against it.

After riding for two hours longer Mr. Hardy consulted the Gauchos if there were any stream near, but they said that it would be at least two hours' riding before they reached another, and that that was a very uncertain supply. Mr. Hardy therefore decided to halt at once, as the men knew this part of the plain thoroughly, from hunting ostriches on it, and from frequent expeditions in search of strayed cattle. They had all lived and hunted at one time or another with the Indians. Many of the Gauchos take up their abode permanently with the Indians, being adopted as members of the tribe, and living and dressing like the Indians themselves. These visits are generally undertaken to avoid the consequences of some little difficulty- -a man killed in a gambling quarrel, or for rivalry in love. Sometimes they make their peace again, satisfy the blood-relations with a bull, secure absolution readily enough by confession and a gift of a small sum to the Church, and return to their former life; but as often as not they remain with the Indians, and even attain to the rank of noted chiefs among them.

The men who accompanied the expedition were all of the former class. All had taken to the pampas to escape the consequences of some crime or other, but had grown perfectly sick of it, and had returned to civilized life. In point of morals they were not, perhaps, desirable companions; but they were all brave enough, thoroughly knew the country further inland, and, if not enthusiastic in the adventure, were yet willing enough to follow their respective masters, and ready to fight for their lives upon occasion.

Just as they halted Mr. Herries thought that he caught sight of some deer a short way ahead. He therefore started at once for a stalk, several of the others going off in other directions. Mr. Herries proceeded very cautiously, and the wind being fortunately toward him, he was enabled to creep up tolerably close. The animals, which are extremely shy, had, however, an idea that danger was about before he could get within a fair shot. As he knew that they would be off in another instant, he at once practiced a trick which he had often found to be successful.

He threw himself on his back, pulled a red handkerchief from his neck, tied it to one of his boots so as to let it float freely in the air, and then threw up both legs in the form of a letter V. Then he began moving them slowly about, waving them to and fro. The deer, which were upon the point of flight, paused to gaze at this strange object; then they began to move in a circle, their looks still directed at this unknown thing, to which they gradually kept approaching as they moved round it. At last they were fairly in shot, and Herries, whose legs were beginning to be very weary, sprang to his feet, and in another instant the foremost of the deer lay quivering in death.

Taking it upon his shoulders, he proceeded to the camp, where his arrival was hailed with acclamation. A fire was already alight, made of grass and turf, the former being pulled up in handfuls by the roots, and making a fierce but short-lived blaze. A large quantity had been collected at hand, and the ducks were already cut up. Half a one was handed to each; fur every man is his own cook upon the pampas.

The other hunters shortly returned, bringing in another of the little deer; for the stag of the pampas is of small size. They were speedily skinned by the Gauchos, and cut up, and all the party were now engaged in roasting duck and venison steaks on their steel ramrods over the fire.

When all were satisfied, a double handful of tea was thrown into the kettle, which was already boiling, pipes were lighted, and a general feeling of comfort experienced. The horses had been picketed close at hand, each man having cut or pulled a heap of grass and placed it before his beast; beside which, the picket ropes allowed each horse to crop the grass growing in a small circle, of which he was the center.

Mr. Hardy chatted apart for some time with the Gauchos, anxious to know as much as possible of the country into which he was entering. The others chatted and told stories. Presently Mr. Hardy joined again in the general conversation, and then, during a pause, said, "Although, my friends, I consider it most improbable that any Indians are in the neighborhood, still it is just possible that they may have remained, on purpose to fall at night upon any party who might venture to pursue. At any rate, it is right to begin our work in a businesslike way. I therefore propose that we keep watches regularly. It is now nine o'clock. We shall be moving by five: that will make four watches of two hours each. I should say that three men in a watch, stationed at fifty yards from the camp upon different sides would suffice."

There was a general assent to the proposal.

"To save trouble," Mr. Hardy went on, "I suggest that we keep watch in the alphabetical order of our names. Twelve of us will be on to-night, and the next twelve to-morrow night."

The proposal was at once agreed to; and the three who were first on duty at once rose, and, taking their rifles, went off in various directions, first agreeing that one of them should give a single whistle as a signal that the watch was up, and that two whistles close together would be a warning to retreat at once toward the center.

The watch also ascertained which were the next three men to be roused, and these and the succeeding watches agreed to lie next to each other, in order that they might be roused without awakening their companions.

In a few minutes there was a general unrolling of ponchos, and soon afterward only sleeping figures could be seen by the dim light of the smoldering fire. Mr. Hardy, indeed, was the only one of the party who did not fall to sleep. Thoughts of the events of the last twenty-four hours, of the best course to be adopted, and of the heavy responsibility upon himself as leader of this perilous expedition, prevented him from sleeping. He heard the watch return, rouse the relief, and lay down in their places. In another half hour he himself rose, and walked out toward the sentry.

It was a young man named Cook, one of the new settlers to the east of Mount Pleasant. "Is that you, Mr. Hardy?" he asked, as he approached. "I was just coming in to wake you."

"What is it, Mr. Cook?"

"It strikes me, sir, that there is a strange light away to the southwest. I have only noticed it the last few minutes, and thought it was fancy, but it gets more distinct every minute."

Mr. Hardy looked out anxiously into the gloom and quickly perceived the appearance that his friend alluded to.

For a minute or two he did not speak, and then, as the light evidently increased, he said, almost with a groan, "It is what I feared they would do: they have set the prairie on fire. You need not keep watch any longer. We are as much separated from the Indians as if the ocean divided us."

Cook gave the two short whistles agreed upon to recall the other men on guard, and then returned with Mr. Hardy to the rest of the party. Then Mr. Hardy roused all his companions. Every man leaped up, rifle in hand, believing that the Indians were approaching.

"We must be up and doing," Mr. Hardy said cheerfully; "the Indians have fired the pampas."

There was a thrill of apprehension in the bosom of many present, who had heard terrible accounts of prairie fires, but this speedily subsided at the calm manner of Mr. Hardy.

"The fire," he said, "may be ten miles away yet. I should say that it was, but it is difficult to judge, for this grass does not flame very high, and the smoke drifts between it and us. The wind, fortunately, is light, but it will be here in little over half an hour. Now, let the four Gauchos attend to the horses, to see they do not stampede. The rest form a line a couple of yards apart, and pull up the grass by the roots, throwing it behind them, so as to leave the ground clear. The wider we can make it the better."

All fell to work with hearty zeal. Looking over their shoulders, the sky now appeared on fire. Flickering tongues of flame seemed to struggle upward. There was an occasional sound of feet, as herds of deer flew by before the danger.

"How far will it go, papa, do you think?" Hubert asked his father, next to whom he was at work.

"I should say that it would most likely stop at the stream where we halted to-day, Hubert. The ground was wet and boggy for some distance on the other side."

The horses were now getting very restive, and there was a momentary pause from work to wrap ponchos round their heads, so as to prevent their seeing the glare.

The fire could not have been more than three miles distant, when the space cleared was as wide as Mr. Hardy deemed necessary for safety. A regular noise, something between a hiss and a roar, was plainly audible; and when the wind lifted the smoke the flames could be seen running along in an unbroken wall of fire. Birds flew past overhead with terrified cries, and a close, hot smell of burning was very plainly distinguishable.

Starting about halfway along the side of the cleared piece of ground, Mr. Hardy set the dry grass alight. For a moment or two it burned slowly, and then, fanned by the wind, It gained force, and spread in a semicircle of flame.

The horses were already unpicketed, and half of the party held them at a short distance in the rear, while the rest stood in readiness to extinguish the fire if it crossed the cleared space.

Over and over again the fire crept partially across--for the clearing had been done but roughly--but it was speedily stamped out by the heavy boots of the watchers.

The spectacle, as the fire swept away before the wind, was fine in the extreme. The party seemed includes between two walls of fire. The main conflagration was now fearfully close, burning flakes were already falling among them, and the sound of the fire was like the hiss of the surf upon a pebbly beach.

"Now," Mr. Hardy said, "forward with the horses. Every one to his own animal. Put your ponchos over your own heads as well as your horses."

In another minute the party stood clustered upon the black and smoking ground which the fire they had kindled had swept clear. There, for five minutes, they remained without moving unscorched by the raging element around them, but half-choked with the smoke.

Then Mr. Hardy spoke: "It is over now. You can look up."

There was a general expression of astonishment as the heads emerged from their wrappers, and the eyes recovered sufficiently from the effects of the blinding smoke to look round. Where had the fire gone? Where, indeed! The main conflagration had swept by them, had divided in two when it reached, the ground already burned, and these columns, growing further and further asunder as the newly kindled fire had widened, were already far away to the right and left, while beyond and between them was the fire that they themselves had kindled, now two miles wide, and already far in the distance.

These fires in the pampas, although they frequently extend over a vast tract of country, are seldom fatal to life. The grass rarely attains a height exceeding three feet, and burns out almost like so much cotton. A man on horseback, having no other method of escape, can, by blindfolding his horse and wrapping his own face in a poncho, ride fearless through the wall of fire without damage to horse or rider.

It was only, therefore, the young hands who had felt any uneasiness at the sight of the fire; for the settlers were in the habit of regularly setting fire to the grass upon their farms every year before the rains, as the grass afterward springs up fresh and green for the animals. Care has to be taken to choose a calm day, when the flames can be confined within bounds; but instances have occurred when fires so commenced have proved most disastrous, destroying many thousands of animals.

"There is nothing to do but to remain where we are until morning," Mr. Hardy said. "The horses had better be picketed, and then those who can had better get a few hours' more sleep. We shall want no more watch to-night." In a few minutes most of the party were again asleep; and the young Hardys were about to follow their example, when Mr. Hardy came up to them and said quietly, "Come this way, boys; we are going to have a council."

The boys followed their father to where some eight or nine men were sitting down at a short distance from the sleepers, and these the boys made out, by the glow from their pipes, to consist of Herries and Farquhar, the two Jamiesons, Mr. Percy, and the four Gauchos.

"This is a terribly bad business," Mr. Hardy began, when he and his sons had taken their seats on the ground. "I expected it, but it is a heavy blow nevertheless."

"Why, what is the matter, papa?" the boys exclaimed anxiously. "Have we lost anything?"

"Yes, boys," Mr. Hardy said; "we have lost what is at this moment the most important thing in the world--we have lost the trail."

Charley and Hubert uttered a simultaneous exclamation of dismay as the truth flashed across their minds. "The trail was lost!" They had never thought of this. In the excitement of the fire, it had never once occurred to them that the flames were wiping out every trace of the Indian track.

Mr. Hardy then went on, addressing himself to the others: "Of course this fire was lit with the especial intent of throwing us off the scent. Have you any idea how far it is likely to have come?" he asked the Gauchos. "That is, are you aware of the existence of any wide stream or damp ground which would have checked it, and which must therefore be the furthest boundary of the fire?"

The Gauchos were silent a minute; then Perez said, "The next stream is fifteen miles further; but it is small, and would not stop the fire going with the wind. Beyond that there is no certain stream, as far as I know of."

"The ground rises, and the grass gets thinner and poorer thirty miles or so on. I should say that they would light it this side of that," Martinez said. The other Gauchos nodded assent.

"We took the bearings of the track by our compass," Farquhar said. "Could we not follow it on by compass across the burned ground, and hit it upon the other side?"

Mr. Percy and Mr. Hardy both shook their heads. "I do not pretend to say where the trail is gone," the former said, "but the one place where I am quite sure it is not, is on the continuation of the present line."

"No," Mr. Hardy continued. "As you say, Percy, there it certainly is not. The Indians, when they got to some place which is probably about half across the burned ground, turned either to the right or left, and traveled steadily in that direction, sending one or two of their number in the old direction to light the grass, so as to sweep away all trace of the trail. They may have gone to the right or to the left, or may even have doubled back and passed us again at only a few miles' distance. We have no clew whatever to guide us at present, except the certainty that sooner or later the Indians will make for their own camping-ground. That is the exact state of the affair." And Mr. Hardy repeated what he had just said in Spanish to the Gauchos, who nodded assent.

"And in which direction do the Gauchos believe that their camping-ground lies?" Mr. Jamieson asked after a pause; "because it appears to me that it is a waste of time to look for the trail, and that our only plan is to push straight on to their villages, which we may reach before they get there. And in that case, if we found them unguarded, we might seize all their women, and hold them as hostages until they return. Then we could exchange them for Ethel; and when we had once got her, we could fight our way back."

"Capital, capital!" the other English man exclaimed. "Don't you think so, papa?"

Hubert added, seeing that Mr. Hardy did not join in the general approval.

"The plan is an admirably conceived one, but there is a great difficulty in the way. I observed yesterday that the trail did not lead due south, as it should have done if the Indians were going straight back to their camping ground. I questioned the Gauchos, and they all agree with me on the subject. The trail is too westerly for the camping-grounds of the Pampas Indians; too far to the south for the country of the Flat-faces of the Sierras. I fear that there is a combination of the two tribes, as there was in the attack upon us, and that they went the first day in the direction which would be most advantageous for both; and that, on reaching their halting-place--perhaps twenty or thirty miles from here--they made a division of their booty, and each tribe drew off toward its own hunting-grounds. In this case we have first to find the two trails, then to decide the terrible question, which party have taken Ethel?"

Again the Gauchos, upon this being translated to them, expressed their perfect accordance with Mr. Hardy's views, and some surprise at his idea as having been so identical with their own upon the subject.

As for the six young men, they were too dismayed at the unexpected difficulties which had started up in their way to give any opinion whatever. This uncertainty was terrible, and all felt that it would have a most depressing effect upon themselves and upon the whole expedition; for how could they tell, after journeying for hundreds of miles, whether every step might not take them further from the object of their search?

In this state of depression they remained for some minutes, when Perez the Gaucho said, in his broken English, "Most tribe take most plunder, most cattle, most sheep--take girl."

"Well thought of, Perez!" Mr. Hardy exclaimed warmly. "That is the clew for us, sure enough. As you say, the tribe who has furnished most men will, as a matter of course, take a larger share of the booty; and Ethel being the only captive, would naturally go to the strongest tribe."

The rest were all delighted at this solution of a difficulty which had before appeared insuperable, and the most lively satisfaction was manifested.

The plans for the day were then discussed. Propositions were made that they should divide into two parties, and go one to the right and the other to the left until they arrived at unburned ground, the edge of which they should follow until they met. This scheme was, however, given up, as neither party would have seen the trail inspected by the other and no opinion could therefore be formed as to the respective magnitude of the parties who had passed--a matter requiring the most careful examination and comparison, and an accurate and practiced judgment.

It was finally resolved, therefore, to keep in a body, and to proceed, in the first place, to search for the trail of the party to the south. A calculation was made, upon the supposition that the Indians had traveled for another twenty-five miles upon their old course, and then separated, each party making directly for home. To avoid all mistakes, and to allow for a detour, it was determined to shape a direct course to a point considerably to the east of that given by the calculation, to follow the edge of the burned ground until the trail was arrived at, and then to cut straight across, in order to find and examine the trail of the western Indians.

As this conclusion was arrived at, the first dawn of light appeared in the east, and Mr. Hardy at once roused the sleepers.

He then gave them a brief account of the conclusions to which he had arrived in the night, and of his reason for so doing. There was a general expression of agreement, then the girths were tightened, and in five minutes the troop was in motion.

How great was the change since the preceding evening! Then, as far as the eye could reach stretched a plain of waving grass. Birds had called to their mates, coveys of game had risen at their approach; deer had been seen bounding away in the distance; ostriches had gazed for an instant at the unusual sight of man, and had gone off with their heads forward and their wings outstretched before the wind.

Now, the eye wandered over a plain of dingy black, unbroken by a single prominence, undisturbed by living creatures except themselves. As Hubert remarked to his father, "It looked as if it had been snowing black all night."

Both men and horses were anxious to get over these dreary plains, and the pace was faster, and the halts less frequent, than they had been the day before.

It was fortunate that the fire had not taken place at an earlier hour of the evening, as the horses would have been weakened by want of food. As it was, they had had five hours to feed after their arrival.

Both men and horses, however, suffered much from thirst; and the former had good reason to congratulate themselves on having filled every water-skin at the first halting-place of the preceding day.

Clouds of black impalpable dust rose as they rode along. The eyes, mouth, and nostrils were filled with it, and they were literally as black as the ground over which they rode.

Twice they stopped and drank, and sparingly washed out the nostrils and mouths of the horses, which was a great relief to them, for they suffered as much as did their masters, as also did Dash, who, owing to his head being so near the ground, was almost suffocated; indeed, Hubert at last dismounted, and took the poor animal up on to the saddle before him.

At last, after four hours' steady riding, a gleam of color was seen in the distance, and in another quarter of an hour they reached the unburned plains, which, worn and parched as they were, looked refreshing indeed after the dreary waste over which they had passed.

The Gauchos, after a consultation among themselves, agreed in the opinion that the little stream of which they had spoken was but a short distance further, and that, although the channel might be dry, pools would no doubt be found in it. It was determined, therefore, to push on, and half an hour's riding by the edge of the burned grass brought them to the spot, when, following the course of the channel, they soon came to a pool, from which men and horses took a long drink.

At their approach an immense number of wild duck rose, and, as soon as the horses were picketed Charley again started with the gun, taking Terence with him to assist in bringing home the birds. They soon heard his gun, and Terence presently returned with six brace of ducks and a goose, and a request that another man would go back with him, for that the birds were so abundant, and so apparently stupefied from flying over the smoke and flame, that he could bring in any quantity.

One of the Jamiesons and Herries therefore went out, and returned in less than an hour with Charley, bringing between them four more geese and eighteen brace of ducks.

Charley was greeted with a round of applause, and was I soon at work with his friends upon the meal which was now ready.

After breakfast there was a comparison of opinion, and it was at last generally agreed that they had ridden nearly forty miles since daybreak, and that they could not be far from the spot where the Indians ought to have passed if they had kept the direction as calculated. It was also agreed that it would be better to let the horses remain where they were till late in the afternoon, when they might accomplish another fifteen miles or so.

Mr. Hardy then proposed that those who were inclined should accompany him on a walk along the edge of the burned ground. "We cannot be very far off from the trail," he said, "if our calculations are correct; and if we can find and examine it before it is time to start, we may be able to-night to cross to the other side, and thus gain some hours."

Herries, Farquhar, the two Jamiesons, Cook, and the young Hardys at once volunteered for the walk, and shouldering their rifles, started at a steady pace.

They had not walked much over a mile when a shout of pleasure broke from them, as, upon ascending a slight rise, they saw in the hollow below them the broad line of trampled grass, which showed that a large body of animals had lately passed along. All hurried forward, and a close and anxious examination took place.

Opinions differed a good deal as to the number that had passed; nor, accustomed as they all were to seeing the tracks made by herds of cattle and flocks of sheep, could they come to any approximate agreement on the subject. Had the number been smaller, the task would have been easier; but it is a question requiring extreme knowledge and judgment to decide whether four hundred cattle and two thousand sheep, or six hundred cattle and three thousand sheep, have passed over a piece of ground.

Mr. Hardy at last sent Charley back, accompanied by Mr. Cook, to request Mr. Percy to come on at once with the Gauchos to give their opinion. Charley and his companions were to remain with the horses, and were to request those not specially sent for to stay there also, as it would be imprudent in the extreme to leave the horses without a strong guard.

Pending the arrival of Mr. Percy, Mr. Hardy and his friends followed up the trail for some distance, so as to examine it both in the soft bottoms and on the rises. They returned in half an hour to their starting place, and were shortly after joined by Mr. Percy and the Gauchos. Again a careful and prolonged examination, took place, and a tolerably unanimous opinion was at last arrived at, that a very large number of animals had passed, apparently the larger half, but that no positive opinion could be arrived at until a comparison was made with the trail on the western side.

Although this conclusion was arrived at unanimously, it appeared to be reluctantly conceded to by most of them, and the reason of this became apparent as they were walking back toward the horses. "I have little doubt that the conclusion we have arrived at is correct," Herries remarked, "although somehow I am sorry for it; for ever since our talk last night I have made up my mind that she was most likely to be taken to the west. I suppose because the Indians there are more warlike than those of the pampas, and therefore likely to have furnished a larger contingent. Of course I had no reason for thinking so, but so it was."

"That was just what I thought," Hubert said; and I the other Englishmen admitted that they had all entertained a somewhat similar idea.

At four in the afternoon they were again in the saddle, having taken the precaution of filling their water-skins, and of watering the horses the last thing.

"How far do you think it is across, papa?" Hubert asked.

"It cannot be very far, Hubert. We are so much nearer the place where the fire began that I do not think it can have spread more than ten miles or so across."

Mr. Hardy's conjecture proved to be correct. An hour and a half's riding brought them to the other side of the burned prairie, striking a point which they felt sure was to the south of the place where the trail would have left it.

As they had done more than fifty miles since the morning, and the horses were much distressed with the effect of the dust, it was resolved to encamp at once. The horses received a little water, and were picketed out to graze. The fire was soon lit, and the ducks cut up and spitted upon the ramrods.

All were so much exhausted with the heat, the ashes, the fatigue, and the want of sleep of the previous night that, the tea and pipes finished and the watch posted, the rest lay down to sleep before the sun had been an hour below the horizon.

All rose at daybreak, refreshed with their quiet night's rest, and were soon in the saddle and on their way northward.

They had nearly an hour's ride before they came upon the trail.

There it was unmistakably--at first sight as broad and as much trampled as the other; but after a careful examination of it there was but one opinion, namely, that the number of animals who had passed was decidedly less than those who had gone south.

One of the Gauchos now told Mr. Hardy that he knew that at a short distance further to the west there was a spring of water much used by the Indians, and where he had no doubt they had halted on the night of the fire. Finding that it was not more than half an hour's ride, Mr. Hardy, after a brief consultation, determined to go over there to water the horses and breakfast, before retracing their footsteps across the burned prairie.

In little over the time named they came to a small pool of bright water, from which a little stream issued, running nearly due north across the plain. After drinking heartily themselves, and filling the water-skins and kettle, the horses were allowed to drink; and Dash plunged in with the greatest delight, emerging his usual bright chestnut color, whereas he had gone into the water perfectly black.

After he had come out and had shaken himself, he commenced hunting about, sniffing so violently that Hubert's attention was attracted to him. Presently the dog ran forward a few paces and gave a sharp bark of pleasure, and Hubert, running forward, gave so loud a cry that all the party rushed up.

Hubert could not speak. There, half-buried in the ground, and pointing west, was an Indian arrow, and! round the head was twisted a piece of white calico, with little blue spots upon it, which Mr. Hardy instantly recognized as a piece of the dress Ethel had worn when she left home.

Surprise kept all quiet for awhile, and then exclamations of pleasure and excitement broke from all, while Mr. Hardy and his sons wore greatly affected at this proof of the recent presence of their lost one. The arrow was deeply sunk in the ground, but it was placed at a spot where the grass happened to be particularly short, so that any one passing outward from the spring could hardly have failed to notice the piece of calico upon the grass. There was a perfect shower of congratulations; and it was some time before they were recovered sufficiently to renew their preparations for breakfast.

At last they sat down round the fire, all their faces radiant with excitement.

Perez and Martinez, however, sat somewhat apart, talking in an animated undertone to each other. They did not even approach the fire to roast their food; and Mr. Hardy's attention being attracted by this circumstance, he asked what they were talking so earnestly about.

Neither of them answered him, and he repeated the question. Then Perez replied: "Martinez and I think same. All trick; girl gone other way."

Conversation and eating were alike suspended at these ominous words, and each looked blankly into the others' faces.

Now that their attention was called to it, the whole circumstances of the case rushed to their minds; and as they felt the probable truth of what Perez said, their hopes fell to zero.

Mr. Percy was the first who, after a long silence, spoke. "I am afraid, Hardy, that what Perez says is right, and that we have been very nearly thrown off the scent by a most transparent trick. Watched as Ethel must have been, is it probable that she could have possessed herself of that arrow, and have fastened a strip of her dress to it, without being noticed? Still more impossible is it that she could have placed the arrow where we found it. No one could have passed without noticing it; so unless we suppose that she was allowed to linger behind every one, which is out of the question, the arrow could not have been put there by her."

"Too true, Percy," Mr. Hardy said with a sigh, after a short silence; "it is alto-gether impossible, and I should call it a clumsy artifice, were it not that it deceived us all for awhile. However, there is one comfort; it decides the question as we had ourselves decided it: Ethel is gone with the larger party to the south."

Breakfast was continued, but with a very subdued feeling. Hubert had now finished his, and, being a lad of restless habit, he took up the arrow which lay beside him, and began toying with it. First he untied the piece of stuff, smoothed it, and put it into his pocketbook, while his eyes filled with tears; then he continued list-lessly twisting the arrow in his fingers, while he listened to the conversation around him.

Presently his eyes fell upon the arrow. He started, a flush of excitement rushed across his face, and his hands and lips trembled as he closely examined the feather.

All-gazed at him with astonishment.

"Oh, papa, papa," he cried at last, "I know this arrow!"

"Know the arrow!" all repeated.

"Yes, I am quite, quite sure I know it. Don't you remember, Charley, the day that those wounded Indians started, as we were taking the quivers down to them, I noticed that one arrow had two feathers which I had never seen before, and could not guess what bird they came from. They were light blue, with a crimson tip. I pulled one off to compare it with my others. It is at home now. I remember that I chose the one I did because the other one had two of the little side feathers gone. This is the feather, I can most solemnly declare, and you see the fellow one is gone. That arrow belongs to one of the men we recovered."

All crowded round to examine the arrow, and then Mr. Hardy said solemnly, "Thank God for his mercy, He has decided our way now. Undoubtedly, as Hubert says, one of the men we aided is of the party, and wishes to show his gratitude. So he has managed to get a piece of Ethel's dress, and has tied it to this arrow, hoping that we should recognize the feather. Thank God, there is no more doubt, and thank Him, too, that Ethel has at least one friend near her."

All was now joy and congratulation, and Hubert rubbed his hands, and said triumphantly, "There, Charley, you were always chaffing me, and wanting to know what was the good of my collection, and now you see what was the good. It has put us on the right trail for Ethel, and you will never be able to laugh at me about my collection again."

CHAPTER XVI.
AT THE STAKE.

It was on the evening of the fifth day after her capture by the Indians that Ethel Hardy rode into a wide valley in the heart of the mountains. It was entered by a narrow gorge, through which ran a stream. Beyond this the hill receded, forming a nearly circular basin a mile in diameter, from the sides of which the rocks ascended almost perpendicularly, so that the only means of entering it was through the gorge. Clumps of trees were scattered everywhere about, and nearly in the center stood a large Indian village, numbering about three hundred lodges, the population of which, consisting almost entirely of women and children, came out with shrill cries of welcome to meet the returning band. This was two hundred strong. Before them they drove about four hundred cattle and fifteen hundred sheep. In the midst of the band Ethel Hardy rode, apparently unwatched, and forming part of it.

The girl was very pale, and turned even more so at the wild yells of triumph which rose around her, when those who had been left behind learned how signal had been the success of their warriors, and heard that the captive in their midst was one of the family which had inflicted such terrible loss upon the tribe two years previously. Fortunately she could not understand the volleys of threats and curses which the women of the tribe heaped upon her, although she could not mistake their furious ejaculations.

Ethel had cried at first until she could cry no more, and had now nerved herself for the worst. She had heard that the Indians have neither mercy nor pity for any one who may exhibit fear of death; she knew that no entreaties or tears would move them in the slightest, but that courage and firmness would at any rate command their respect and admiration. She had therefore schooled herself to show no emotion when the time came; and now, except that she had given an involuntary shudder at the sight of the gesticulating throng, she betrayed no sign whatever of her emotion, but looked round so calmly and unflinchingly that the violent abuse and gesticulations died away in a murmur of admiration of the pale-faced child who looked so calmly on death.

Nevertheless, as the troop drew up in front of the council hut, and alighted, the women pressed round as usual to heap abuse upon the prisoner; but one of the Indians stepped up to her, and waved them back, and saying, "She is the child of a great chief," took her by the arm, and handed her over to the care of the wife of one of the principal chiefs. The selection was a good one; for the woman, who was young, was known in the tribe as the Fawn for her gentle disposition. She at once led the captive away to her lodge, where she bade her sit down, offered her food, and spoke kindly to her in her low, soft, Indian tongue. Ethel could not understand her, but the kindly tones moved her more than the threats of the crowd outside had done, and she broke down in a torrent of tears.

The Indian woman drew the girl to her as a mother might have done, stroked her long fair hair, and soothed her with her low talk. Then she motioned to a pile of skins in the corner of the hut; and when Ethel gladly threw herself down upon them the Indian woman covered her up as she would have done a child, and with a nod of farewell tripped off to welcome her husband and hear the news, knowing that there was no possibility of the captive making her escape.

Exhausted with fatigue and emotion, Ethel's sobs soon ceased, and she fell into a sound sleep.

Of that terrible catastrophe at the Mercers' she had but a confused idea. They were sitting round the table talking, when, without the slightest notice or warning, the windows and doors were burst in, and dozens of dark forms leaped into the room. She saw Mr. Mercer rush to the wall and seize his pistols, and then she saw no more. She was seized and thrown over the shoulder of an Indian before she had time to do more than leap to her feet. There was a confused whirl of sounds around her--shrieks, threats, pistol shots, and savage yells--then the sounds swam in her ears, and she fainted.

When she recovered consciousness she found that she was being carried on a horse before her captor, and that the air was full of a red glare, which she supposed to arise from a burning house. On the chief, who carried her, perceiving that she had recovered her senses, he called to one of his followers, who immediately rode up, bringing a horse upon which a side-saddle had been placed. To this Ethel was transposed, and in another minute was galloping along by the side of her captor.

Even now she could hardly persuade herself that she was not dreaming. That instantaneous scene at the Mercers'--those confused sounds--this wild cavalcade of dark figures who rode round her--could not surely be real. Alas! she could not doubt it; and as the thought came across her, What would they say at home when they heard it? she burst into an agony of silent tears. Toward daybreak she was often startled to hear the words, "Hope, Ethel, hope!" in Spanish distinctly spoken close to her. She turned hastily, but there rode the dark forms as usual. Still she felt sure that she was not mistaken. Her own name she had distinctly heard; and although she could not form a conjecture who this unknown friend could be, still it was a great consolation to her to feel that she had at any rate one well-wisher among her enemies. He had told her to hope, too; and Ethel's spirits, with the elasticity of youth, rose at the word.

Why should she not hope? she thought. They were sure to hear it at home next morning, even if no one escaped and took them the news earlier; and she was certain that within a few hours of hearing it her father and friends Would be on their trail. Before the night fell, at latest, they would be assembled. Twenty-four hours' start would be the utmost that the Indians could possibly obtain, and her friends would travel as fast or faster than they could, for they would be free from all encumbrances. How far she was to be taken she could not say, but she felt sure that in a week's traveling her friends would make up for the day lost at starting. She knew that they might not be able to attack the Indians directly they came up, for they could not be a very strong party, whereas the Indians were several hundred strong; but she believed that sooner or later, in some way or other, her father and brothers would come to her rescue. Ethel from that time forward did not doubt for a moment. Trusting thus firmly in her friends, she gained confidence and courage; and when the troops halted at nine in the morning, after nine hours' riding, Ethel was able to look round with some sort of curiosity and interest.

It was here that an incident occurred, which, although she knew it not at the time, entirely altered her destination and prospects.

She was sitting upon the ground, when a man, who by his bearing appeared to be the principal chief present, passed in earnest talk with another chief. In the latter she recognized at once one of the wounded Indian prisoners.

"Tawaina," she said, leaping to her feet.

He paid no attention to her call, and she repeated it in a louder tone.

The principal chief stopped; Tawaina did the same. Then he walked slowly toward the captive.

"Save me, Tawaina," she said, "and send me back again home."

Tawaina shook his head.

"Not can," he said. "Tawaina friend. Help some time--not now." And he turned away again.

"Does the Raven know the White Bird," the chief asked him, "that she sings his name?"

Tawaina paused and said:

"Tawaina knows her. Her father is the great white brave."

The Indian chief gave a bound of astonishment and pleasure.

"The white brave with the shooting flames?"

Tawaina nodded.

The Raven's meeting with Ethel had been apparently accidental, but was in reality intentional. Her actual captor was one of the chiefs, although not the principal one, of the Pampas Indians; and in the division of the spoil, preparations for which were going on, there was no doubt that she would be assigned to that tribe, without any question upon the part of the Raven's people.

Now, however, that the Stag knew who the prisoner I was, he determined to obtain her for his tribe. He therefore went direct to the chief of the Pampas Indians, and asked that the white girl might fall to his tribe.

The chief hesitated.

"She is our only captive," he said. "The people will like to see her, and she will live in the lodge of the Fox, who carried her off."

"The Stag would like her for a slave to his wife. He will give fifty bullocks and two hundred sheep to the tribe, and will make the Fox's heart glad with a present."

The offer appeared so large for a mere puny girl that the chief assented at once;

and the Fox was content to take a gun, which proved part of the spoil, for his interest in his captive.

The Indians of Stag's tribe murmured to themselves at this costly bargain upon the part of their chief. However, they expressed nothing of this before him, and continued the work of counting and separating the animals in proportion to the number of each tribe present--the tribes from the plains being considerably the more numerous.

Not until four o'clock were they again in motion, when each tribe started for home.

In three hours' riding they reached the spring, and then the Stag ordered a small tent of skins to be erected for Ethel's accommodation. From this she came out an hour later to gaze upon the great wave of fire which, kindled at a point far away by their scouts, now swept along northward, passing at a distance of three or four miles from the spring.

It was when sitting gravely round the fire later on that the Stag deigned to enlighten his followers as to his reasons for giving what seemed to them so great a price for a pale-faced child.

The delight of the Indians, when they found that they had the daughter of their twice victorious enemy in their hands was unbounded. Vengeance is to the Indian even more precious than plunder; and the tribe would not have grudged a far higher price even than had been paid for the gratification of thus avenging themselves upon their enemy. The news flew from mouth to mouth, and triumphant whoops resounded throughout the camp; and Ethel inside her tent felt her blood run cold at the savage exultation which they conveyed.

She was greatly troubled by the fire, for she saw that it must efface all signs of the trail, and render the task of her friends long and difficult, and she felt greatly depressed at what she looked upon as a certain postponement of her rescue. She lay thinking over all this for a long time, until the camp had subsided into perfect quiet. Then the skins were slightly lifted near her head, and she heard a voice whisper:

"Me, Tawaina--friend. Great chief come to look for girl. Two trails--eyes blinded. Tawaina make sign--point way. Give piece dress that great chief may believe."

Ethel at once understood. She cautiously tore off a narrow strip from the bottom of her dress, and put it under the skin to the speaker.

"Good," he said. "Tawaina friend. Ethel, hope."

Greatly relieved by knowing that a clew would be now given to her friends, and overpowered by fatigue, Ethel was very shortly fast asleep.

At daybreak they set off again, having thus thirty hours' start of their pursuers. They traveled six hours, rested from eleven till three, and then traveled again until dark. Occasionally a sheep lagged behind, footsore and weary. He was instantly killed and cut up.

For four days was their rate of traveling, which amounted to upward of fifty miles a day, continued, and they arrived, as has been said, the last evening at their village.

During all this time Ethel was treated with courtesy and respect. The best portion of the food was put aside for her, the little tent of skins was always erected at night, and no apparent watch was kept over her movements.

The next morning she was awake early, and had it not been for the terrible situation in which she was placed she would have been amused by the busy stir in the village, and by the little copper-colored urchins at play, or going out with the women to collect wood or fetch water. There was nothing to prevent Ethel from going out among them, but the looks of scowling hatred which they cast at her made her draw back again into the hut, after a long, anxious look around.

It was relief at least to have halted, great as her danger undoubtedly was. She felt certain now that hour by hour her father must be approaching. He might even now be within a few miles. Had it not been for the fire, she was certain that he would already have been up, but she could not tell how long he might have been before he recovered the trail.

Toward the middle of the day two or three Indians might have been seen going through the village, summoning those whose position and rank entitled them to a place at the council.

Soon they were seen approaching, and taking their seats gravely on the ground in front of the hut of the principal chief. The women, the youths, and such men as had not as yet by their feats in battle distinguished themselves sufficiently to be summoned to the council, assembled at a short distance off. The council sat in the form of a circle, the inner ring being formed of the elder and leading men of the tribe, while the warriors sat round them.

Struck by the hush which had suddenly succeeded to the noise of the village, Ethel again went to the door. She was greatly struck by the scene, and was looking wonderingly at it, when she felt a touch on her shoulder, and on looking round saw the Fawn gazing pityingly at her, and at the same time signing to her to come in.

The truth at once flashed across Ethel's mind. The council had met to decide her fate, and she did not doubt for a moment what that decision would be. She felt that all hope was over, and retiring into the hut passed the time in prayer and in preparation for the fearful ordeal which was at hand.

After the council had met there was a pause of expectation, and the Stag then rose.

"My brothers, my heart is very glad. The Great Spirit has ceased to frown upon his children. Twice we went out, and twice returned empty-handed, while many of our lodges were empty. The guns which shoot without loading were too strong for us, and we returned sorrowful. Last year we did not go out; the hearts of our braves were heavy. This year we said perhaps the Great Spirit will no longer be angry with his children, and we went out. This time we have not returned empty-handed. The lowing of cattle is in my ear, and I see many sheep. The white men have felt the strength of our arms; and of the young men who went out with me there is not one missing. Best of all, we have brought back a captive, the daughter of the white chief of the flying fires and the guns which load themselves. Let me hand her over to our women; they will know how to make her cry; and we will send her head to the white chief, to show that his guns cannot reach to the Indian country. Have I spoken well?"

A murmur of assent followed the chief's speech; and supposing that no more would be said upon the matter, the Stag was about to declare the council closed, when an Indian sitting in the inner circle rose.

"My brothers, I will tell you a story. The birds went out to attack the nest of an eagle, but the eagle was too strong for them; and when all had gone he went out from his nest with his children, the young eagles, and he found the raven and two other birds hurt and unable to fly, and instead of killing them, as they might have done, the eagles took them up to their nest, and nursed them and tended them until they were able to fly, and then sent them home to their other birds. So was it with Tawaina and his two friends." And the speaker indicated with his arm two Indians sitting at the outer edge of the circle. "Tawaina fell at the fence where so many of us fell, and in the morning the white men took him and gave him water, and placed him in shelter, and bandaged his wound; and the little White Bird and her sister brought him food and cool drinks every day and looked pitifully at him. But Tawaina said to himself, The white men are only curing Tawaina that when the time comes they may see how an Indian can die. But when he was well they brought horses, and put a bow and arrows into our hands and bade us go free. It is only in the battle that the great white chief is terrible. He has a great heart. The enemies he killed he did not triumph over. He laid them in a great grave. He honored them, and planted trees with drooping leaves at their head and at their feet, and put a fence round that the foxes might not touch their bones. Shall the Indian be less generous than the white man? Even those taken in battle they spared and sent home. Shall we kill the White Bird captured in her nest? My brothers will not do so. They will send back the White Bird to the great white chief. Have I spoken well?"

This time a confused murmur ran round the circle. Some of the younger men were struck with this appeal to their generosity, and were in favor of the Raven's proposition; the elder and more ferocious Indians were altogether opposed to it.

Speaker succeeded speaker, some urging one side of the question, some the other.

At last the Stag again rose. "My brothers," he said, "my ears have heard strange words, and my spirit is troubled. The Raven has told us of the ways of the whites after a battle; but the Indians' ways are not as the whites' ways, and the Stag is too old to learn new fashions. He looks round, he sees many lodges empty, he sees many women who have no husbands to hunt game, he hears the voices of children who cry for meat. He remembers his brothers who fell before the flying fire and the guns which loaded themselves, and his eyes are full of blood. The great white chief has made many wigwams desolate: let there be mourning in the house of the white chief. Have I spoken well?"

The acclamations which followed this speech were so loud and general that the party of the Raven was silenced, and the council at once broke up.

A cry of exultation broke from the women when they heard the decision, and all prepared for the work of vengeance before them.

At a signal from the Stag two of the young Indians went to the hut and summoned Ethel to accompany them. She guessed at once that her death was decided upon and, pale as marble, but uttering no cry or entreaty, which she knew would be useless, she walked between them.

For a moment she glanced at the women around her, to see if there was one look of pity or interest; but faces distorted with hate and exultation met her eyes, and threats and imprecations assailed her ears. The sight, though it appalled, yet nerved her with courage. A pitying look would have melted her--this rage against one so helpless as herself nerved her; and, with her eyes turned upward and her lips moving in prayer, she kept along.

The Indians led her to a tree opposite the center of the village, bound her securely to it, and then retired.

There was a pause before the tragedy was to begin. Some of the women brought fagots for the pile, others cut splinters to thrust under the nails and into the flesh. The old women chattered and exulted over the tortures they would inflict; a few of the younger ones stood aloof, looking on pityingly.

The men of the tribe gathered in a circle, but took no part in the preparations--the torture of women was beneath them.

At last all was ready. A fire was lit near; the hags lit their firebrands and advanced. The chief gave the signal, and with a yell of exultation they rushed upon their victim, but fell back with a cry of surprise, rudely thrust off by three Indians who placed themselves before the captive.

The women retreated hastily, and the men advanced to know the reason of this strange interruption. The Raven and his companions were unarmed. The Indians frowned upon them, uncertain what course to pursue.

"My brothers," the Raven said, "I am come to die. The Raven's time is come. He has flown his last flight. He and his brothers will die with the little White Bird. The Raven and his friends are not dogs. They have shed their blood against their enemies, and they do not know how to cry out. But their time has come, they are ready to die. But they must die before the little White Bird. If not, her spirit will fly to the Great Spirit, and will tell him that the Raven and his friends, whom she had sheltered and rescued, had helped to kill her; and the Great Spirit would shut the gates of the happy hunting grounds against them. The Raven has spoken."

There was a pause of extreme astonishment, followed by a clamor of voices.

Those who had before espoused the cause of the Raven again spoke out loudly, while many of the others hesitated as to the course to be pursued.

The Stag hastily consulted with two or three of his principal advisers, and then moved forward, waving his hand to command silence. His countenance was calm and unmoved, although inwardly he was boiling with rage at this defiance of his authority. He was too politic a chief, however to show this. He knew that the great majority of the tribe was with him; yet the employment of force to drag the Raven and his companions from their post would probably create a division in the tribe, the final results of which none could see, and for the consequences of which he would, in case of any reverse, be held responsible and looked upon with disapproval by both parties.

"The Ravens and his friends have great hearts," he said courteously. "They are large enough to shelter the little White Bird. Let them take her. Her life is spared. She shall remain with our tribe."

The Raven inclined his head, and taking a knife from a warrior near, he cut the cords which bound Ethel, and beckoning to the Fawn, handed the astonished girl again into her charge saying as he did so, "Stop in hut. Not go out; go out, bad." And then, accompanied by his friends, he retired without a word to one of their huts.

A perfect stillness had hung over the crowd during this scene; but when it became known that Ethel was to go off unscathed a murmur broke out from the elder females, disappointed in their work of vengeance. But the Stag waved his hand peremptorily, and the crowd scattered silently to their huts, to talk over the unusual scene that had taken place.

The Raven and his friends talked long and earnestly together. They were in no way deceived by the appearance of friendliness which the Stag had assumed. They knew that henceforth there was bitter hatred between them, and that their very lives were insecure. As to Ethel, it was, they knew, only a short reprieve which had been granted her. The Stag would not risk a division in the tribe for her sake, nor would attempt to bring her to a formal execution; but the first time she wandered from the hut she would be found dead with a knife in her heart.

The Raven, however, felt certain that help was at hand. He and his friends, who knew Mr. Hardy, were alone of the tribe convinced that a pursuit would be attempted. The fact that no such attempt to penetrate into the heart of the Indian country had ever been made had lulled the rest into a feeling of absolute security. The Raven, indeed, calculated that the pursuers must now be close at hand, and that either on that night or the next they would probably enter the gorge and make the attack.

The result of the council was that he left his friends and walked in a leisurely way back to his own hut, taking no notice of the hostile glances which some of the more violent of the Stag's supporters cast toward him.

On his entrance he was welcomed by his wife, a young girl whom he had only married since his return from the expedition, and to whom, from what he had learned of the position of women among the whites, he allowed more freedom of speech and action than are usually permitted to Indian women. She had been one of the small group who had pitied the white girl.

"The Raven is a great chief," she said proudly; "he has done well. The Mouse trembled, but she was glad to see her lord stand forth. The Stag will strike, though," she added anxiously. "He will look for the blood of the Raven."

"The Stag is a great beast," the Indian said sententiously; "but the Raven eat him at last."

Then, sitting down upon a pile of skins, the chief filled his pipe, and made signs to his wife to bring fire. Then he smoked in silence for some time until the sun went down, and a thick darkness closed over the valley.

At length he got up, and said to his wife, "If they ask for the Raven, say that he has just gone out; nothing more. He will not return till daybreak; and remember," and he laid his hand upon her arm to impress the caution, "whatever noise the Mouse hears in the night, she is not to leave the hut till the Raven comes back to her."

The girl bowed her head with an Indian woman's unquestioning obedience; and then, drawing aside the skin which served as a door, and listening attentively hear if any one were near, the Raven went out silently into the darkness.

CHAPTER XVII.
RESCUED.

In spite of their utmost efforts Mr. Hardy's party had made slower progress than they had anticipated. Many of the horses had broken down under fatigue; and as they had no spare horses to replace them as the Indians had in like case done from those they had driven off from Mr. Mercer, they were forced to travel far more slowly than at first. They gained upon the Indians, however, as they could tell by the position of the camping ground for the night.

At three o'clock on the afternoon of the last day they passed the place their enemy had left that morning; but although they kept on until long after sunset, many of them having led their horses all day, they were still more than thirty miles away from the mountains among which they knew that the Indian village was situated,

None of the Gauchos had ever been there, but they knew its situation and general features by report. There had been no difficulty in following the trail since they had struck it. The broad line of trodden ground and the frequent carcasses of sheep sufficiently told the tale.

That was a night of terrible anxiety to all. They knew that already Ethel was in the Indian village, and they thought with a sickening dread of what might happen the next day. Nothing, however, could be done. Many of the party were already exhausted by their long day's walk under a burning sun. It was altogether impossible to reach the village that night.

Before lying down for the night, Mr. Hardy asked all the party to join in a prayer for the preservation of his daughter during the following day; and it was a strange and impressing sight to see the group of sunburned, travel-worn men standing uncovered while their leader offered up an earnest prayer.

Mr. Hardy then said for that night it was unnecessary to keep watch as usual.

The Indians had pushed on and could no longer dread pursuit, and therefore there was no risk of a night attack. Besides which, there was little chance of his sleeping. This proposition was a most acceptable one, and in a very short time a perfect silence reigned in the camp.

Before daybreak they were again on the march, all on foot and leading their horses, in order to spare them as much as possible should they be required at night. Speed was now no object. It was, they knew, hopeless to attack in broad daylight, as the Indians would be probably more than a match for them, and Ethel's life would be inevitably sacrificed. They walked, therefore, until within six or seven miles of the gorge, nearer than which they dared not go, lest they might be seen by any straggling Indian.

Their halting-place was determined by finding a stream with an abundance of fresh grass on its banks. They dared not light a fire, but chewed some of the tough charqui, and watched the distant cleft in the hill which led to the ardently wished-for goal.

As evening fell they were all in the saddle, and were pleased to find that the horses were decidedly fresher for their rest. They did not draw rein until the ground became stony, and they knew that they must be at the mouth of the gorge. Then they dismounted and picketed the horses. Two of the Gauchos were stationed with them as guards, and the rest went stealthily forward--the rockets being interested to the care of Terence, who fastened them tightly together with a cord, and then hung them by a loop, like a gun, over his shoulder, in order that he might have his hands free.

It was still only eight o'clock--dangerously early for a surprise; but the whole party were quite agreed to risk everything, as no one could say in what position Ethel might be placed, and what difference an hour might make. Their plan was to steal quietly up to the first hut they found, to gag its inmates, and compel one of them, under a threat of instant death, to guide them to the hut in which Ethel was placed.

Suddenly Mr. Hardy was startled by a dark figure rising from a rock against which he had almost stumbled, with the words: "White man good. Tawaina friend. Come to take him to child."

Then followed a few hurried questions; and no words can express the delight and gratitude of Mr. Hardy and his sons, and the intense satisfaction of the others, on finding that Ethel was alive and for the present free from danger.

It was agreed to wait now for two hours, to give time for the Indians to retire to rest; and while they waited the Raven told them all that had happened up to the arrival at the village, passing over the last day's proceedings by saying briefly that Ethel had run a great risk of being put to death, but that a delay had been obtained by her friends. Having told his story, he said, "Tawaina friend to great white chief. Gave signal with arrow; save little White Bird to-day. But Tawaina Indian--not like see Indian killed. White chief promise not kill Indian women and children?"

Mr. Hardy assured the Indian that they had no thought of killing women and children.

"If can take little White Bird without waking village, not kill men?" Tawaina asked again.

"We do not want to wake the village if we can help it, Tawaina; but I do not see any chance of escaping without a fight. Our horses are all dead beat, and the Indians will easily overtake us, even if we get a night's start."

"Mustn't go out on plain," the Raven said earnestly. "If go out on plain, all killed. Indian two hundred and fifty braves--eat up white men on plain."

"I am afraid that is true enough, Tawaina, though we shall prove very tough morsels. Still we should fight at a fearful disadvantage in the open. But what are we to do?"

"Come back to mouth of canyon--hold that; can keep Indians off as long as like. Indians have to make peace."

"Capital!" Mr. Hardy said delightedly; for he had reviewed the position with great apprehension, as he had not seen how it would be possible to make good their retreat on their tired horses in the teeth of the Indians. "The very thing! As you say, we can hold the gorge for a month if necessary, and sooner or later they will be sick of it, and agree to let us retreat in quiet. Besides, a week's rest would set our horses up again, and then we could make our retreat in spite of them."

"One more thing," the Raven said. "When great chief got little White Bird safe, Tawaina go away--not fight one way, not fight other way. When meet again, white chief not talk about to-night. Not great Indian know Tawaina white chief's friend."

"You can rely upon us all, Tawaina. They shall never learn from us of your share in this affair. And now I think that it is time for us to be moving forward. It will be past ten o'clock before we are there."

Very quietly the troop crept along, Tawaina leading the way, until he approached closely to the village. Here they halted for a moment.

"Only six of us will go in," Mr. Hardy said; "there will be less chance of detection--Jamieson, Percy, Herries, my boys, and myself. The others take post close to the hut we see ahead. If you find that we are discovered, be in readiness to support us. And, Farquhar, two or three of you get matches ready, and stick a blue light into the straw roof of the hut. We must have light, or we lose all the advantage of our firearms. Besides, as we retreat we shall be in darkness, while they will be in the glare."

Thus speaking, Mr. Hardy followed his guide, the men he had selected treading cautiously in his rear. Presently they stopped before one of the huts, and pointing to the door, Tawaina said, "Little White Bird there;" and then gliding away, he was lost in the darkness.

Mr. Hardy cautiously pushed aside the skin and entered, followed by his friends. It was perfectly dark, and they stood for a moment uncertain what to do. Then they heard a low voice saying, "Papa, is that you?" while at the same instant they saw a gleam of light in the other corner of the tent, and heard a rustling noise, and they knew that an Indian had cut a slit in the hide walls and had escaped; and as Mr. Hardy pressed his child to his heart, a terrific war-whoop rose on the air behind the hut.

"Come," Mr. Hardy said, "keep together, and make a run of it."

Ethel had lain down without taking off even her shoes, so strong had been her hope of her father's arrival. She was therefore no impediment to the speed of their retreat. For a short distance they were unopposed. The Indians, indeed, rushed from their huts like swarms of bees disturbed by an intruder. Ignorant of the nature of the danger, and unable to see its cause, all was for a minute wild confusion; and then guided by the war-whoop of the Indian who had given the alarm, all hurried toward the spot, and as they did so, several saw the little party of whites. Loud whoops gave the intimation of this discovery and a rush toward them was made.

"Now, your revolvers," Mr. Hardy said. "We are nearly out of the village."

Not as yet, however, were the Indians gathered thickly enough to stop them. A few who attempted to throw themselves in the way were instantly shot down, and in less time than it has occupied to read this description they reached the end of the village. As they did so a bright flame shot up from the furthest hut, and the rest of the party rushed out and joined them. The Indians in pursuit paused at seeing this fresh accession of strength to their enemies, and then, as they were joined by large numbers, and the flame shooting up brightly enabled them to see how small was the body of whites, they rushed forward again with fierce yells.

But the whites were by this time a hundred and fifty yards away, and were already disappearing in the gloom.

"Stop!" Mr. Hardy cried. "Steady with your rifles! Each man single out an Indian. Fire!"

A yell of rage broke from the Indians as fourteen or fifteen of their number fell, and a momentary pause took place again. And then, as they were again reinforced, they continued the pursuit.

But the two hundred yards which the whites had gained was a long start in the half a mile's distance to be traversed, and the whites well knew that they were running for their lives; for once surrounded in the plain, their case was hopeless.

Well was it, then, that Ethel was so accustomed to an out-of-door life. Hope and fear lent speed to her feet, and running between her father and brothers, she was able to keep up a speed equal to their own.

Scarce a word was spoken, as with clinched teeth and beating hearts they dashed along. Only once Mr. Jamieson said, "Can Ethel keep up?" and she gasped out "Yes."

The whites had this great advantage in the race, that they knew that they had only half a mile in all to run, and therefore put out their best speed; whereas, although a few of the Indians saw the importance of overtaking the fugitives on the plain, the greater portion believed that their prey was safe in their hands, and made no great effort to close with them at once. The whites, too, had the advantage of being accustomed to walking exercise, whereas the Indians, almost living on horseback, are seldom in the habit of using their feet. Consequently the whites reached the narrow mouth of the gorge a full hundred and fifty yards ahead of the main body of the pursuers, although a party of their fastest runners was not more than half that distance in their rear.

There was a general ejaculation of thankfulness as the parties now halted and turned to face the enemy.

It was now that the full advantage of Mr. Hardy's precaution of firing the Indian hut had become manifest.

The fire had communicated to the next two or three dwellings, and a broad flame rose up, against the glare of which the Indians stood out distinctly, while the whites were posted in deep gloom.

"Now, boys," Mr. Hardy said, "pick off the first lot with your carbines, while we load our rifles. Ethel, get behind that rock. Take shelter all till the last moment. The arrows will soon be among us."

Steadily as if firing at a mark the boys discharged their five shots each; and as the enemy was not more than fifty yards off, every shot told.

The rest of the leading band hesitated, and throwing themselves down, waited until the others came up. There was a momentary pause, then a volley of arrows and musket halls was discharged in the direction of their hidden foe, and then, with a wild yell, the whole mass charged.

Not till they were within thirty yards was there a return shot fired; but as they entered the narrow gorge, the whites leaped to their feet with a cheer, and poured in a volley from twenty-four rifles,

The effect was terrible; and those in front who were unwounded hesitated, but, pressed on from behind, they again rushed forward. Then, as they closed, a desperate combat began.

The boys had hastily handed their carbines to Ethel to fit in the spare chamber, and had taken their place by their father's side. The gorge was so narrow that there was not room to stand abreast, and by previous arrangement those who had no revolvers placed themselves in front, clubbing their rifles, while those with revolvers fired between them.

Mr. Percy, one of the Jamiesons, and Herries stood a pace or two in the rear, with their revolvers in hand, as a reserve.

For a few minutes the contest was terrific. The rush of the Indians partially broke the line, and the whirl of gleaming hatchets, the heavy crash of the blows with the rifles, the sharp incessant cracks of the revolvers, the yells of the Indians, the short shouts of encouragement from the English, and the occasional Irish cry of Terence, made up a total of confusion and noise which was bewildering.

Scarce a shot of the whites was thrown away, and a heap of dead lay across the pass.

Still the Indians pressed on.

The fight was more silent now, the cracks of the revolvers had ceased, and the whites were fighting silently and desperately with their rifles. They had not given way a foot, but the short panting breath told that the tremendous exertion was telling, as they stood in a line at short intervals, and their weapons rose and fell with a force and might that the Indian hatchets could seldom stem or avert.

Not bloodless on their part had the fight been up to this time. Most of them had received gashes more or less severe, and Martinez the Gaucho and Cook lay dead at their feet.

Charley and Hubert, upon emptying their revolvers, had fallen back and taken their carbines, and now stood with the reserve upon a flat rock a few paces in the rear, all burning with impatience to take part in the strife.

At this moment they were joined by the two Gauchos who had been left with the horses, but who now, hearing the firing, had arrived to take part in the fray.

At last Mr. Hardy judged that the time had come, and shouted:

"Take aim into the middle of the mass, and fire as quick as you can, then all charge together. Now!"

In less than half a minute the four barrels of the Gauchos' guns, and the thirty shots from the revolvers, had been discharged into the densely packed throng; then the seven men leaped from the rock, and with a cheer the whites threw themselves upon the Indians, already recoiling and panic-struck by the tremendous and deadly fire.

The Indians in front, surprised and confused, were mown down by the long rifles like grass before the mower, and those behind, after one moment's hesitation, broke and fled; in another two minutes the fight was over, and the Indians in full flight to their village. After a few words of hearty congratulation the whites threw themselves on the ground, panting and exhausted, after their tremendous exertions.

Their first care, upon recovering a little, was to load their revolvers; as for the rifles, there was not one, with the exception of those of the three men who had formed the reserve, and the boys' carbines, which were not disabled. The stocks were broken, the hammers wrenched off, and the barrels twisted and bent.

The party now crowded round Ethel, with whom not a single word had yet been exchanged since her rescue, and warm and hearty were the congratulations and welcome bestowed upon her. There was then an examination of wounds.

These had been many, and in some cases severe. Mr. Farquhar was completely disabled by a deep wound in the shoulder. Mr. Percy had received a fearful gash on the arm. Charley had one ear nearly cut off, and the side of his face laid completely open with a sweeping blow. Four others were seriously wounded, and six had less important wounds. All, however, were too much elated with their success to make anything but light of their hurts.

"You seem fated to have your beauty spoiled, Charley," Mr. Hardy said, as he bandaged up his son's face. "A few more fights, and you will be as seasoned with scars as any Chelsea pensioner."

Charley joined in the general laugh at his own expense.

"Yes, papa, if I go on like this, I shall certainly get rid of my looking-glass."

"You have not lost the rockets, I hope, Terence?" Mr. Hardy asked.

"Sure and I've not, your honor. I put them down behind a big rock before the little shindy began."

"We will fire them off," Mr. Hardy said. "They will heighten the impression, and make the Indians more anxious to come to terms, when they see that we can reach their village. We will not let them off all at once; but as we have four of each sort, we will send off a pair every half hour or so, as they may think, if we fire them all at once and then stop, that we have no more left. We may as well give them a few shots, too, with our carbines and the rifles that remain serviceable. They will carry as far as half a mile if we give them elevation enough, and it is well to impress them as much as possible."

Mr. Hardy's suggestion was carried out. The first signal rocket showed the village crowded with Indians, over whose heads the cracked rocket slowly whizzed. The light of the next rocket did not disclose a single person, and it was apparent that the place was deserted. The third rocket happened to strike one of the roofs, and exploding there, set the thatch on fire.

"Good!" Mr. Percy said. "We shall have them asking for terms to-morrow."

Four of the unwounded men were now placed as a guard at the mouth of the gorge, the others retiring further into it, so as to be beyond the dead Indians, who lay there literally in piles.

The morning broke over the white men occupied in the burial of their two fallen companions, and upon the Indians assembled at a short distance beyond the village. The men sat upon the ground in sullen despair; the women wailed and wrung their hands.

Now that it was day, they could see how terrible had been their loss. Upward of sixty of their number were missing. The Stag had fallen, as had several of the most valiant braves of the tribe.

Presently the Raven rose from the midst of the warriors. His absence the preceding evening had not been noticed; and although all knew that he had taken no part in the fight, this was considered natural enough, when his advice to give up the captive had been rejected.

"My brothers," he began, "the Great Spirit is very angry. He has hidden his face from his children. Yesterday he blinded their eyes and made them foolish; last night he made them as water before the white men. Why were the ears of the chiefs closed to the words of the Raven? If the Raven had set out with the little White Bird, the great white chief would have been glad, and the hatchet would have been buried in peace. But the chiefs would not hear the words of the Raven. The Stag said, Kill! and the war chiefs shouted, Kill! and where are they now? Their wigwams are empty, and their women have none to bring in the deer for food. The Great Spirit is angry."

The Raven then took his seat; but, as he anticipated, no one rose to speak after him. The depression was too general; and the fact that, had the Raven's advice been followed, the evils would have been avoided, was too manifest for any one to attempt to utter a word.

After a profound silence of some minutes' duration, the Raven again rose.

"What will my brothers do? The flying fires will burn down our village, and there is no retreat. The guns that shoot without loading carry very far. We are as water before them. We are in the hands of the white chief, and our bones will feed the crows. What will my brothers do?"

There was still a profound silence, and then he continued: "The Raven is a great chief, and he will tell them what to do. The Raven has stood by the side of the little White Bird, and the great white chief will listen to his voice. He will say, Let there be peace between us. The men who would have harmed the Little White Bird are dead; there is no more cause of quarrel. Let us bury the hatchet. Take horses and cattle for your journey, and forgive us if we have done wrong. If the white men were on the plains, the Raven would say, Let my young men charge; but they hold the pass, and the guns that shoot without loading are too strong. Have I spoken well?"

There was a low murmur of applause. The feeling that the position of the white men was impregnable was general; and they all felt convinced that those terrible enemies would devise some unknown scheme which would end in the total annihilation of the tribe. The Raven's proposition was therefore unanimously assented to. The Raven then laid aside his arms, and attended by six of the principal chiefs, carrying green boughs in token of amity, advanced toward the mouth of the gorge. Mr. Hardy, with five of the whites, and with Perez to interpret, advanced to meet him. When the two groups met the Raven commenced gravely, in the Indian language: "The white chief of the flying fire is mighty, and the Great Spirit has blinded his children. They carried off the little White Bird, but they did not harm her. Bad men would have harmed her, but the Raven stood by her side. The great white chief has taken back his little White Bird, and he has killed the men whom the Great Spirit blinded. Why should there be any more war? The Indians are brave; they have cattle, and sheep, and water. They can live out of reach of the white chief's guns, and can fight if the white chief comes out against them. The white chief is strong, and he can defend the pass, but he cannot venture out to attack. They are equal. There is no cause of quarrel any longer. Let us bury the hatchet. The white chief's young men can take horses--for the Indians have many--to take them back to their homes. They can take cattle to eat. Let there be peace."

This address of the Raven was a very politic one. He already knew that Mr. Hardy was willing to grant terms, but he wished to show the other chiefs that he supported the honor of the tribe by boasting of their power and resources, and by making the peace as upon equal terms.

When the Gaucho had translated their proposal, Mr. Hardy spoke, using the phraseology which would be most intelligible to the Indians.

"The Raven is a great chief; he has spoken wisely. The little White Bird has sung in the white chief's ear that the Raven stood by her side when bad Indians would have hurt her. The bad Indians are dead. The Great Spirit frowned upon them. The white chief has no quarrel with the Raven and his friends. Let there be peace."

A general expression of satisfaction pervaded both parties when it was known that peace was arranged; and one of each side hurrying back with the news, the rest went into the village, where, sitting down before the principal hut, the pipe of peace was solemnly smoked.

The two parties then mingled amicably, mutually pleased at the termination to the hostilities; and no one would have guessed that a few hours before they had met in deadly strife. The Raven courteously invited the whites to stop for a night at the village; but the invitation was declined, as all were very anxious to return home.

Some Indians were dispatched by the Raven, who had now naturally assumed the position of chief of the tribe, to catch horses to take the place of those which had broken down upon the journey. The offer of cattle was declined, as they were confident that they should be able to procure game. They took, however, as large a supply of fresh meat as their horses could carry.

Mr. Hardy saw that the Raven wished to avoid any private conversation with him. He therefore drew the boys aside, and made a proposal to them, to which they cordially agreed. As the horses were brought up, and the whole tribe assembled, he advanced toward the Raven with one of the boys' carbines in his hand.

"The Raven is a great chief," he said. "He has a great heart, and stood by the side of the little White Bird. But he has not a good rifle. The white chief gives him a rifle which will shoot many times. Let him promise that he will never use it in fight against the white men."

This gift the Raven received with great pleasure, and readily gave the required promise, adding, on behalf of his tribe, that the hatchet which was buried should never again be dug up against the whites. An extra chamber and all the spare ammunition was given to him, and a further supply promised when he chose to send for it; instructions were also given to him in the use of the weapon, then a solemn farewell was exchanged, and the party of whites turned their faces toward home.

CHAPTER XVIII.
AND LAST.

With this memorable conflict, and the lesson taught to the Indians, that even in the heart of their own country they could not consider themselves secure from retaliations and from the vengeance of the white settlers, the Indian troubles of the Hardys were over. Occasionally, indeed, raids were made upon the outlying settlements, and the young Hardys were summoned to beat off their savage foes. Upon the estate of Mount Pleasant, however, hostile foot was not again placed. Occasionally the Raven, with two or three of his braves, would pay a visit for a day or two, and depart with presents of blankets, and such things as his tribe needed. Upon the first of these visits Hubert questioned him respecting the bird whose remarkable feather had been the means of saving Ethel's life. At his next visit the chief brought two very perfect skins of the bird. It turned out, to Hubert's great delight, to be a new species; and one of them is now, with many other hitherto 'unknown birds which had fallen to his gun, in the British Museum, with the specific names of Hardiensis, in compliment to their discoverer. The Raven's tribe honorably performed their agreement with Mr. Hardy, and never joined in any subsequent attacks upon the whites. Being much weakened by the loss of so many of their fighting men, they would probably have been exterminated by hostile tribes; but Mr. Hardy subsequently furnished them with a supply of military muskets, which he had bought chiefly for the purpose, together with ammunition, and they were then able to oppose a resolute front to their enemies, and to support themselves by hunting. The Raven is now one of the most powerful and respected chiefs upon the plains of the pampas.

The return of the expedition, after the rescue of Ethel and the chastisement of the Indians in the heart of their own country, caused quite a sensation throughout the Republic. Of Mrs. Hardy's and Maud's joy we need not speak, but the adventure was considered a matter of congratulation and joy throughout the whole district. It was felt that a signal blow had been struck to the Indians, and that for a long time life and property would be secure. There was, in consequence, quite a rush to the neighborhood and land was taken up and occupied in all directions.

It was well for Mrs. Hardy and the girls that they were to sail by the next mail for England. The effect of those terrible four days upon Ethel, and of that week of anxiety upon her mother and sister, had so shaken them that the change, even if it had not been previously determined upon, would have been imperatively necessary. It is not too much to say that Mrs. Hardy and Maud had suffered even more than Ethel. She at least had known and seen her danger, and was sustained, except during that morning when she was fastened to the stake, with a strong hope and belief of rescue. Those left behind could do nothing but picture up scenes of horror, and pass their time in alternately praying and weeping. They were all sadly shaken and nervous during the short time that remained for them at Mount Pleasant; but the sea voyage and the fresh breezes soon brought health and color into their cheeks, and none of them ever after felt any bad effects from that terrible week.

And now our story is drawing to a close. The stormy period of the Mount Pleasant settlement was over. The hard work, the difficulties and dangers of the life of a new settler on the extreme edge of civilization, had been passed, and nothing remained but to continue to devote attention and energy to the estate, and to reap the fruits of the labor.

For two years after the departure of his wife and daughters Mr. Hardy remained at his post. It was now nearly six years since he had left England, and he longed to return to it. He felt that he could do so without any uneasiness as to the future. Rosario was, according to his anticipation, rising into a large and important town; the country was fairly settled for leagues beyond the estate; land was rapidly rising in value; and there was now no fear whatever of Indian attacks. His flocks and herds had multiplied greatly, and were doubling every two years. The income obtained by the sale of cattle fatted on the alfalfa, and upon the sale of wool and other farm produce, was considerable. The dairy alone brought in a large yearly amount. Charley was now twenty-two, Hubert a year younger; both were as capable of managing the estate as he was himself.

He one day, therefore, unfolded his plans to them. "As you know, boys, I am going to England shortly; and although I shall perhaps now and then come over here, I shall make England my permanent home. You boys will therefore jointly manage the estate. The income this year will reach six thousand dollars, and would be much more did we not keep the greater portion of our animals to increase our stock. I have now twelve thousand five hundred dollars in the bank. After the busy life I have led here, I could not remain inactive. My present intention is to take a large farm upon a long lease with the option of purchase. My object will be to obtain a lease upon large acreage and poor land, but improvable with irrigation or drainage and an outlay of capital. I shall risk no more than twelve thousand five hundred dollars in this, and also the income I draw from here for the next two years. The profits will increase each year. I shall therefore in two years have sunk twenty-five thousand dollars in the farm--a portion being devoted to building a suitable house. You will, of course, during the two years spend whatever money you may require; but, in fact, it is impossible for you to spend much money here. At the end of two years I propose that first you, Charley, as the elder, shall come home to England for a year, and then that Hubert shall take his turn. You will then stay a year here together, and again have each a year in England, and so on regularly. From the end of this two years I shall draw half the income of this estate, and you will take the other half between you, to invest or use as you may think fit. At the end of six years I calculate that the estate will be stocked with as many cattle and sheep as it can support. Fifteen thousand cattle, say, and thirty thousand sheep. You will then sell all your annual increase, and the profits will be greater every year. At the end of ten years from this time, if, as I think probable, you will have had enough of this life, we will sell the estate. By that time it will be the center of a populous district, the land will be greatly increased in value, and will be equal to any in the country--so much so, indeed, that it will probably be out of the question to find a purchaser for the whole. We could therefore break it up to suit purchasers, dividing it into lots of one, two, three, or four square miles, or a square league, and dividing the stock in proportion. The house would, of course, go with the arable land and a mile or two of pasture beyond it. My share of the yearly income I shall devote to buying my estate. Say the price is fifty thousand dollars. This I shall, with my income from here and my income from the estate itself, probably be able to make in ten years. The estate, with the twenty-five thousand dollars I propose to risk in drainage, etc., ought then to be worth one hundred thousand dollars. The value of this estate of fifty thousand acres, with the flocks and herds, ought to be at least double that amount; so that at the end of ten years I shall be a rich man. You, with care, can certainly save twenty-five thousand dollars each in the ten years, and will receive another fifty thousand dollars each as your share of the estate. You will consequently, boys, at the age of thirty-one and thirty-two, be able to settle down in England in very comfortable circumstances. Your sisters will of course be provided for out of my share. Do you approve of my plans?"

The boys warmly expressed their satisfaction at the plan, and their gratitude to their father for his intentions.

And so things were carried out.

Six months after Mr. Hardy's arrival in England, the boys heard of Maud's marriage to Mr. Cooper, now, by the death of his father, a wealthy country gentleman. Charley, during his first visit to England, also married--an example which Hubert followed the next year.

The two now took it by turn to manage the estate--the one in England always passing a considerable portion of his time at Mr. Hardy's, and spending the rest in traveling.

Ethel was married the year after Hubert to a rising barrister in London.

Everything prospered at Mount Pleasant, and at the sale it was broken up into lots and fetched rather a larger sum than Mr. Hardy had calculated.

Mr. Hardy's own plan had been fully carried out, but by the end of the ten years he began to wish for a quiet town life. He therefore made an arrangement with Charley, whereby the latter, who had obtained some money with his wife, has taken his place as master of the estate, and has settled down into the life of a country gentleman, which exactly suits him. Hubert lives in London. His income is sufficient for his wants, he has become a member of a number of scientific societies, and his collection of the fauna of the pampas of America is considered to be unequaled. The girls are very happy with the men of their choice; and Mr. and Mrs. Hardy have always some of their children or grandchildren staying with them, and often amuse the young ones with tales of how their fathers or mothers fought the Indians on the pampas of South America.

The Codes Of Hammurabi And Moses
W. W. Davies

QTY

The discovery of the Hammurabi Code is one of the greatest achievements of archaeology, and is of paramount interest, not only to the student of the Bible, but also to all those interested in ancient history...

Religion   **ISBN:** *1-59462-338-4*   Pages:132
MSRP $12.95

The Theory of Moral Sentiments
Adam Smith

QTY

This work from 1749. contains original theories of conscience amd moral judgment and it is the foundation for systemof morals.

Philosophy **ISBN:** *1-59462-777-0*   Pages:536
MSRP $19.95

Jessica's First Prayer
Hesba Stretton

QTY

In a screened and secluded corner of one of the many railway-bridges which span the streets of London there could be seen a few years ago, from five o'clock every morning until half past eight, a tidily set-out coffee-stall, consisting of a trestle and board, upon which stood two large tin cans, with a small fire of charcoal burning under each so as to keep the coffee boiling during the early hours of the morning when the work-people were thronging into the city on their way to their daily toil...

Pages:84

Childrens   **ISBN:** *1-59462-373-2*   *MSRP $9.95*

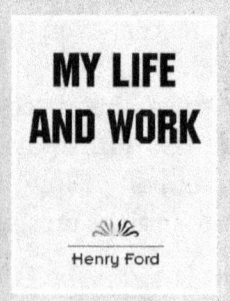

My Life and Work
Henry Ford

QTY

Henry Ford revolutionized the world with his implementation of mass production for the Model T automobile. Gain valuable business insight into his life and work with his own auto-biography... "We have only started on our development of our country we have not as yet, with all our talk of wonderful progress, done more than scratch the surface. The progress has been wonderful enough but..."

Pages:300

Biographies/   **ISBN:** *1-59462-198-5*   *MSRP $21.95*

The Art of Cross-Examination
Francis Wellman

QTY

I presume it is the experience of every author, after his first book is published upon an important subject, to be almost overwhelmed with a wealth of ideas and illustrations which could readily have been included in his book, and which to his own mind, at least, seem to make a second edition inevitable. Such certainly was the case with me; and when the first edition had reached its sixth impression in five months, I rejoiced to learn that it seemed to my publishers that the book had met with a sufficiently favorable reception to justify a second and considerably enlarged edition. ..

Reference   **ISBN:** *1-59462-647-2*

Pages:412

MSRP $19.95

On the Duty of Civil Disobedience
Henry David Thoreau

QTY

Thoreau wrote his famous essay, On the Duty of Civil Disobedience, as a protest against an unjust but popular war and the immoral but popular institution of slave-owning. He did more than write—he declined to pay his taxes,   and was hauled off to gaol in consequence. Who can say how much this refusal of his hastened the end of the war and of slavery ?

Law   **ISBN:** *1-59462-747-9*

Pages:48

MSRP $7.45

Dream Psychology Psychoanalysis for Beginners
Sigmund Freud

QTY

Sigmund Freud, born Sigismund Schlomo Freud (May 6, 1856 - September 23, 1939), was a Jewish-Austrian neurologist and psychiatrist who co-founded the psychoanalytic school of psychology. Freud is best known for his theories of the unconscious mind, especially involving the mechanism of repression; his redefinition of sexual desire as mobile and directed towards a wide variety of objects; and his therapeutic techniques, especially his understanding of transference in the therapeutic relationship and the presumed value of dreams as sources of insight into unconscious desires.

Pages:196

Psychology   **ISBN:** *1-59462-905-6*

MSRP $15.45

The Miracle of Right Thought
Orison Swett Marden

QTY

Believe with all of your heart that you will do what you were made to do. When the mind has once formed the habit of holding cheerful, happy, prosperous pictures, it will not be easy to form the opposite habit. It does not matter how improbable or how far away this realization may see, or how dark the prospects may be, if we visualize them as best we can, as vividly as possible, hold tenaciously to them and vigorously struggle to attain them, they will gradually become actualized, realized in the life. But a desire, a longing without endeavor, a yearning abandoned or held indifferently will vanish without realization.

Pages:360

Self Help   **ISBN:** *1-59462-644-8*

MSRP $25.45

QTY

The Rosicrucian Cosmo-Conception Mystic Christianity *by Max Heindel*   ISBN: *1-59462-188-8*   **$38.95**
The Rosicrucian Cosmo-conception is not dogmatic, neither does it appeal to any other authority than the reason of the student. It is: not controversial, but is: sent forth in the, hope that it may help to clear..   New Age/Religion Pages 646

Abandonment To Divine Providence *by Jean-Pierre de Caussade*   ISBN: *1-59462-228-0*   **$25.95**
"The Rev. Jean Pierre de Caussade was one of the most remarkable spiritual writers of the Society of Jesus in France in the 18th Century. His death took place at Toulouse in 1751. His works have gone through many editions and have been republished...   Inspirational/Religion Pages 400

Mental Chemistry *by Charles Haanel*   ISBN: *1-59462-192-6*   **$23.95**
Mental Chemistry allows the change of material conditions by combining and appropriately utilizing the power of the mind. Much like applied chemistry creates something new and unique out of careful combinations of chemicals the mastery of mental chemistry...   New Age Pages 354

The Letters of Robert Browning and Elizabeth Barret Barrett 1845-1846 vol II   ISBN: *1-59462-193-4*   **$35.95**
by Robert Browning and Elizabeth Barrett   Biographies Pages 596

Gleanings In Genesis (volume I) *by Arthur W. Pink*   ISBN: *1-59462-130-6*   **$27.45**
Appropriately has Genesis been termed "the seed plot of the Bible" for in it we have, in germ form, almost all of the great doctrines which are afterwards fully developed in the books of Scripture which follow...   Religion/Inspirational Pages 420

The Master Key *by L. W. de Laurence*   ISBN: *1-59462-001-6*   **$30.95**
In no branch of human knowledge has there been a more lively increase of the spirit of research during the past few years than in the study of Psychology, Concentration and Mental Discipline. The requests for authentic lessons in Thought Control, Mental Discipline and...   New Age/Business Pages 422

The Lesser Key Of Solomon Goetia *by L. W. de Laurence*   ISBN: *1-59462-092-X*   **$9.95**
This translation of the first book of the "Lernegton" which is now for the first time made accessible to students of Talismanic Magic was done, after careful collation and edition, from numerous Ancient Manuscripts in Hebrew, Latin, and French...   New Age/Occult Pages 92

Rubaiyat Of Omar Khayyam *by Edward Fitzgerald*   ISBN:*1-59462-332-5*   **$13.95**
Edward Fitzgerald, whom the world has already learned, in spite of his own efforts to remain within the shadow of anonymity, to look upon as one of the rarest poets of the century, was born at Bredfield, in Suffolk, on the 31st of March, 1809. He was the third son of John Purcell...   Music Pages 172

Ancient Law *by Henry Maine*   ISBN: *1-59462-128-4*   **$29.95**
The chief object of the following pages is to indicate some of the earliest ideas of mankind, as they are reflected in Ancient Law, and to point out the relation of those ideas to modern thought.   Religiom/History Pages 452

Far-Away Stories *by William J. Locke*   ISBN: *1-59462-129-2*   **$19.45**
"Good wine needs no bush, but a collection of mixed vintages does. And this book is just such a collection. Some of the stories I do not want to remain buried for ever in the museum files of dead magazine-numbers an author's not unpardonable vanity..."   Fiction Pages 272

Life of David Crockett *by David Crockett*   ISBN: *1-59462-250-7*   **$27.45**
"Colonel David Crockett was one of the most remarkable men of the times in which he lived. Born in humble life, but gifted with a strong will, an indomitable courage, and unremitting perseverance...   Biographies/New Age Pages 424

Lip-Reading *by Edward Nitchie*   ISBN: *1-59462-206-X*   **$25.95**
Edward B. Nitchie, founder of the New York School for the Hard of Hearing, now the Nitchie School of Lip-Reading, Inc, wrote "LIP-READING Principles and Practice". The development and perfecting of this meritorious work on lip-reading was an undertaking...   How-to Pages 400

A Handbook of Suggestive Therapeutics, Applied Hypnotism, Psychic Science   ISBN: *1-59462-214-0*   **$24.95**
by Henry Munro   Health/New Age/Health/Self-help Pages 376

A Doll's House: and Two Other Plays *by Henrik Ibsen*   ISBN: *1-59462-112-8*   **$19.95**
Henrik Ibsen created this classic when in revolutionary 1848 Rome. Introducing some striking concepts in playwriting for the realist genre, this play has been studied the world over.   Fiction/Classics/Plays 308

The Light of Asia *by sir Edwin Arnold*   ISBN: *1-59462-204-3*   **$13.95**
In this poetic masterpiece, Edwin Arnold describes the life and teachings of Buddha. The man who was to become known as Buddha to the world was born as Prince Gautama of India but he rejected the worldly riches and abandoned the reigns of power when...   Religion/History/Biographies Pages 170

The Complete Works of Guy de Maupassant *by Guy de Maupassant*   ISBN: *1-59462-157-8*   **$16.95**
"For days and days, nights and nights, I had dreamed of that first kiss which was to consecrate our engagement, and I knew not on what spot I should put my lips..."   Fiction/Classics Pages 240

The Art of Cross-Examination *by Francis L. Wellman*   ISBN: *1-59462-309-0*   **$26.95**
Written by a renowned trial lawyer, Wellman imparts his experience and uses case studies to explain how to use psychology to extract desired information through questioning.   How-to/Science/Reference Pages 408

Answered or Unanswered? *by Louisa Vaughan*   ISBN: *1-59462-248-5*   **$10.95**
Miracles of Faith in China   Religion Pages 112

The Edinburgh Lectures on Mental Science (1909) *by Thomas*   ISBN: *1-59462-008-3*   **$11.95**
This book contains the substance of a course of lectures recently given by the writer in the Queen Street Hall, Edinburgh. Its purpose is to indicate the Natural Principles governing the relation between Mental Action and Material Conditions...   New Age/Psychology Pages 148

Ayesha *by H. Rider Haggard*   ISBN: *1-59462-301-5*   **$24.95**
Verily and indeed it is the unexpected that happens! Probably if there was one person upon the earth from whom the Editor of this, and of a certain previous history, did not expect to hear again...   Classics Pages 380

Ayala's Angel *by Anthony Trollope*   ISBN: *1-59462-352-X*   **$29.95**
The two girls were both pretty, but Lucy who was twenty-one who supposed to be simple and comparatively unattractive, whereas Ayala was credited, as her Bombwhat romantic name might show, with poetic charm and a taste for romance. Ayala when her father died was nineteen...   Fiction Pages 484

The American Commonwealth *by James Bryce*   ISBN: *1-59462-286-8*   **$34.45**
An interpretation of American democratic political theory. It examines political mechanics and society from the perspective of Scotsman James Bryce   Politics Pages 572

Stories of the Pilgrims *by Margaret P. Pumphrey*   ISBN: *1-59462-116-0*   **$17.95**
This book explores pilgrims religious oppression in England as well as their escape to Holland and eventual crossing to America on the Mayflower, and their early days in New England...   History Pages 268

QTY

The Fasting Cure *by Sinclair Upton*   ISBN: *1-59462-222-1*   **$13.95** ☐
In the Cosmopolitan Magazine for May, 1910, and in the Contemporary Review (London) for April, 1910, I published an article dealing with my experi-
ences in fasting. I have written a great many magazine articles, but never one which attracted so much attention... New Age/Self Help/Health Pages 164

Hebrew Astrology *by Sepharial*   ISBN: *1-59462-308-2*   **$13.45** ☐
In these days of advanced thinking it is a matter of common observation that we have left many of the old landmarks behind and that we are now pressing
forward to greater heights and to a wider horizon than that which represented the mind-content of our progenitors...   Astrology Pages 144

Thought Vibration or The Law of Attraction in the Thought World   ISBN: *1-59462-127-6*   **$12.95** ☐

by William Walker Atkinson   *Psychology/Religion Pages 144*

Optimism *by Helen Keller*   ISBN: *1-59462-108-X*   **$15.95** ☐
Helen Keller was blind, deaf, and mute since 19 months old, yet famously learned how to overcome these handicaps, communicate with the world, and
spread her lectures promoting optimism. An inspiring read for everyone...   Biographies/Inspirational Pages 84

Sara Crewe *by Frances Burnett*   ISBN: *1-59462-360-0*   **$9.45** ☐
In the first place, Miss Minchin lived in London. Her home was a large, dull, tall one, in a large, dull square, where all the houses were alike, and all the
sparrows were alike, and where all the door-knockers made the same heavy sound...   Childrens/Classic Pages 88

The Autobiography of Benjamin Franklin *by Benjamin Franklin*   ISBN: *1-59462-135-7*   **$24.95** ☐
The Autobiography of Benjamin Franklin has probably been more extensively read than any other American historical work, and no other book of its kind
has had such ups and downs of fortune. Franklin lived for many years in England, where he was agent...   Biographies/History Pages 332

Name	
Email	
Telephone	
Address	
City, State ZIP	

☐ **Credit Card**   ☐ **Check / Money Order**

Credit Card Number	
Expiration Date	
Signature	

Please Mail to: Book Jungle
PO Box 2226
Champaign, IL 61825
or Fax to: 630-214-0564

ORDERING INFORMATION

web: *www.bookjungle.com*
email: *sales@bookjungle.com*
fax: *630-214-0564*
mail: *Book Jungle PO Box 2226 Champaign, IL 61825*
or PayPal *to sales@bookjungle.com*

Please contact us for bulk discounts

DIRECT-ORDER TERMS

**20% Discount if You Order
Two or More Books**
Free Domestic Shipping!
Accepted: Master Card, Visa,
Discover, American Express